ARCHER

A NOVEL

MIRA JEFFREYS

BWP
Better World Press
Gardner, Kansas 66030

Copyright © 2020 Mira Jeffreys
Print Edition: ISBN 978-1-0983044-1-6
Library of Congress Control Number: 2020903526

All rights reserved. This book or any portion thereof may not be reproduced or used in any manner whatsoever without the express written permission of the publisher except for the use of brief quotations in a book review.

Archer is a work of fiction. Names, characters, locations, business, events and incidents are the products of the author's imagination. Any resemblance to actual persons, living or dead, or actual events is purely coincidental.

Printed & Bound in the United States of America

First Printing, 2020
Cover Design by JennJ Designs jennjdesigns.com
Book illustrations by Desiree Taylor

Dedicated to my Mom & Dad

"You don't have to be famous.
You just have to make your mother and father proud of you." ~Meryl Streep

And also, for C.L.J.
Without your friendship and love, I wouldn't be the person I am today. Thank you.

"I would rather walk with a friend in the dark, than alone in the light."

HELEN KELLER

Chapter 1

Lena added the last meatball to the plate and garnished it with a piece of fresh parsley. She smiled approvingly. Placing the plate in the lightbox, she reached for her camera and captured a series of photos for her next Instagram post.

"Which one of these looks best?" she asked, switching between the five photos she had taken.

Nadia peeked over her shoulder. "Umm, I hate to tell you this, but they all look alike to me."

"No, they don't. They're all different."

"Says you. But to me, they look the same."

Lena cut her eyes over at her. "You're no help at all."

"Don't ask for my opinion if you don't like what I have to say." Nadia chuckled while grabbing the plate from the lightbox. "May I eat my dinner now?"

"Sure, go ahead."

Nadia wasted no time devouring the meal. "Your meatballs are the best."

"Thanks, sweetie." Lena cycled through her pictures until she found the one. "This one is perfect for my next IG post."

"Hey, are you done traveling for a while?"

"Maybe. Why?"

"I don't know. The house gets lonely without you."

"Are you trying to say you miss me?"

Nadia sipped her water in silence. "Even though work keeps me busy, when I'm here, I still miss you. I miss your company."

"I thought this day would never come," Lena joked, "You actually miss me!"

Nadia couldn't resist Lena's humor. Their shared laughter quickly evaporated into silence. "I know we laugh about it, but I really mean it. I do miss you."

Lena nodded. "I know you do." She reached for a piece of parsley and popped it into her mouth. "My next commission is sending me to the Redwoods. Isn't that great?"

"When?"

"In two weeks."

"How long will you be gone?"

"I don't know. Probably three weeks, maybe less."

Nadia stabbed at her food and avoided her eyes. "That's a long time."

Lena took her hand. "Honey, is there something wrong?"

"No."

Lena could tell something was wrong by the way Nadia vacantly twirled the noodles over her fork. "This will be a great boost for the bank account, and if I do a good job, someone will give me a more permanent, higher-paying contract."

"Someone like who?"

"I don't know, National Geographic or maybe even Smithsonian."

Nadia turned her attention back to her plate. "I'm working too, and I get a regular paycheck every week."

"I understand, but you aren't responsible for taking care of me. I am responsible for taking care of you."

"You're not responsible for me. I'm a grown woman."

Lena scooted her chair closer and put her arm around her. "Yes, you are. You're a brilliant and talented, grown woman. You can do anything you want to do, but you don't need to take care of me, sweet pea."

"At least let me help."

"I appreciate your willingness to help me, but the money you make is yours for when you finally spread your wings and fly the coop."

"Oh, not this again."

"What? Do you really expect to live with me for the rest of your life?"

"I'd thought about it."

Lena laughed. "I love you. I only want what's best for you."

"I know you do, but you've been working your entire life for me. Isn't it time for you to relax and enjoy yours?"

Lena chuckled. "You make it seem like I'm old."

"Well, you are about to hit the big four-oh."

"Shh. Don't say that too loud." Lena pushed herself out of the chair. Her body felt like it was on the brink of eighty instead of forty. She strolled over to the cupboard and grabbed a wine glass. She poured a generous amount of Roscato and brought it to her lips.

"What's wrong?" Nadia asked, interrupting her much needed sip.

She shrugged. "It just seems weird that I'm about to turn forty. It seems like only yesterday I was starting high school." Lena's mind drifted into the past where her thoughts lingered for a few quiet moments, while she sipped from her wine glass. She turned her back and gazed out of the window. The sun was just dipping below the horizon. Another day gone.

"Will you ever tell me?"

Nadia's voice startled her out of her thoughts. "Tell you what, sweet pea?"

"Will you ever tell me what happened to you?"

Lena sighed and turned around. "Every day, I tell myself that I will, but it still hurts. I guess I've never really had closure."

Nadia got up and walked over to her, draping her hand over Lena's shoulder, "I love you, Mom," she whispered.

Reluctant tears pricked the backs of Lena's eyes. "I love you too, sweet pea."

"I need to get ready for work. I'm working a double tonight," she said before leaving the room.

Lena sighed with relief when she disappeared from the room. She had become an expert at hiding her pain, but the more Nadia aged, the harder it was to conceal it. Some days, she couldn't bear to look into her own daughter's eyes. Everything about her reminded Lena of the ones she once loved. She occupied her mind by loading the dishwasher. Five minutes into the task, she heard her phone ringing.

Perhaps this was finally her big break! She hoped for an answer from the online submission she made a month ago. She dashed across the room and grabbed the phone. She glanced at the caller ID. "Of course, no major magazine would want my work!" she grumbled. She answered the call. "Hello?"

"Magdalena?"

"Hey, Big Mama. This is the first time in history you're late calling."

"I know, baby. I'm sorry." Maybelle "Big Mama" Curtis called Lena at noontime, every day. But today she was hours late. Maybelle coughed, her voice was heavy and wheezy. "I'm not good at all."

Lena's heart dropped into her stomach. Maybelle sounded nothing like her usual self, bursting with enthusiasm from the first hello. "You don't sound like it. What's going on?" Lena asked.

Maybelle whispered something indecipherable, perhaps a prayer, and held the line briefly. "The doctors found some cancer in me."

"What? What kind? Where?"

"In my lungs."

"Cancer?" Lena couldn't breathe. "Lung cancer?" she repeated quieter.

"Yes, baby."

"But how is this possible? You don't even smoke!" As soon as she asked the question, she realized how. Years working for and around smokers had finally caught up with her. Her knees felt like they were about to buckle. She grabbed the edge of the table and sat down. "How bad is it?"

"It's pretty bad. I was calling to see if you could come down and help me for a little. Zeke is too old to help me with things around the house."

Lena felt numb. There was more to the news than Maybelle was sharing at the moment. She was certain of it. She heard Nadia walking back into the kitchen. She glued her eyes to the table. Her nerves were on edge. Tears streamed down her face as the world as she knew it came to a screeching halt.

"I know you have to work, but I will make sure you have enough money to live on when you're finished. I just need a little help."

Lena cleared the lump from her throat as Nadia sat across from her. Nadia stilled Lena's trembling hand with her own. She glanced across the table, only to find

Nadia's haunting eyes staring back at her. "Of course, I'll come, Big Mama. You're more important than work."

"Thank you."

"You're welcome. I'm going to make some arrangements and come as soon as I can. I'll call and let you know when I'll be leaving."

"All right." Maybelle went silent.

"I promise I'll come as soon as I can."

"I know you will." Maybelle finally responded.

"I love you," Lena whispered. "I love you so much."

"I love you too, my sweet Magdalena." Maybelle's voice hung with sadness. "Come home and see me soon, okay?"

"I will."

"I'm mighty tired. I need to rest my voice."

"Okay. Goodbye."

The line disconnected. Lena couldn't move, her entire system was stunned and confused. Her heart clenched inside of her chest. She placed her phone down on the table and looked up at Nadia. It was then she realized that Nadia was holding her hand, caressing it gently between her hands.

"Oh, sweet pea, I'm sorry."

Nadia moved her chair closer. "What's wrong?"

Lena shook her head; she found it a challenge repeating the heartbreaking news she'd just received. She couldn't breathe, she couldn't think, and with each passing minute, the pain in her heart grew more intense.

Nadia jumped up and retrieved Lena's pills from the cabinet. She measured out a dosage and a half and brought it to her. She ran a glass of water and handed it to her. "Take this," she said, reseating herself beside her mother.

Fifteen minutes later, Lena sat motionless, cradling her half-empty glass of water with nothing but silence filling the space between them. She thought she would have more time, more time to plan and be ready. Twenty-four years should have been long enough. She hid Nadia from everyone. It was imperative for her safety. She hid her from a world that was far too cruel for her sweet pea. She dreamed of one day taking Nadia back home and letting everyone know of her existence, but she knew most of them could not handle the truth about her.

Nadia would never be accepted by them.

As she gazed into the eyes of her only child, she felt a sadness unlike any she had ever experienced before. Nadia was the only innocent person in this whole mess. Lena knew the day in which she would be forced to tell her the truth was quickly approaching. "I need to go back home to Georgia."

"Okay. What's happening?"

She recounted all that Maybelle told her. She paused several times when her heart choked the words from her throat. "Big Mama needs some help around the house."

Nadia nodded quickly. "What do you need me to do?"

"I don't know yet, sweet pea. I'm just trying to wrap my mind around this, you know?"

"I know," Nadia whispered. She glanced at her watch and cursed.

"I know you need to get to work. I'll be okay. I just need to start making some plans."

Nadia sighed and got up from the table. She walked over to the fridge and retrieved her lunch from it. She walked cautiously back over to her. "I would like to go with you."

Lena shook her head slowly. "I don't think that's a good idea."

"Why not?"

"Because I haven't had time to plan."

"Time to plan for what?"

"Could we please not talk about this right now?" Lena's body trembled. Her mind wanted to escape from the reality of this moment.

Nadia sat down beside her. "Are you ashamed of me?"

"What? No."

"It seems like you are."

"I can't argue with you right now, Nadia."

"I'm not trying to start an argument. I would just like to go and support you."

"You don't know how those people are!" Lena struggled to stay composed. The way Nadia looked right now, made her heart clench tighter inside. "You don't know what's waiting back there. I do!"

"Maybe I don't, but I just want to go with you. And if I meet them, great. If not, that's fine too."

"We both know that as soon as you set foot in Archer, you're going to be snooping around, trying to find out things you're not ready for. Just like you did when you were sixteen."

"That was a long time ago. I'm almost twenty-four."

"I am very aware of how old you are."

"Then give me the benefit of the doubt. Please."

Lena ran her hands over her face. "Christ! Why do you have to be so stubborn?"

Nadia shrugged. "I guess I get it from you."

Lena nodded slowly, "Okay," she surrendered, "Okay, I'll think about it. What are you going to do about your job?"

"I have some vacation time built up. I'll use as much as I can."

"I don't know about this, Nadia."

"It'll be okay. I promise. Trust me."

Lena trusted her. More than anyone else alive at the moment. Her secrets, the ones waiting for her back home, were far too devastating to reveal. She kept Nadia in the dark for the majority of her life, but deep down, she knew Nadia deserved to know who she was. "All right. I'll take you with me," she finally surrendered.

A gentle smile swept across Nadia's face. "Thank you so much."

"You're welcome, sweet pea."

Nadia wrapped her up in a tight hug, "I promise I won't be Sherlock Holmes."

"Yeah, right," she chuckled.

Nadia got up and headed for the front door. "I'll request the time off tonight. Are we flying or driving?"

"Driving." She answered blankly. Lena dreaded the sixteen-hour drive from Kansas to rural South Georgia, but it was the most reasonable option.

"Okay. I have about three weeks' vacation. How much do you want me to request?"

By now, Lena's heart clenched with grief. Memories of Maybelle's love flooded through her mind. She knew what her Big Mama's request to come back home meant. Her heart wasn't ready. "Go ahead and take all of it. Because I think she's gonna…" Her heart choked the words right out of her mouth. She turned away from Nadia, hiding the pain on her face. "Bye, sweet pea," she whispered.

"All right, I'll take care of it tonight." She left Lena sitting at the table and went to work.

Lena remained in the same spot. Time stood still. Nothing but echoes from the past filled the void in her mind. She always heard them. Over time she managed to quiet them to mere whispers, but now with this news, they overwhelmed her. Paralyzed her.

"That was the past. They can't hurt you anymore," she reminded herself. "That was the past." She had to pull it together for Big Mama's sake. Finally, she found the wherewithal to open her laptop and begin preparations to go back home.

Time waited for no one. Especially her.

Chapter 2

Janine wanted to end it all. Mostly, she wanted an end to the pain that ate away at her day after day, and month after month, and year after year. From this high up, death would be instant. She didn't want to suffer anymore. She told herself it would get better, but it didn't.

It was just some lie her brain had invented to deceive her heart. Every promise that anyone had ever made to her, went unfulfilled. She swallowed hard, watching the tiny figures below her carry on with their lives, completely unaware of the danger lurking above them. The urge to jump was intense tonight. And relentless.

A warm southeasterly breeze gusted through the window, carrying with it the scent of a distant rainstorm. Flashes of lightning lit up the horizon. Janine leaned her head against the windowsill. She wished she could talk to her, and then maybe she could explain what really happened. This is what her heart hoped for all these years, but her brain knew that no explanation in the world could bring back what they once had. The loneliness she felt every day was punishment enough for what she had done. Betrayal came at a high cost.

Her phone rang, startling her out of her thoughts. Who could that be? No one ever called this late. She let it ring. Probably the wrong number. The chime of a new voicemail piqued her interest. She closed the window and swiped her phone from the nightstand.

Perhaps it was the doctor calling with another proposition for her. She hated him more and more each day. He sickened her, the very thought of him turned her stomach. She wasn't sure how many more of his advances she could take before she completely snapped on him. She felt it coming. Years of suppressing it had her on the verge.

She glanced down at the phone and tapped the voicemail button. She listened. It was a message from her grandmother. Her heart sunk, she sounded extremely ill. Janine quickly redialed the number. Her heart raced. Her mind spun with thoughts of what could be wrong. Two months ago, when Janine last spoke to her, she didn't sound anything like this! Janine chewed her lip, waiting for the line to finally connect.

"Hello?"

Janine sighed with relief. "Big Mama? It's me, Janine."

"Hey, baby."

"Are you okay?"

"I can't say that I am."

Janine sat down on the edge of the bed. Maybelle Curtis was always all right, and when she wasn't, you didn't know about it. "What is it?" Janine asked. Her voice was calm, although inside she begged of a silent god who no longer recognized her voice.

"The doctors found some cancer in me."

"What? Where?"

"There's a big spot on my lungs. They think I might have some in my stomach, too."

Janine allowed two months to go by without calling and checking on her. She knew better. At eighty-four years of age, Maybelle needed someone to check on her regularly.

"Oh no," Janine gasped. She wanted to say more, but she couldn't get the words past the lump in her throat.

"Don't you worry now. I have lived a good long life, baby. When it's my time, I will be ready."

"But, I won't."

"Now, now. Don't you fret."

"How much time did they say, Big Mama?"

Maybelle went silent on the other line. The silence was deafening.

"How long?" she repeated.

"Two months, give or take."

"Two months!" she shouted. "Christ!"

"If you can, I need some help."

Janine ran her trembling fingers through her hair. When she glanced around her bedroom, nothing looked the same anymore. What used to be her favorite Picasso painting hanging above her bed, now looked like an eerie representation of the pain she felt inside of her heart. She wanted to scream. "Sure, what do you need help with?"

"Do you still know how to do medical stuff?"

"Like what?"

"Shots, taking blood pressure, and things like that?"

"Yes, ma'am."

"I need you to be here to help me with my meds. One of my medicines, I need shots, and I can't do it myself."

"Of course, Big Mama. Do you need more medicine?"

"Yes, maybe something for pain. The pain is awful."

Janine swallowed hard, forcing the lump in her throat down into her chest. She always wondered why bad things happen to good people. Maybelle was the most good-natured person she had ever met. "Yes, ma'am. I'll be sure to pack enough for you."

"Thank you so much."

"When do you need me to come?"

"As soon as you can. I would be happy with a weekend if that's all you can do."

"Yes. All right. I'll come right away." Janine squeezed the tears out of her eyes. She meditated over what Maybelle was asking of her. Thoughts of the duties that lie ahead tugged at her heart. She cursed herself for being so weak. Weakness is what got her where she is now. She needed to be stronger.

Maybelle held the line, not saying a word, while she gave Janine time to wrap her mind around what she just told her. "I wish it didn't have to be like this."

"I do too."

"I have a caretaker, but I would much rather have my girls here with me."

"I understand," Janine said.

"Have you spoken to your sister lately?"

"No, ma'am."

"Did you call the number I gave you or write her?"

"No."

"Why not, baby? I thought you wanted to talk to her again."

"I did... I do, but I am just afraid."

"Of what?"

"I'm not really sure. I just feel like she could never feel the same way about me ever again, and she's better off without me in her life." Janine sighed and held the phone. "Yeah, her life is better without me in it."

"She needs you as much as you need her," Maybelle said.

"I doubt she needs me."

Maybelle started coughing and wheezing. "I need to rest my voice."

"All right. Get some rest, Big Mama."

"I'll try."

"I love you, Big Mama."

"I love you too. Come and see me."

"I will, I promise. Goodbye."

Maybelle disconnected the line without saying goodbye. Still, down to this very day, she would never say goodbye on the phone. Janine sat frozen, dazed, and confused. After some time, she got up and walked back over to the window. A train of memories crossed her mind, one after another, endlessly assaulting her mind. She squeezed her eyes shut, forcing her tears to remain inside. She would not mourn for her right now. Not while she was still alive.

Chapter 3

Janine had already prepared herself for what the doctor might say. Lately, he'd been pissing her off—more than usual. It was the way he undressed her with his eyes and in the way he would "accidentally" brush up against her. Rumors around the office placed her in his bed, but that was the furthest thing from the truth. Perhaps if he wasn't a womanizing narcissist, she might have actually entertained the idea of dating him. She steered clear of his handsome face. She knew too many like him and they all broke her heart.

"You're requesting how much time?"

"At least three weeks, Dr. Newsome."

"That's a long time, Janine. What would I do without you?"

Her stomach turned. "I'm sorry, but this cannot be avoided. Could you temporarily authorize me to telecommute, and I'll work from my computer?"

Dr. Newsome leaned against Janine's filing cabinet and crossed his arms. "That may be possible. What, a week of telecommuting, and then you come back?"

Janine groaned. He reminded her so much of her father it made her sick. It was obvious that he wasn't going to let her go without complicating matters more. "No, sir. I need three weeks total time."

He shut the door and glided over to her desk. He sat on the edge and picked at his fingernail. "I don't think I can let you have so much time all at once, Janine."

"I need to go home and help my grandmother. It's terminal."

He leaned in closer, tracing figure eights on her desk. "You see, I'm terribly sorry about your grandmother's sickness, but this office would fall apart without you."

"That's hardly true," she pushed away from her desk and stood up. "Why are you being so difficult about this? I work hard for this office every single day!"

"It wouldn't have to be so difficult if you'd just give me what I want."

Janine bit her tongue, her jaw trembled as she fought back the words that so desperately needed to come out. "And what exactly is it you want from me, Doctor?"

"Let me take you out, wine and dine you, and maybe a little bit more, and then you can have all the vacation time you want."

She knew it was coming, so when his proposition came, she was prepared for it. "I will not go out with you. And quite frankly, for you to hold my deserved vacation time hostage in exchange for a date is not only morally wrong, but it's also ethically wrong." She walked over to the door and swung it open. Several coworkers were gathered around the front desk, chit-chatting about the usual office nonsense.

"Keep your voice down, Janine."

"I will not keep my voice down. I am highly offended that you would even have the audacity to proposition me this way!" Instantly, the office went silent. "My answer to you is no, Dr. Newsome. No, I will not allow you to take me on a date. No, I will not allow you to wine and dine me, and absolutely no way whatsoever, will I ever agree to a sexual relationship with you!"

"Janine!" he said with a hushed whisper.

Her face blazed with indignation. "No, I will not accept your offer in exchange for the authorization of my vacation time." She stormed over to her desk and grabbed her purse, laptop bag, and cell phone. "In fact, you can keep my vacation time, because I quit!" She heard gasps and muffled speech from her coworkers from outside of the door. The doctor had pushed her one inch too far.

"You don't mean that."

"You best believe I mean every word. You'll be hearing from my lawyer. Goodbye." She slammed the door behind her and avoided the eyes of everyone who watched her leave. Hopefully, the stance she took with him gave others the courage to do the same. At least this was one thing she could do right. She ignored her office mates and stormed out of the front door. And she never looked back.

***

Lena tucked the last pair of jeans into her suitcase and zipped it shut. She looked around the room, taking a mental picture of everything gathered for the trip. She had three bags full of clothing and two carry-ons full of other necessities. She made sure to pack everything that she thought she would need. That way, she reduced the odds of needing to run into town and inadvertently into someone she didn't want to see.

For years, she prepared her mind for this. For the time when she would go home and see the same people who had hurt and betrayed her. Oddly enough, she realized that even if her mind was ready for this, her heart wasn't. She yanked the last suitcase off the bed and placed it with the others by the door. Her cell phone chimed with a text message:

Nadia: Are you sleeping?

Lena: I wish. Aren't you supposed to be working?

She placed her phone on the nightstand and pulled the suitcases into the living room. She knew she should be sleeping, but sleep was a luxury that would just have to wait. She glanced around the room and nodded approvingly at her own progress at such short notice. She returned to her room and picked up her phone.

Nadia: I'm on my lunch break. I was worried about you.

Lena sat on the edge of the bed, her eyes burned from fatigue and sleep deprivation. Last night was another sleepless night. She was so busy making submissions that she forgot to take her sleep medication, and she paid dearly for it. Her anxiety was at an all-time high. She could hear her nerves vibrating in her ears. Her entire body, even down to the molecular level, hummed with anxiety.

Lena: I'm okay right now. Just packing.
Nadia: Have you slept at all?
Lena: Nope

She closed her eyes and laid her head on the pillow. She couldn't lie, it was incredibly refreshing to relax for a brief minute. The pillow wrapped her head in a warm embrace, one that she so desperately needed. "Just five minutes," she told herself. "Give me just five minutes." Her body willed for sleep, but her mind raced with thoughts and voices from the past. Voices she knew she would soon hear again. Was five minutes of peace too much to ask for? She turned over and opened her eyes to see bouncing dots in Nadia's message box.

Nadia: Try to get some sleep. I'll drive the first leg.
Lena: You worked a double tonight. I think you need the rest more than I do.
Nadia: Sleep well. I'll be home in an hour.

Lena slipped her phone underneath her and closed her eyes again. The next thing she knew, she was awakened by a loud crashing sound. "What was that?" she gasped, sitting straight up in the bed. She grabbed her phone and checked the time. It was almost four o'clock in the morning.

"Sorry!" Nadia yelled from the front room. "I dropped a plate."

Lena got up and joined Nadia in the front room. "You didn't hurt yourself, did you?"

"Nope."

"Good. How was work tonight?"

"Sucked. As usual." The microwave buzzer chimed. Nadia yanked open the door and grabbed the plate inside. She sat down at the table and stabbed at her meal, "Chris, the new supervisor from Zone 4, tried to give me a hard time about my request."

"Oh, really?" Lena took a seat beside her and caressed her shoulder. "Were you approved?"

"Yeah, but I literally had to state reasons why he was legally required to approve my request."

Lena chuckled lightly. "I bet he didn't like that, did he?"

"He sure didn't. He threatened to write me up. I told him I would like to see him try because my many years of service with the company was spotless."

"You pulled rank on him?"

"You know I did."

They shared a laugh before silence settled over them. "I'm surprised you haven't accepted a promotion by now. You would be what, a regional manager by now?"

Nadia chuckled. "Not quite a regional, but close."

"Why haven't you reached out for more?" Lena had asked this question before, on numerous occasions, but Nadia only shrugged off a response. She did it again this time.

"I know what you're thinking, Mother."

"You don't know what I'm thinking."

Nadia shook her head. "You think that I lack the ambition, enthusiasm and desire to better myself."

Lena cleared her throat softly. "That's not what I'm thinking."

"I'm happy doing what I'm doing. I go to work, work, and come home. I don't need anything more." Nadia was an introvert. If she was given the options of going out with her friends or staying home, she would most likely choose the latter.

Lena kept her close, perhaps too close, protecting her from the horrible world that waited for her outside. It was supposed to be a foolproof plan to protect her from evil, but as she sat and looked at her daughter, Lena came to the realization that maybe she had shielded her a little too well. "Don't you need your friends?"

"I'm good."

"What about Richard?"

"What about him?"

"When was the last time you two went out on a date? I thought he wanted to go steady?"

Nadia glared at her. "Really?"

"What?"

"My personal life is not up for discussion right now. We're talking about work."

Lena sat back in her seat and nodded. "I know we were talking about work, but I wanted to know about Richard."

Nadia pushed away from the table and took her plate back to the microwave. She nuked it for another minute. She stood there silent, watching the plate revolve around inside. After the buzzer sounded, she retrieved the plate and retook her seat across from Lena. "He dumped me."

"What? Why?"

Nadia laughed. "For the same reason why I'm always getting dumped."

Lena's heart dropped in her chest. "Oh, sweet pea, I'm so sorry."

"Don't be. That just proves that he wasn't the one. No matter how much I thought he was."

"How long have you been broken up?"

"Two months now." She shoved a meatball into her mouth and held Lena's gaze. Tears twinkled in her eyes, but they never fell.

"I know it hurts to break up. But someone else will come along."

Nadia blinked away her tears and inhaled deeply. "I want my first time to be special and with someone I'm going to be with forever."

"I can understand that." Lena reached over and took her hand, squeezing it gently. "I am so proud of you for making this decision for yourself."

"Thanks."

"And I'm sorry I set you up with a jerk."

Nadia laughed. "He got over me really quick."

"Oh?"

"Um-hmm. Word got back to me that he slept with Meghan a week later. They're together now."

"Wait. Meghan from the Tomahawk Diner?"

"Yep."

"Oh, wow."

"They deserve each other." She twirled the spaghetti onto her fork and shoved the last bit of it into her mouth. "Good riddance," she mumbled.

Lena smiled and got up from the table. She noticed that Nadia had already packed up the cooler with the perishables. A quick inspection of the kitchen revealed that she didn't need to do anything else to get ready for this long haul. Nadia had taken care of everything on the list. "Thanks for packing the food, sweet pea."

"No problem. It wouldn't be a road trip without snacks along the way, right?"

"Right." Lena answered vacantly as she dragged the cooler over to the front door. She checked her phone again. "If we can leave by six, that would be great."

"Are we driving straight through?"

"I'm afraid so unless it gets too rough and we need to sleep."

"How long will it take to get there?"

"Figuring in stops to fill up, to eat, and stretch our legs," she ran a shaky hand through her hair, "Probably about sixteen and a half hours. Give or take."

"Oh my God!"

"Hey, you're the one begging to come. Changing your mind already?"

"Not really. That's just a long drive."

"I know." Lena's voice trailed off. Her conscience beat her for staying away from Big Mama for so long. So many years had gone by. Valuable years that she couldn't get back.

"Mom?"

"Huh?" Lena blinked away her thoughts and glanced up at her.

"I said, if you want to go now, we can go."

"Oh..." She looked around the room one more time before nodding, "All right. We should hit the road. What about the mail?"

"I can request a mail hold or temporary mail forward to a Georgia address."

"Hmm," Lena mused. Something as simple as deciding what to do with the mail proved to be too difficult at the moment.

"Or we can decide what to do on one of our stops? I'll just download the app," Nadia added in.

"Sure." Lena's heart drummed in her chest. She was about to leave the safety of the place she called home and venture out into the world, back to a place where her worst nightmares occurred. A place where no matter how hard she ran, and no matter which corner she turned, she could never escape the boogeyman who chased after her. And by some weird twist of fate, she was going to drag her daughter right into the middle of it. She smiled at Nadia and Nadia smiled back at her. She hoped Nadia would forgive her for the secrets she had kept from her.

Chapter 4

Maybelle gazed out of the window while her caretaker finished drawing her blood. Daisy was gentle with her technique, being careful not to injure Maybelle's delicate skin. She smiled as Daisy looked up at her and patted her gently on the arm.

"Almost done, Mrs. Curtis."

"How much blood does the doctor want from me today?"

"Just one more vial, and I'll be finished." Daisy was very attentive, going far above and beyond her job description to make Maybelle feel comfortable. She was Maybelle's personal favorite from the many who were sent from the home care service. Daisy's presence was warm and welcoming, a real joy to be around.

But now, as Maybelle's condition worsened, she needed to be with family more than anything. "My granddaughters are coming."

"I remember you telling me that you asked them to come. I'm so happy to hear they agreed."

"They are a stubborn bunch, but they both are coming."

"That's wonderful." Daisy smiled. She released the rubber band from Maybelle's arm and pulled the needle out. "There, finished." She placed the last vial of blood specimen into the sample bag and removed her gloves. "When will they be arriving?"

Maybelle glanced at the clock. "Anytime now. One of them is coming all the way from Kansas. Last time she called she was just passing through Birmingham."

"Oh, that's exciting."

"It sure is. Magdalena hasn't been home in ages." Her voice lowered with a twinge of sadness.

"Why hasn't she been home?"

Maybelle wiped the sweat off her brow with her sleeve. "People and their evil ways chased my baby away."

Daisy acknowledged with a nod and continued to pack up her utensils.

"The other one lives in Alpharetta."

"Does she visit often?"

"Yes. She comes to see me every now and then when she comes to town."

"That's good."

"I just hate they have to come home with me like this."

Daisy zipped up her bag and knelt down beside Maybelle. "Don't say that, Mrs. Curtis. I'm sure if they minded, they wouldn't be coming."

"It's not so much I worry about them minding, I just worry the sicker I get, the harder it will be on them."

Daisy caressed her gently on the arm. "I understand your concerns, but right now, we all want what's best for you."

Maybelle's eyes danced across her wall of pictures. Dozens of frames decorated the wall, telling the story of her family's life. So many years were represented. Some great years, many good years, and then the empty years after Lena left.

"I wish it didn't take me getting sick to bring them home."

"I know," Daisy whispered. "But the important thing is they're coming back, right?"

Maybelle nodded and touched Daisy lightly on the chin. "You've been so good to me. The Lord will take good care of you, too."

Daisy chuckled. "Thanks, Mrs. Curtis. I need all the help I can get."

"Do you need more money?"

"I could always use more money."

They shared a laugh. "No, I mean, do you need more pay for what you are doing for me?"

"You pay me enough to take care of my immediate needs."

"Do you need more money for yourself? You're taking care of that little boy, so you need to be able to do it."

"Mrs. Curtis, you have given me more than anyone has ever given me to take care of them. You're very generous."

"Will you just answer my question?" Maybelle knew that she would never ask her for more money. But she has noticed that Daisy's work pants are a little worn and she's gone without lunch several days in a row.

Daisy eventually lowered her head. "Yes, ma'am, I do need a little more money."

"All right, then." Maybelle patted her hand softly. "Hand me my checkbook over there," she said, pointing to the heavy chest dresser by the front door.

Daisy retrieved it and handed it to her.

"You should've told me before if you needed more, honey."

"I know, but I was ashamed. I've just had a lot of medical bills because I don't have insurance."

"I understand that." Maybelle scribbled on the check and ripped it out. She glanced over it one last time before handing it to her. "This should help, even long after I'm gone."

Daisy took the check and gazed at it. Her eyes immediately filled with tears. "Oh, Mrs. Curtis, I can't accept this!"

"Why not?"

"It's too much! I mean, I could never repay this."

"I'm not going to be here for you to repay it, now stop fretting. It's for you and your baby boy."

Daisy cupped her mouth and shook her head. "But—"

"No buts, please accept it as a gift of gratitude."

After some time, Daisy finally nodded in agreement and embraced her. "Thank you so much!"

"It's my pleasure. You've taken care of me so well for the past few months, I want to repay you."

Daisy held on to her for a while before she finally pulled away. "I should get your afternoon dosages ready."

"All right now."

Daisy folded the check and slid it into her pocket before disappearing into the kitchen. Maybelle smiled, happy that she could ease the stress of someone who'd taken such good care of her.

She heard a car pulling up outside. She got up as quickly as she could and shuffled to the window, catching a glimpse of Lena as she was getting out of the car.

"Oh! My baby's home!" she shouted with joy. "Daisy, my baby's home!"

Maybelle walked briskly to the front door and opened it. She couldn't hide her excitement even if she tried.

"Oh, my baby's home!" she repeated as she outstretched her arms towards her. She held back her tears as she watched Lena approach her. She'd dreamed of this moment for years, the moment when her baby came back home to her. It was finally happening.

Lena stepped up onto the porch and pulled Maybelle into a loving embrace. As Lena tightened her grip around her beloved grandmother, she lifted her just a bit from the ground. She was so light now.

"I'm so sorry, Big Mama." Lena choked out, "I should've come home sooner."

"Shh, it's okay, baby." Maybelle patted her softly on the back, "You're home now. That's all that matters."

Lena buried her face into Maybelle's shoulder and cried softly. Maybelle comforted her by whispering soft reassurances into her ear. Eventually, Lena pulled away and swiped her tears away with the backs of her hands.

"Just look at you," Maybelle said. "You haven't changed, not one bit. Just a little older."

"And wiser," Lena added.

Maybelle chuckled and then she grabbed her chest and coughed hard. Daisy appeared at the door and came to her side. Maybelle touched her gently on the arm, reassuring her that she was okay. She was just a bit excited.

"I'm okay," Maybelle said as she peeked around Lena's shoulder to see Nadia walking up behind her. "Is this who I think it is?" A smile as bright as the morning sun graced her face.

"Yes, ma'am," Lena said, "This is Nadia. My daughter."

Nadia stepped up to Lena's side and took Maybelle's hand. It was then that the tears that she had been holding back came out.

"Oh, my heavens!" Maybelle gasped. "I have waited so long to see your face, baby."

Nadia smiled and tightened her grip on Maybelle's hand. She glanced over at Lena, who gave her a look of approval. "It's so nice to finally meet you, Mrs. Curtis."

Maybelle's eyes widened, and she shot Lena a look of hot displeasure.

"Mrs. Curtis? The only people who call me Mrs. Curtis are salesmen and Daisy here," she said, nudging Daisy with her elbow. This solicited a light chuckle from her. "And the only reason why she calls me Mrs. Curtis is because she feels weird calling me Big Mama."

Nadia nodded and smiled. "I'm sorry."

"Don't be. You call me Big Mama, you got that, baby?"

"Yes, ma'am."

Maybelle pulled her in for another embrace; this time, she held her tightly and kissed her gently on the cheek.

"My heart almost burst out of my chest when I saw your Mama here, but when I finally laid my eyes on you... the Good Lord as my witness, I can't tell you how much joy I feel."

"Thank you," Nadia said.

"No. Thank you. Thank you both for coming."

Lena came to Maybelle's side and put her arm around her. "Let's go sit inside. It's hot out."

"Good idea," Maybelle said.

They all went inside and took seats around the kitchen table. Inside wasn't any cooler than outside. A box fan sat in the window above the sink. It was going at high speed and blowing that hot Georgia air into the room.

Maybelle always reasoned that as long as the fan was blowing, it was cooling off the room, but in reality, it was just pulling the humid air inside faster.

"I see you never broke down and got the house wired with central air," Lena said as she picked up a paper plate and started fanning herself.

"There was no point in wasting all that money to do such a thing. You survived all those years here in the heat of the summer and the cold of winter."

"Just barely."

Daisy arrived at the table and placed a glass of ice water in front of Maybelle.

"Would you girls like Daisy to make you something?"

"Sure," Lena said. "What do you have?"

"You haven't been gone that long that you can't remember what Big Mama keeps in her icebox, now have you?" Maybelle asked.

Lena laughed lightly and nodded. "We'll take some iced tea."

While Daisy busied herself at the island preparing the drinks, Lena and Maybelle sat quietly and looked at each other.

"I can't believe you're here, baby." She reached over and took Lena's hand.

"I'm sorry it took me so long to come back. And," Lena lowered her head. "I'm sorry it's under these circumstances. I should've done better."

"Now, now. There ain't no sense in crying over spilled milk."

"Yeah."

Daisy brought the glasses of tea back to the table and placed them down. She patted Maybelle on the shoulder and disappeared into the front room.

Lena sipped on her beverage and kept her eyes glued to the table. Her hands trembled slightly as she cupped them around the glass in an attempt to hide the fact. But of course, Maybelle noticed.

"Magdalena?" Maybelle said her name the same way she always had when she was a young girl. The way she called her name left Lena with no doubt in her mind that her Big Mama loved her.

"Yes, ma'am?" Lena glanced up; her eyes were filled to the brim with tears.

"I mean it. Don't worry about what you think you should've done. What really matters to me is that you are here now, okay?"

Lena nodded briskly. "All right."

Maybelle smiled warmly and tugged at Lena's hands. "I am so happy you're finally home."

Lena got up from her seat and knelt down in front of Maybelle and embraced her. Maybelle pulled her in close to her heart, resting Lena's head safe in her bosom.

"I love you," Lena whispered.

"I know you do, baby. I love you more than you could ever know."

Maybelle took a few minutes to comfort Lena. There was no rush. Nothing at the moment was more important than sharing this tender moment with her. Eventually, Lena pulled away from her and took her seat back at the table.

She looked over at Nadia, who reached out and touched her lightly on the arm.

"I got most of the rooms cleaned out. You can have your old room, Lena. And your baby can stay in the room next to mine."

"Okay," Lena said.

"I need help getting the room connecting to yours cleaned."

"Oh, really? Why?"

"Some more family is coming to stay to help ease the load on you girls."

"Oh." Lena frowned at her. "Who's coming?"

Maybelle smiled and fanned herself with the newspaper circular. "You'll see."

Lena narrowed her eyes at her and processed what she said. She only said two words, but the way she smiled and looked as if her mind was replaying memories made Lena extremely nervous. She knew her Big Mama well. And she knew that Big Mama was up to something.

"Hmm, okay." Lena took her glass and finished off the tea in one gulp. She then rose from her seat. "I'm going to go get our bags so we can get settled in and help you clean."

"All right, baby."

Lena motioned for Nadia to join her, and they walked out to the car. Her mind raced with thoughts of who Big Mama had invited to come. It could have been anyone. An aunt or a cousin or anyone. But her heart began to burn with the realization of the one person whom she'd most likely invited.

For years, Maybelle had kept in touch with Lena. She'd asked her to come home every year for Mother's Day, Thanksgiving, and Christmas. But Lena couldn't ever see herself going back to celebrate with the same family who'd banished her. If she'd gone back, a scarlet letter would be hung around her neck for all of Archer to see.

She wanted to do it for Big Mama. But the fear she had was too strong to take the first step. Every year when she'd told her that she couldn't come back home, Maybelle would express her desire to see her girls together again.

Her girls...

Lena's heart clenched in her chest. She knew she was coming. And she wasn't ready for her.

"Mom?"

Nadia's voice snapped her out of her panicked thoughts. "Huh?"

"I said, do you want me to bring everything in?"

"Uhm..." Lena ran her fingers through her hair and eyed the stuffed Equinox. "No, we'll just bring in our suitcases, laptops. The other stuff can wait until morning."

"Okay." Nadia reached in and started grabbing the suitcases. Those suitcases were as light as pillows in comparison to the packages that she handled on a nightly basis at UPS. She had no problem carrying in four bags with one trip.

Lena leaned against the car and took a deep breath to still her racing heart.

"This is about Big Mama, and not you." She told herself. "We are here to care for Big Mama."

Her words calmed her heart enough for her to grab the last of the suitcases and drag them inside. Once inside, she sat down next to Maybelle and watched Nadia finish the task. Maybelle just smiled and watched her walk back and forth.

Lena took Maybelle's leathery hand and held it. "I'm going to take my things to my room."

"All right."

Lena took the handle of her two suitcases and rolled them into her old bedroom. She was amazed that it looked the exact same way it did when she left twenty-four years ago. It almost seemed like Maybelle had locked the door and thrown away the key. Nothing was touched.

A flood of memories hit her as she walked further into the room. Echoey voices and sounds that she'd so long ago tucked away and forgotten bounced around in her head. She caught a faint scent of her old favorite perfume, which made her gag.

She sat down on the bed and sighed when she saw a handwritten note still sitting on her nightstand. She picked it up. The memories of the day she received it and of the events surrounding it, assaulted her mind. She brought it to her nose and inhaled. It still smelled like him.

Her heart quivered inside. She placed it back in its original place and then picked up a stack of her old drawings. She smiled, thinking about when she drew each picture. She was happy then, in love and innocent.

Her first instinct when she walked into the room was to turn right back around and get the heck out of dodge. But this wasn't about her. She was here for Big Mama. She was sick and dying, and her last wish was for her to come home. It was the least that she could do since she'd stayed hidden away like a coward for so long.

There was a light knock on the door. She glanced up and saw Nadia standing there. "Hey. What's up?" She placed the stack of drawings back down on the nightstand.

Nadia stepped in and brought her a garment bag full of her shirts. "Here's the stuff that needs to be hung up."

"Thanks, sweet pea." Lena's voice was low and emotionless.

"You okay?"

"Yes, I am. Being here brings back a lot of memories."

"I imagine," Nadia said looking around the room.

It was a regular-sized room. It was decorated with posters of Lena's favorite singers at the time; Boyz-II-Men, Prince, and Mariah Carey. In the corner, was a single bookshelf stocked with a full Encyclopedia Britannica set, and various other books.

Nadia scanned over the entire room in a matter of seconds, her eyes settling on Lena's dresser by the window. She walked over to it, transfixed by something that had caught her eye. She picked up a small pink bootie that looked to have been made from hobby yarn.

"What's this?"

"I made it."

"I didn't know you crocheted?"

"Yeah, one of the many things Big Mama taught me."

"It's a sock?"

Lena laughed softly and sighed. "Actually, it's a bootie that I made for you. I was planning on making a full set of booties, mittens and a beanie, but I didn't have time."

"Have time?"

Lena nodded and joined her at the dresser. She took the bootie from her and toyed with it.

"Yeah," She cleared her throat softly. "I wanted to complete it so it would be ready when you were born, but..." Her voice trailed off as she stared at the delicate little item in her hands.

"But what?"

Lena gave the bootie back to her. "But I was forced to leave home."

Nadia gasped. "Because of me? Big Mama made you leave?"

Lena shushed her gently and caressed her face. "No, baby, not because of you. And no, it wasn't Big Mama. She wanted me to stay."

Nadia just stared at her, her eyes already brimming with tears. She didn't utter the question that Lena could see floating around in her eyes.

"I promise you; you will get your answers while we are here. But right now, I just need to focus on helping Big Mama." She nodded and waited for Nadia to agree with her.

"May I keep this?" Nadia asked, clenching the bootie close to her heart.

"Of course. I made it for you."

"How did you know I was going to be a girl?"

Lena shrugged. "I didn't really know. We just hoped. And if you turned out to be a boy, you'd just have to wear pink."

"We?"

Lena nodded slowly. "Yes." She reached and toyed with the bootie again. "Your father wanted a little girl, and I wanted whatever he wanted."

Nadia just stared at her. This was the first time Lena spoke about him with such warmth and affection.

"You both wanted me?"

Lena nodded; a veil of sadness fell over her face. "More than anything," she whispered.

Nadia opened her mouth to respond, but she was interrupted by another knock at the door. Lena peeked around to see Daisy standing at the door.

"Hey Daisy," Lena greeted her.

"Hi. Mrs. Curtis asked if you would mind cooking dinner tonight?"

Lena chuckled lightly. "Of course, I don't mind. Is there something in particular she would like?"

"She's supposed to be on a special diet, but she hasn't been keeping to it. So, her doctor allows her to have whatever she wants, just in moderation."

"Gotcha. So, what would she like tonight?"

"She would like meatloaf, mashed potatoes, corn, and cornbread," She read from the piece of paper in her hand. "With sweet potato pie for dessert."

"Wow, I'm almost sorry I asked. What, no tea?"

Daisy glanced down at her notes and then, "And a gallon of tea." She winked and disappeared out of the doorway.

Lena stood there, thankful for the interruption, but realizing that Nadia was still hanging on to her last statement. She knew Nadia wanted her to give her more to work with. She could feel it, but she wasn't ready to dive into that sea of emotions just yet. Although that time was coming.

She glanced down at her watch. "I better get dinner started. Would you like to help me?"

Her question met no response. She turned around and saw Nadia gazing down at the bootie, playing with it in her hands.

"Sweet pea?"

Nadia glanced up, "Oh. If you don't mind, I'll start cleaning out that room she needs if that's okay."

"Oh, well, sure."

"That way, it'll be cleaned up when the other company gets here."

Lena nodded. "Great idea. Good looking out."

Nadia tucked the bootie into her pocket and headed for the door. Lena took one last glance around her room. Her heart warmed slowly with thoughts and memories that she'd long ago locked away.

Chapter 5

Janine couldn't believe how much her mother had aged since the last time she'd seen her. She looked about ten years older, frailer, and sadder. The hollowed look in her eyes revealed the reason. She was a product of her environment. Living with the burden of loving a man who is incapable of loving in return. A man full of hate and contentiousness. He was draining the life out of her.

"How long are you in town for, honey?" Linda Chamberlain's voice was softer than usual.

"A couple of months. Maybelle is not doing too well."

"Oh?" She took a seat in the recliner by the fireplace and lifted her cup of tea to her lips. "What's happening with her?"

Janine lowered her eyes. "She's got cancer."

"Oh, my stars," she said, shaking her head slowly. "How are you going to be able to help?"

Janine shrugged. "She has specific medical requests and I believe she just needs my practical help around the house."

Linda sipped quietly. "Who else is going to be there?"

Janine sat down next to her in her father's chair. "I don't know yet. Perhaps a caretaker."

"Hmm," she said, sitting the cup down. "Is there a possibility that she might come?"

"She who?"

Linda chuckled softly. "Why are you playing ignorant, honey?"

"Oh..." Janine grazed her fingers lightly through her hair, pulling out the kinks of frustration as they mounted. "I'm not certain. Maybe."

"When was the last time you spoke to her?"

"I haven't. Not since the day she left, and I haven't seen her either."

"Are you hoping she comes?"

"What kind of question is that, Mother?"

"I'm just curious."

Janine rolled her eyes towards the kitchen and caught sight of her father standing and listening to their conversation. His eyes were still dark with hatred and contempt.

She turned her attention back to her mother. "No, I'm not hoping that she comes because, quite frankly, I cannot handle the guilt of knowing what I did to her."

Linda nodded vacantly and took another sip of tea. "I wish you would stop blaming yourself for what happened. You did the right thing."

"The right thing?"

"Yes."

"If it was the right thing, then why did so many people have to get hurt? If it was the right thing, then why did we do what we did to her?"

Linda winced in response to Janine's question and looked over her shoulder. Janine's father approached them. She turned and met his angry gaze. She stood to greet him. She would not be caught off guard this time.

"We are never to speak of that girl in this house," he said.

"That girl?"

"Yes."

"That girl is my best friend! At least she was until you interfered with our lives," Janine snapped back.

"If my memory serves me correctly, you volunteered the information," he said with a smile.

"But I didn't know you were going to hurt her like that! I didn't know you were going to hurt them like you did!"

Roger Chamberlain's nostrils flared angrily as his face turned almost crimson in color. He took her by the arm and yanked her closer. "It's been twenty something years, Janine. Get over it."

She pulled her arm from his grip and pushed him away. "You don't intimidate me, Dad. I'm not a child anymore."

"I never said you were a child."

"Don't ever touch me like that again. Do you understand?"

Roger crossed his arms; a smirk creasing his mouth as he shook his head. He glanced over at Linda, who immediately looked away from him. "I see living in the city has made you forget where you come from."

"Oh, I remember where I come from. But I will not be disrespected or manhandled by anyone. Especially not by my father."

"I see." Roger rubbed his hand over his perfectly trimmed goatee and sat down in his chair. He reached into his pocket and pulled out a cigar.

Janine backed away from him. After he lit it, he took a few deep puffs and exhaled a massive plume above his head. "Do you need money or something? Is that why you're here?" he asked.

Janine stared at him in disbelief. She couldn't believe two things. One, that he was her father and, two, that her mother has stayed with him for so long.

"No, I don't need money."

"How's your savings?"

"Why is that important?"

"Because money is important."

Janine sighed and ran her fingers through her hair. "My savings is fine, Dad. I've doubled it since I got established."

"Why not tripled?"

"Because I have to live and work in an expensive town."

"Are you still working for the dentist?"

"What's with the third degree?"

"Just making sure you can handle life."

Janine chuckled and grabbed her purse. "I can handle life just fine, Dad. Especially the financial aspect of it."

"No boyfriend yet? You know your mother and I would like to have grandchildren one day. And we all know your brother ain't gonna give us none." He smiled at her, and the very act made her stomach lurch inside.

The thought of bringing a child into this world and having it bear the legacy of the Chamberlain's name was something that had always struck panic inside of her. She had already made up her mind that she would never have a child. She didn't want it to carry the burden that the Chamberlain name forced her to bear.

"No, no boyfriend," She walked over and gave her mother a kiss on the cheek, "I'm content being alone."

She wished her mother was as strong as her name sounded, but she was just a weak shell of a human being. Thanks to her father.

"I'll come by in a couple days, Mom. Maybe we can go to lunch."

"Oh, can't you stay longer?"

Janine glanced down at her watch, but she knew she wasn't going to stay. She couldn't stay in a home where the air was as thick and suffocating as this.

"It's already getting late, and I want to get to Maybelle's and get settled before nightfall."

"Why don't you stay here?" Linda asked.

"Because I've already promised her that I would stay there. And I plan on keeping my promise."

"Very well."

Janine reached down and embraced her. "When I go home, you and Jack are coming with me." Her mother nodded and continued to nurse her cup.

Janine waved goodbye to her father and exited the house. Outside, she could finally breathe. She wasn't sure if it was just her imagination, but it really felt like she couldn't breathe in there. The house was full of memories. More bad ones than good. Some of those memories could never be erased from her mind.

She was just about to get into her car when she heard footsteps running up behind her. She spun around, sure that her father was behind her. "Stop right there!"

The shadowy figure stopped and put his hands up in mock surrender. "Janine?"

Instantly her heart relaxed. She outstretched her arms and walked over to him. "Jack!"

Jackson, or Jack as his friends and family called him, came over and embraced her with a tight bear hug. He picked her up and spun her around several times before setting her back down on her feet.

He towered over her, standing at six feet, four inches tall. He was a gentle giant. She took his hand and led him back over to the porch so she could see him in the light. This was the first time she'd seen him in a few months. The last time she visited, he was away with Roger on a fishing trip.

"How are you, Janine?" Jack asked.

She just smiled at him and stared up into his piercing blue eyes. She reached and caressed his cheek. "I'm better now that I've seen my big brother's handsome face."

He laughed happily and smiled. According to Janine, he was still the most handsome guy in the world.

"What? You're growing a beard now?"

"You like it?"

Janine ran her fingers over a scar that traveled from the edge of his ear down to his cheek. The hair that he'd already grown covered it somewhat. A little more length and the scar that became his scarlet letter would be concealed.

"I absolutely love it." She swallowed her heart back down into her chest. The memories of that night came alive in her mind as she gazed at him.

Looking up into his eyes, she saw nothing but love and happiness. She wished that she could have the same peace that he had. And his innocence.

"Mom told me you were leaving. You just got here."

"Oh, I'm not leaving leaving. I'll be in town for a couple of months."

He nodded and shifted his weight on his feet. "You don't want to stay here with me?"

"I'm sorry, Jack, but I can't stay here."

"Why not?"

She sighed and shoved her hands in her pockets. Explaining to Jack why she couldn't stay at the Chamberlain estate was harder than she thought.

"Dad and I don't get along well enough for me to stay for an extended length of time."

"Oh, okay."

"I'm sorry, big brother."

"It's okay. I got a new job."

"You did? Where?" she asked, turning and walking back to her car. He followed in her steps carefully, almost walking on her heels.

"Bailey's."

"What? That's awesome! What are you doing? I bet they have you working as a manager."

He laughed, "No, no. I'm just a bagger. I help people to their cars."

"Aww, congratulations. Do you like it?"

"Yes. Mr. Bailey thinks I'm too slow to be manager, but he says I have strength to bag groceries."

"He said you were too slow?"

He lowered his head. "Yeah. But it's okay. I know it's true."

Janine's heart burned inside. "No, it's not true."

"You're just saying that because you're my sister," he laughed.

"I am biased, but in this case, Mr. Bailey is also wrong. You could be anything you want to be. Even police chief!"

"Wow, police chief?"

"Yep. You know Uncle Ty can't be chief all his life. He's getting old."

Jack laughed. "I would be a cool chief."

"You sure would. I think you would clean up this old town really well."

"Yeah, and I wouldn't let nobody hurt anybody or bully them."

"See, you already have my vote." She smiled at the way his eyes seemed to glaze over as he contemplated being police chief one day. Her parents always told her to stop giving him false hopes and goals too far for him to reach. But in her mind, he could achieve anything.

Even the office of chief. It would be a new age for Archer when an uncorrupt Chamberlain finally took office.

He reached for the handle and opened the door for her. "Maybe I can come over and we can play video games or walk? I can bring my PlayStation."

"Oh... Jack, that would be nice, but I'll let you know about that, okay? Let me get settled first and assess the situation."

"Oh, okay." She could hear the sadness in his voice. She hugged him tightly and patted him on the back.

"You look so good, Jack."

"Thanks."

And she meant it, too. The burdens that they carried because of the Chamberlain legacy were two entirely different entities. Hers could be lifted with therapy maybe, but his would remain on his shoulders an entire lifetime. Somehow, he looked as if he was at peace.

She slipped into her car and waited for him to shut the door. "Text me, okay?"

"Okay."

"Goodnight, Jack."

"Night." He backed away from the car.

She turned the ignition and drove off down the long driveway lined with dogwood trees. She glanced up into the rearview mirror. She felt tears stinging the backs of her eyes as she watched him wave goodbye.

She'd already made it up in her mind that once she'd finished her promised stay with Maybelle, she was going to take him back home with her. Her mother could stay if she wanted, but she was going to take Jack.

She waited at the end of the drive before turning onto the main roadway. There were so many things that needed to be accomplished. She needed to get to Maybelle's and take her into her arms and hug her. That's all she wanted to do at this moment.

Without further hesitation, she turned off onto the main road and headed to Maybelle's house.

Chapter 6

Lena had just placed the last dish onto the countertop when Nadia came into the room. She heard her hum with delight over the intoxicating aromas. "Something smells absolutely delicious!" she said.

Lena glanced over her shoulder. "Well, I hope it's as good as it smells."

"I'm sure it will be."

"What have you been up to, sweet pea?"

Nadia sat down at the table. "I finished cleaning up the room and then I helped Big Mama sort through some old papers."

"Oh, that was nice of you."

"It's the least I could do." Nadia toyed with the saltshaker on the table. "Hey, did she say who is coming?"

Lena shook her head slowly. "No, she didn't say, but I think I know."

"Who?"

Lena continued at the stove and temporarily ignored the question. In time, she came and sat down across from Nadia and removed her apron.

"More than likely she invited Janine."

"Who is Janine?"

Lena shrugged. "She was my childhood best friend. We were inseparable. Big Mama thought of her as a daughter."

"Why are you using past tense?"

Lena smiled half-heartedly and cleared her throat. "Because she was all those things to me. She was like my sister. But she betrayed me, and we had a falling out."

"How did she betray you?"

She knew Nadia was going to ask the question. It was the next logical one, but she didn't want to answer it. It was the source of some of the most bitter feelings that she'd ever felt in her life. Janine is the reason why she trusts no one today and she is the reason why she's afraid to love and let someone in.

"That bad, huh?" Nadia yanked a napkin from the holder in the middle of the table and handed it to her.

Lena took it and daubed her eyes. She didn't get emotional often, but whenever she thought about Janine's betrayal, the tears came easy.

"Yeah, it's bad and just plain sad. I got hurt pretty badly because of it. But not just that. It was the principle of the matter. I thought we were closer than that. But blood proved to be thicker than water."

"Wow, I'm sorry, Mom."

"It's okay."

"How are you going to deal with it if it is her?"

Lena shrugged. "I'm here for Big Mama, and no one else."

Nadia nodded with understanding. She touched her lightly on the arm and got up from her seat. "Should I go tell Big Mama that dinner is ready?"

"Yes. And while you're doing that, I'm going to make a plate for Uncle Zeke."

"Uncle Zeke?"

Lena chuckled. "Yes, Uncle Zeke basically lives in his room," she said pointing to the right of the kitchen. "You won't see him much, but he does need to be fed."

"Okay. Gotcha."

Lena took a nicely portioned plate to her uncle in the back room and returned before Maybelle and Nadia had made it to the kitchen. Maybelle walked extremely slow. She could tell that she was tired.

"Are you ready to eat, Big Mama?" Lena asked.

"My, oh heavens. Something smells good in here."

Lena placed a prepared plate down in front of her. She went light on the portion size but gave her everything she asked for.

"Per your request, Big Mama."

Maybelle smiled and bent down to smell the aroma of the meal. "Everything looks delicious, baby. I sure taught you well."

"Yes, you sure did."

Nadia sat down at her place, and Lena served her meal. After serving herself a modest portion, she sat with them and dined. They really didn't say much to each other. Lena and Nadia watched her attempt to eat her food. She didn't seem to have much of an appetite.

After about fifteen minutes, Maybelle pushed away from the table and reached for Nadia's hand.

"Can you help me to my chair, Magdalena?" she asked Nadia.

Nadia glanced over at Lena and frowned. Lena reached over and touched Maybelle lightly on the arm.

"Big Mama?" Lena said softly.

Maybelle looked over at her and then back at Nadia. "Oh, Lord. I'm sorry, baby, you just look so much like your Mama, I got confused."

"It's quite all right," Nadia said, rising from her chair, "I consider it a compliment when someone mistakes me for my mother."

Lena laughed out loud. "You're full of it."

Nadia winked and took Maybelle's hand. "Let's get you in your chair, Big Mama."

She walked with her to the living room, where she helped her down gently into her chair. Maybelle sighed with contentment and glanced at the clock. It was nearing eight-thirty.

"Would you like to watch T.V?"

"No, come sit and talk to me while your Mama cleans up the kitchen."

Lena called out from the kitchen something about being a guest and also being worked like a slave.

"There are no guests in this house, baby," Maybelle replied.

Lena could be heard clanging pots and noisily straightening up the room. She was unhappy, and she wasn't afraid to show it.

Maybelle leaned over and nodded her head towards the kitchen. "Your mama always hated doing dishes. She'd fuss and fuss while she was doing them, but she always got it done."

Nadia laughed and sat down on the ottoman beside Maybelle's chair.

"Tell Big Mama about yourself."

Nadia took a deep breath and smiled. "Well, what would you like to know? My mom hasn't told you anything about me?"

"Not much, no."

"Oh... wow."

"She called me when you were born, and I saw you for about thirty minutes before they took you back to the nursery. Then your mama moved away with you. And I didn't get to see you at all."

"Earlier, Mom said that she was forced to leave home because of me."

Maybelle nodded slowly and glanced into the kitchen. By now, Lena had calmed down and was singing a song while cleaning.

"What has your mama told you?"

"Nothing at all. I ask, but she won't tell me anything."

"It's no wonder. She endured some things that not many people are strong enough to endure."

"What happened?"

"Let's just say your mama is one of the strongest women I know."

Nadia watched Lena pace back and forth. She'd always felt that Lena's secrets would be hard to bear. What Maybelle said was just a confirmation of the fact.

"Do you know who my father is?"

Maybelle didn't answer her, so she turned her gaze towards her. Maybelle was looking at her with a warm expression on her face.

"Yes, I do."

Nadia moved closer and took her hand. "Please tell me about him. Is he still alive?"

Maybelle nodded.

"Please tell me about him."

When Maybelle's eyes cut over behind her, Nadia turned around to see Lena standing behind her. Her expression gave clear indication that she'd heard what she had requested of Maybelle.

"Oh, hey," Nadia said rising to her feet.

Lena came closer and stood in front of her. "Who are you asking Big Mama to tell you about?"

Nadia glanced down at Maybelle and then back at her mother. "I... uhm," she stammered.

"We haven't been here even a day, and you're starting it already." Lena forced through her tightly clenched teeth. "Don't go around asking questions of my family, please, Nadia."

Nadia lowered her head and nodded. "I'm sorry." She glanced down at Maybelle. "I'm sorry, Big Mama."

"It's okay, baby."

"No, it's not okay." Lena snapped.

"It sure is okay. There's no secrets in this house. Nadia has a right to know about her daddy."

"Not now, Big Mama."

"Maybe not now, but she will know about him before I leave this Earth. Secrets are what brought us to this place right now. It's time for it all to end. It's time for my babies to start living again."

Lena cupped her mouth and quickly turned away from them. Her shoulders trembled slightly, and she took several deep breaths before she turned back around to face them.

"She's not ready, Big Mama."

"Why don't you let her be the judge of that?"

Lena swiped the tears out of her eyes and glanced over at Nadia. "The truth is too horrible, sweet pea."

Nadia opened her mouth to reply, but headlights from a car pulling in the driveway caught her attention. "Looks like your other company has arrived, Big Mama."

A smile crossed Maybelle's face, and she reached for Nadia's arm so she could stand up. Lena raced to the kitchen window and peeked out. The headlights were directly in her eyes so she couldn't see a thing.

"Go bring them in, Magdalena," Maybelle said.

Lena stayed glued in her spot. She couldn't move, didn't want to move.

"Magdalena?"

Lena turned and looked at Maybelle.

"Please, go bring them in," she repeated softly.

Slowly, Lena nodded. "Yes, ma'am," she said, opening the kitchen door. "I'll be right back."

***

Once outside, she walked up to the car. She approached cautiously as if the driver might pull a gun on her. That would have been easier.

She covered her eyes, trying to shield them from the lights as she approached. Suddenly the headlights went off, and Lena was surrounded by darkness. The car door swung open, and she could see the silhouette of a feminine figure step out of the car and approach her just as cautiously as she had approached earlier.

Lena's first instinct was to run away and hide. Long before her eyes recognized this person, her heart already knew who she was. Janine stepped into the light and closed the distance between the two of them. When Lena realized that it was her, she stumbled back onto the first step of the porch.

Janine instinctively reached out, catching her before she could fall. Lena yanked her arm from her and stared at her as if she saw an apparition. Janine looked the same, just older. Still beautiful.

Janine gave her the quick glance up and down, her head shaking slowly in disbelief. "Hello, Lena," Janine finally broke the awkward silence.

Lena swallowed hard. Her tongue felt like it had swelled to the size of a grapefruit and was dry as sandpaper. Even if she wanted to talk, she couldn't.

She slowly backed up the stairs and pushed through the door, leaving Janine standing at the bottom of the steps. She rushed inside straight to the kitchen sink and dry heaved over it. She felt sick. She couldn't breathe. Her heart spazzed in her chest. She trembled. And she felt like she was going to pass out.

Nadia and Maybelle were standing there in the kitchen when Janine entered the house. Maybelle walked over to Janine and embraced her.

"Welcome home, Janine." Maybelle said.

Janine hugged her tightly, glancing over and meeting Lena's penetrating gaze head on. Lena held the gaze for a few moments before she eventually turned away from them.

"Let's give Magdalena some privacy. Come sit with me." She pulled Janine into the living room and sat down in her chair.

Janine kneeled down beside Maybelle's chair. She looked up at Maybelle with tear filled eyes.

Maybelle cupped Janine's chin and kissed her tenderly on the forehead. "Now, now, baby. Save those tears until there's something to cry about."

She glanced up to see Nadia entering the room. Nadia sat down on the loveseat next to them and observed this very tender moment. She was curious about this woman and why she had invoked such a strong reaction in her mother.

Janine squeezed her eyes shut. "I don't deserve to be here," she whispered. "I didn't know she would be here. I'm sorry."

"You have every bit as much right to be here as anyone. This is your home."

"Not after what I did."

"You did nothing wrong."

Janine opened her eyes. "I wish I could believe that."

"That's why you're here. So, you can start believing it."

"I don't understand."

"You will. Eventually. But for now, let's feed you."

Janine rose to her feet and dried her tears with a handkerchief from her pocket. She turned to look towards the kitchen. It was then that she caught sight of Nadia sitting on the loveseat. She smiled at her.

"Hi," Janine greeted her.

"Hi," Nadia said standing to greet her. She outstretched her hand. "My name is Nadia."

"I'm Janine. Janine Chamberlain."

"It's nice to meet you," she said. Her attention went towards the kitchen when Lena appeared in the doorway. She was staring at them with a blank expression on her face.

Maybelle stood and took Janine by the arm and then motioned for Lena to come closer. When Lena was again standing in front of her, Janine greeted her once more.

"Hey," Lena said dryly. She turned to Maybelle. "What's going on, Big Mama?"

Maybelle shrugged and put her arms around the both of them. "Well, it seems that I've invited you both to come and stay with me."

"That's obvious," Lena said.

"Now you girls have two choices. Either you stay and make amends before I die, or you can walk out that door."

"Why would you do this to me?" Lena asked. She closed her hand into a tight fist and trembled in Maybelle's arms.

"Baby..." Maybelle's soft and soothing voice calmed her. "My sweet Magdalena. I did not bring y'all here to cause pain. I brought you here because I need to know my girls are going to be okay after I'm gone."

Lena groaned and clenched her chest tightly. Maybelle looked over at Janine and nodded at her.

Janine blinked the tears out of her eyes and put her head on Maybelle's shoulder. Maybelle kissed her tenderly on the head and inhaled deeply.

"Y'all are tearing up an old woman's heart. I hope you know that." She stood there, holding her "babies" like she always had. Lena to her right and Janine to her left.

In time, Janine pulled away. "I'll stay."

Maybelle sighed contentedly and squeezed her tighter. "Thank you."

They both looked over at Lena. And Lena stared at Janine. All the years of practicing what she would say to her flew out the window the moment she looked into her eyes. Memories flooded Lena's mind. Memories of their life together, of their adventures, and their promises. But Janine had betrayed her and there was no going back. She clenched her eyes shut, trying her best to banish the childhood memories from her mind.

She felt a soft hand on her shoulder and turned to see Nadia standing behind her. Even though Maybelle hadn't included Nadia in the choice, she knew Nadia wanted to stay. Nadia slipped her hand around Lena's arm and tugged her gently.

"Let's stay," she whispered to her.

Lena shook her head slowly and gazed into her daughter's eyes. Perhaps all these years of running and trying her best to protect her had been futile. She ran so far and for so long, she eventually ended up in the same place where it all began.

"Please, Mom?" In Nadia's eyes, Lena saw someone who needed to know the truth about herself. And she knew that it was wrong of her to have kept Nadia in the dark for so long, but she had to protect her. She turned her gaze back to Janine, who held hers in return.

Janine was always the only one who was able to withstand her penetrative stare. That hadn't changed. Finally, she nodded. "All right. I'll stay."

Maybelle sighed with relief and squeezed her in for a tight hug. "Thank you so much, Magdalena."

Lena said nothing. She couldn't believe that she had just agreed to stay and make nice with her. After all she'd done to her! She slowly pulled away from them and smoothed out her clothes.

"Well, I'm going to bed."

"So soon?" Maybelle asked.

Lena opted not to answer. She was extremely irritated, and she didn't want to disrespect Maybelle with an attitude. But what did Maybelle expect? She kept the fact that she'd invited Janine along too, and then she makes a request that they make amends before she dies.

It was all too uncomfortable and too forced for Lena to feel "good" about anything. She had agreed and she was a woman of her word; so, she would make amends. It just wouldn't be tonight. She turned to Nadia, "Nite, sweet pea."

"Goodnight," Nadia said.

Without another word, Lena shoulder checked Janine on her way out of the room. Janine sighed and glanced down the hallway in the direction Lena had gone.

Maybelle put her arm around her again and pulled her closer. "Give her some time, baby."

"I'm not too sure this is a good idea."

"It's a wonderful idea."

"How can you be so sure?"

Maybelle smiled and stroked her face with the back of her hand. "She's been needing to see you for a long time. Now she can start healing."

"Did you see the way she looked at me?"

Maybelle nodded.

"She hates me!"

"She ain't capable of hating anybody. Her heart is too good."

"I'm the exception," Janine laughed to herself. She looked up and noticed Nadia watching her.

"She doesn't hate anybody, baby. Especially, not you." Maybelle said guiding her to the kitchen. "Are you hungry?"

"Um, I'm not sure. What do you have?"

"Meatloaf, mashed potatoes, some corn and cornbread, sweet potato pie."

"Oh my God. All of my favorites! Sure, I can't say no to my favorites, now can I?"

"It would be a crime." Maybelle said. She tipped her head to Nadia. "Make Janine a plate, please, baby?"

Nadia nodded quickly and joined them by the kitchen table. "Yes, of course, Big Mama." She motioned for Janine to sit down at the table as she quickly made her a heaping helping of their dinner. She poured her a glass of tea and placed everything down in front of her.

Janine's eyes grew wide and a smile crossed her face. "This looks delicious. Did you make this?" she asked Nadia and immediately started stuffing her face with mashed potatoes.

"It's very delicious. No, my mother made it," she said proudly.

Janine paused mid-bite and looked up at her. A slight frown creased her face. "Your mother?"

Nadia nodded and smiled. "Yes."

"Lena is your mother?"

"Yes."

She swallowed what she had in her mouth and chased it with nearly the entire glass of tea. She looked at her again, this time with a little more scrutiny than before.

Suddenly, Nadia felt like she was under a microscope, Janine's eyes scanned her almost expertly in a matter of seconds. Her green eyes penetrated the layer that Nadia had spent many years fortifying. She'd never seen this woman before in her life, yet she seemed so familiar.

Janine shook her head slowly, "I'm sorry. You must forgive me for staring. I'm just shocked."

"Shocked? Why?"

"Because you're so old."

"Well, geez thanks," she laughed. She was used to it. Almost everyone she'd come in contact with had the same reaction. Shocked that she could be so old and also be Lena's daughter.

"How old are you?" Janine asked, her eyebrow craned just slightly in anticipation of her answer. Janine's face was clear of any particular emotion as she stared at her.

Nadia cleared her throat softly, "Twenty-three."

Janine took another sip of her tea, "Wow."

"Wow what?"

Janine frowned and shook her head, "Nothing." She clasped her hands in front of her and smiled, "I was just thinking of how much you look like her. That's all."

"Thanks. That's a very nice compliment."

Janine kept silent and toyed with the food on her plate. An awkward silence settled over the room. Maybelle rocked slowly in her chair and watched the two of them. Janine stole glances at Nadia and Nadia pretended not to notice.

"Nadia?" Janine broke the uncomfortable silence.

"Yes?"

Janine sighed, "Forgive me for asking this, but who is your father?"

Nadia sat back in her seat and nibbled lightly on her lip. "Why?"

"I am just curious. Do you know who your father is?"

Nadia narrowed her eyes at her. Janine held her gaze, her eyes never flinching a second. Nadia could see that Janine's personality was strong like her mother's. If not stronger. When she couldn't hold her gaze any longer, her eyes fell away shamefully. "No. I do not know who he is. Why do you ask?"

"I am curious."

"Yes, you've already said that, but why? Why ask me if I know who my father is? Do you know who he is?"

Janine tightened her jaw and looked down at her plate. Suddenly, the environment had turned hostile and neither one of them knew how they got here.

"You know who he is, don't you?"

"No, I do not."

"I find that hard to believe."

"Excuse me?"

Nadia pushed away from the table, keeping her eyes firmly fixed on Janine as she stood. "For you to ask me if I knew who my father was, makes me think that you actually do know who he is."

"Again, I do not know who he is."

"What, do I resemble him? Can you see him in me?"

Janine shook her head slowly.

"Don't shake your head at me, Ms. Chamberlain. You are the one who started this. You just met me, and you ask me a question that personal?"

"I said that I was sorry." Janine got up from her seat. "Listen, I am not trying to fight with you, sweetheart. And I'm really sorry if I offended you with my question. I really am."

"I don't know anything about my father, but I do know his family hurt my mother in some way. Whatever they did to her was bad. So bad that she can't even live her life without looking over her shoulder. And for that reason, I couldn't care less who he is or who they are. All I care about is her and making sure no one hurts her like that ever again."

Janine lowered her head and nodded.

"So, if you think you know who my father is, don't bother sharing that information with me, because for all I care, both he and his family can go to—"

Janine raised her palms facing Nadia, ending her emotional monologue mid-sentence. "I'm sorry I upset you, sweetheart," she said in a calm voice. "Your mother is so very lucky to have someone like you in her life."

Nadia frowned at her response.

"I am going to go get some of my bags from the car," Janine said before retreating quickly out the door.

Nadia stood in front of Maybelle with shame written all over her face. Janine had triggered a part of her that she kept hidden from most people. She hid it so well, that sometimes she forgot it was even there. It was that part of her that longed to know what really happened between her parents and the family. Lena never talked on the subject of her father, but only alluded to something terrible going down with the family.

So, she was left to guess, and wonder, and hope. Janine touched a nerve. She hated not knowing and asking but only being denied information. She wanted to know what happened. She needed to know. Lena's behavior whenever she was asked about the subject of her pregnancy, gave light to the understanding that something very wrong had happened to her.

Nadia could do the math too. Lena was at the tender age of fifteen when she gave birth to her. Knowing also now that Lena was forced to leave home, left no doubt in her mind that she was likely an unplanned pregnancy.

"I'm so sorry, Big Mama," she whispered, "She didn't deserve to be spoken to like that. Please forgive me for disrespecting your guest." Nadia kept her eyes glued on the floor.

"I understand."

"Does she know who he is?"

Maybelle motioned for her to come closer. She took Nadia's hand and pulled her onto the ottoman beside her. "She doesn't know who your daddy is. There's only three people who know who he is. Your mama, your daddy, and me."

"How do I find him?"

"Why do you want to find him so bad?"

"Because I'll finally know who I am."

"Aren't you happy with who you are now?"

"Yes. Mostly."

"Do you have a sweetheart?"

Nadia shrugged. "I used to, but he didn't want to wait."

"Wait for what?"

Nadia's eyes fell slowly onto her lap. Maybelle tipped her chin gently so her eyes could meet hers again.

"He didn't want to wait for what?"

"For me. I wanted my first time to be with the person whom I planned to be with for the rest of my life."

Maybelle nodded slowly and smiled. Her hand caressed Nadia's chin, "You are so precious. I hope you know that."

"I don't know about precious. I'm just a little old fashioned."

Maybelle laughed and pulled Nadia into an embrace. "What would you do if you found out your daddy was a billionaire with everything he could ever want right at his fingertips? Would that change how you view yourself?"

Nadia thought on the question for a moment. "I don't know. Maybe."

"How so?"

"Maybe it would make me feel like I belong somewhere. Like that other piece of my life's puzzle is finally put into place. And him being a billionaire would be a plus!"

Maybelle laughed softly. "And what if you found him sitting under a bridge with nothing but a pair of holey shoes to his name?"

"In both instances, the key is how he feels about me. If one rejects me, then I wouldn't want anything to do with him. If the other one accepts me, then I would want him in my life, regardless of his life's circumstance."

"Do you truly mean that?"

"Yes, ma'am, I do."

"Your mama has raised you right then. She's definitely raised you right."

Nadia took Maybelle's hand and stroked it. "What's his name?"

"I'm sorry, but I can't tell you that bit of information."

"Why not? I don't understand. You said besides my parents, you were the only one who knew."

"Yes, that's right."

"I'm not asking anything but his name."

Maybelle gazed long and hard into Nadia's eyes. "Your mama needs to be the one to tell you his name."

"Why is it such a secret?"

"Not a secret, but guarded information."

"Why?"

"You've figured out some things on your own, so you know that something terrible happened to your mama, and it was by the grace of God, you survived it."

Nadia ran her fingers through her hair and groaned under her breath. Maybelle wasn't going to crack; she could already see it. And she thought it was hard getting information from Lena.

"All right," she surrendered. "I won't ask about him anymore."

"Sure, you will." Maybelle laughed.

"I think I should go help her with her bags. She's taking a long time."

"Good idea, baby."

"Do you need help getting ready for bed?"

"No but thank you. I'm just going to do a crossword and then hit the hay."

"Hit the hay?"

"That means go to bed."

"Gotcha." She got up and headed towards the kitchen. "Sleep well, Big Mama."

"You too."

Chapter 7

Janine reclined her seat and closed her eyes. She planned to stay outside long enough for everyone to go to bed. That way she'd avoid any confrontations with Lena or her daughter. Looking into her eyes sent chills up her spine. Was it because she looked so much like Lena, or was it because when she looked into her eyes, she saw family?

Janine's stomach lurched and turned at the thought. She swallowed hard and settled her head against the headrest. She was hoping that she'd get to see Lena, but she had no idea that she would come home with a child. A child who undoubtedly belonged to that terrible night.

She opened her eyes and gazed up at the rear-view mirror. Nothing but darkness reflected back at her, but her mind lit up with memories of the past. Images played quickly through her mind. Voices, shadows, and cries.

She squeezed her eyes tightly shut, hoping to force the images out of her head, but they kept coming. Images of her uncle Ty, and of her father and the others, and of Lena. Her heart quivered inside of her chest.

"God, please make it stop!" she begged. She pounded the steering wheel with her open palms and choked on her tears. She clenched her chest with trembling hands and leaned against the wheel and cried.

She heard a light tapping on her driver's side window. She jumped with a start; visibly shaken from the unexpected interruption of her thoughts. She squinted to see Nadia standing outside of the car. She opened the door slowly. It was impossible to hide the fact that she'd been crying hysterically just a minute earlier, so she just pretended like she wasn't.

"Hey," she greeted Nadia.

Nadia came closer and knelt down by the door. "Are you okay?"

"Yes, fine. Why do you ask?"

Janine's heart turned over in her chest as she looked down into Nadia's concerned eyes.

"I am so sorry for the way I spoke to you earlier. You didn't deserve that."

Janine nodded briskly. The warmth in Nadia's voice moved her more than she thought possible. "It's okay, sweetheart. I shouldn't have asked such a personal question."

Nadia touched her hand. "Why are you crying?"

Janine chuckled. "Oh, I see it's your turn now to ask personal questions, huh?"

Nadia shrugged and smiled.

Janine took a deep breath and let it out. She reminded herself that she wasn't talking to a child, but she was talking to a grown woman. "I was thinking about your mother."

"What about her?"

"I guess I didn't realize how much I missed her until I saw her again."

Nadia sighed lightly and stroked Janine's hand gently.

"It's just really awkward being here under these circumstances with her. I mean..." Janine pulled herself out of the car and paced the grounds in front of it. "Our grandmother is dying!"

"I know and I'm sorry it had to be this way."

"It shouldn't have been this way. I was a coward." Janine turned away from Nadia and dried her tears. She could hear Nadia approaching her; cautiously stepping closer. "It was all my fault," she said.

"What was?"

Janine turned and faced her, "Everything."

Nadia stepped a little closer. "I don't understand."

"Everything that happened to her was because of me. And now that I find out about you, the guilt is crushing me. It's too much!"

"What about me?"

Janine clenched her fist against her teeth and started past Nadia, but she caught her by the arm, stilling her escape.

"Tell me what you mean. Please!"

Janine stared into those familiar eyes and her heart trembled inside of her chest. "It's obvious that she hasn't told you anything, and I will not be the one to disclose this to you. I can't be that one."

"Yes, you can. Tell me what you mean!" Nadia demanded.

Janine shook from Nadia's grip and pushed her away. "Don't," she warned.

Nadia took a moment to compose herself. She didn't know what it was about this woman, but she got under her skin easily. She raised her hands up; palms facing Janine and sighed.

"Look, I'm sorry." She lowered her head and strummed her fingers through her hair. "Maybe I shouldn't have come with her, because it seems like everyone knows things about me, but no one wants to tell me anything."

Janine remained silent and watched her.

"If you were me, what would you do?"

"Ask questions."

"You can see where that got me." Nadia laughed lightly and stepped closer. "I apologize for putting my hands on you. That's not me at all."

Janine didn't respond, she just looked at her.

"Why are you looking at me like that?"

"When is your birthday?"

"February 24th."

"What year?"

"1995. Why?"

The kitchen door swung open and Lena appeared into view. They spun and looked at her as if they'd just been caught misbehaving. She stepped slowly down from the porch and came closer to where they stood. Her eyes bounced from Nadia and then to Janine and then back to Nadia.

"What's going on here?" Her voice was cold and devoid of emotion. Her eyes had narrowed, focusing now more on Janine than Nadia.

"I was about to help her with her bags," Nadia offered.

Lena crossed her arms and cut her eyes over towards Nadia. "Really? Because it looked like you two were engrossed in deep conversation."

"Not at all," Janine said walking around to the trunk of the car and popping it open. "Just chit chat."

"About what?" she pushed.

Janine laughed and came back over to her. "Some things never change. I see you're still as bossy as you used to be."

Lena nodded and scoffed. "Do me a favor while we're here and stay away from my daughter, okay?"

Janine crossed her arms and held Lena's terrifyingly intimidating gaze.

"Perhaps if she was a child, you could tell me that. But I happen to like her company."

"I mean it, Jay."

"What's so wrong with me talking to Nadia?"

Lena's jaw clenched tighter and her body started trembling slightly.

"Are you afraid of something?" Janine pressed.

"I'm afraid of nothing."

"Are you afraid of her talking to me and finding out something?"

"I'm warning you."

"Go ahead, Nadia. Now's your opportunity," Janine spoke over Lena's shoulder.

Lena turned slowly and looked at Nadia. There was a look of almost betrayal and sadness on Lena's face. She knew now what they had been talking about. Nadia had been doing exactly what she said she would not do.

As they stood there looking at each other, Nadia finally broke eye contact with Lena and lowered her eyes.

"Listen," Lena said turning back to Janine, "I get that this is all a shock to you, but my daughter will not be pulled into the middle of what we have going on. Keep her out of this."

"I wasn't trying to pull her into the middle of anything."

"I plan on keeping my word to Big Mama, but for this to actually work out, it's best if you keep your distance from Nadia."

Janine shook her head. "Fine."

"Help her with her bags, sweet pea." Lena called over her shoulder.

Nadia obediently walked over to the car and grabbed the bags from the trunk. Janine had packed light; only three carry-ons which she scooped up immediately and carried over to the house.

"Thank you," Janine said. "Just place them inside my room."

When Nadia had disappeared into the house, Janine faced Lena once more. She stepped closer. Lena stood, arms crossed and extremely guarded. Her eyes had narrowed, that much Janine could tell; the cloak of darkness grew ever more intense by the minute.

"Do you hate me?" Janine asked.

"I hate no one."

"Please, I just need to hear you say it. Do you hate me?"

Lena unglued herself from her spot and moved closer to her. "If I had known that you were coming, I would not have come and subjected myself to the memories of what you did to me."

Janine struggled to remained composed. She nodded her head slowly. She understood.

"For all it's worth, I am so sorry."

Lena turned her back to her. "I drove a long way. I'm tired."

She started to walk off towards the house, but Janine caught her by the arm. "Please."

Lena stilled on contact. Feeling her touch after so long had a devastating effect on her. She turned to face her. "What do you want from me, Jay?"

Janine took hold of her other arm and pulled her closer. "Forgiveness."

"Forgiveness?" she said with a laugh.

"Yes. I need it. Please."

Janine attempted to embrace her, but Lena broke free and pushed her away. "You can't do this to me right now."

"Whether you realize it or not, we are going to need to lean on each other in order to help Big Mama. You are going to need me."

"I don't need you for anything!"

"Well, I need you!" Janine snapped back. She expected some resistance to her efforts.

She used to be so easy-going, allowing Janine to have whatever she wanted, but this Lena was different. Janine could tell that she still had a heart of gold, but there were so many layers of protection covering it, she wasn't sure if she would be able to break through.

"This is what Big Mama has wanted for so long. I want so badly to give it to her, don't you?"

Lena shook her head slowly.

"I've wanted to say those words to you; that I was sorry, for so long now, but I was a coward."

The porch light flipped on, illuminating them in a soft orange glow. To Janine's surprise, Lena had tears streaming down her face.

"I am well aware that what I did to us may be unforgiveable in your eyes, and I'm ready to accept that. I just wanted you to know that I have also lived with what happened that night. You weren't the only one."

Lena swiped her tears out of her eyes. "Your reasons for why you did it... That's what made it wrong."

"I know. I just thought I was losing you."

"It sounded ridiculous then and it sounds ridiculous now." Lena sounded bitter and tired.

Janine nodded. "I know," she whispered.

"The only good and pleasant thing that came out of that whole summer was my daughter."

Lena's words floated gently through the air. Janine didn't respond to her statement and Lena added nothing more. They just stood there looking at each other, each one perhaps playing out a coveted memory.

"You look tired, you probably should go to bed," Janine said.

Lena nodded in response and turned back towards the house.

"Even if we had to come together under these circumstances," she called after her, "I am happy that I have had a chance to see you and talk to you at least."

She turned and looked at her. "Goodnight, Jay."

"Goodnight."

Janine watched Lena walk slowly into the house and shut the door. After a minute of quiet reflection, she followed the same path and retired for the night.

Chapter 8

Lena awakened to the feeling of a hand stroking her face. She opened her eyes and saw Maybelle sitting on her bed, smiling down at her. She squinted and yawned as she sat up in bed.

"Big Mama? Are you okay?"

"Yes, I am. I didn't mean to wake you up."

"What time is it?"

"About four-thirty."

Lena groaned. She had completely forgotten that Maybelle gets up around 4 a.m. every morning.

"What are you gonna have me do at this hour?" She already knew it was coming.

"Remember when you were eight and you moved in with me?"

"How could I forget?"

Lena grabbed a hairbrush and brushed her hair quickly.

"All I wanted was for my first granddaughter to feel at home."

"And you did... By making me cook."

They shared a laugh together as Maybelle gently caressed Lena's arm. Her hands trembled slightly. It was barely noticeable, but Lena detected it.

"You're shaking, Big Mama."

Maybelle nodded. "Just a bit."

"Do you need something? Some medicine?"

"The pharmacy is supposed to deliver my pain meds today. I ran out."

"You're in pain?" Lena hopped up quickly and inspected her.

"Yes, but nothing a hot cup of coffee can't fix."

"But, Big Mama?"

Maybelle placed a hand on Lena's shoulder. "Let's make some breakfast. It'll be a good distraction for me."

Slowly Lena agreed. She got up and offered her arm to Maybelle and walked with her to the kitchen. Maybelle walked slower than she did yesterday. When they made it to the kitchen table, Lena placed her gently in her seat.

"Coffee first, right?"

"You got it."

Lena worked quickly at brewing a pot of coffee for Maybelle. She was surprised she remembered where everything was. Maybelle rarely changed things around. She was a creature of habit. After thirty years, some items were still kept in the same places.

It took about ten minutes for the coffee to finish brewing. Lena poured Maybelle a cup and placed it in front of her. She took it and sipped it slowly, humming with delight.

"Now, this is the cure for all."

Lena chuckled lightly. "What would you like for breakfast?"

Maybelle tapped her head slowly and thought about it for a minute or two. "Are you sure you wanna tackle breakfast alone?"

"Who else is going to cook if it's not me?"

"Didn't you teach your baby how to cook?"

"Yes, but I do all the cooking for us."

"Why's that?"

Lena shrugged and toyed with a sugar pack on the table. "I don't know, I guess I don't want her to have to worry about anything. So, I cook and take care of everything."

"Sounds to me like you spoil her." Maybelle glanced at her from over the rim of the cup.

"She is by no means spoiled."

"What is she like?"

Lena smiled. "She's perfect in my eyes."

"Every Mama says the same thing."

"Even when she was a baby, she rarely gave me problems. That made it easier working, you know."

Maybelle nodded slowly and sipped her coffee.

"She's a very kind person. Strong-willed. Thoughtful."

"She wants to know about her daddy."

Lena gazed into Maybelle's eyes. "I know."

"You should tell her before she bumps into him."

Lena got up and made herself a cup of coffee and sat back down at the table. "I'm afraid."

"Of what?"

She took a slow and thoughtful sip. "I'm afraid of how she will view me after she finds out about him."

Maybelle nodded.

"I mean, I was made out to be this horrible person. This whole town ostracized me. My heart can't take it if my own daughter starts to feel the same way about me."

"I understand your fears, but it's better if it comes from you than someone else."

"I know."

"Maybe the Good Lord thinks it's time for everybody to start healing."

"Maybe... Did she ask you about him?"

"You know she did."

"What did you tell her?"

"She had got on Janine's case earlier, because Janine asked her if she knew who her daddy was."

"Oh dear."

"She's got a temper on her."

Lena laughed a little. "Yeah, she does. So, she asked you about him?"

"Oh, yeah. Sorry, you know how my mind wanders."

"That's okay."

"She asked me if Janine knew who her daddy was, and I told her no. That there was only three people who knew who he was. That was you, me, and him."

Lena sipped quietly. "I know she needs to know who she is. She's entitled."

"Everyone has a right to know who they belong to."

"She belongs to me."

"I know she does, but she also belongs to them, too. And that's a secret that won't stay a secret very long. Especially when family finds out she's your baby and starts doing the math."

Lena groaned and clenched her stomach. "His family is the reason why I'm a train wreck today."

"Don't talk about yourself like that, baby. You seem fine to me."

"On the outside, yeah. But inside... A mess."

"That's all of us."

"I don't know if I can handle them knowing about her."

"She is a miracle, you know that."

"Yes, she is."

"It doesn't matter what his family thinks about her. Most of them will shun her. The important ones will accept her."

Lena felt tears stinging her eyes. "I never meant for any of this to happen. She deserves to be accepted by people who love her."

"She is... And she will be."

"This is so hard."

"Once people know she exists, the ones who were involved that night will think she belongs to them."

"I know."

"But we know the truth. And it's by the grace of God, she survived it."

Lena swiped tears from her eyes and sipped on her lukewarm coffee. She glanced over at the clock on the wall. It was nearing 5 a.m.

"I trust you will do what's right for you both. But just remember; all these years, you still had her. He lost you both."

Lena's heart rose into her throat. "How is he doing?"

"The last time I saw him, he was doing fine. But I can see the sadness in his eyes."

"This is all very overwhelming. I wasn't ready for any of this."

"Maybe not, but sometimes when the Lord wants things to happen, we just have to go along with it."

Lena pushed away from the table and went over to the fridge. "What would you like for me to cook?"

"Scrambled eggs, grits, bacon, toast, and maybe some hash browns."

"All right."

Lena wanted to occupy her mind with something other than thoughts of telling Nadia about her father. She'd stressed years over it. Wondering how her beloved daughter would view her once she found out. It didn't really matter anymore. The truth was she had to know.

Maybelle watched Lena as she worked quietly in the kitchen. She worked at a quick pace, whipping the breakfast up in record time. Maybelle got up from the table and poured another cup of coffee. She stood by the stove, inspecting Lena's work.

"All of this looks so good."

"Thanks." Lena stirred the pot of grits vacantly; her mind seemingly millions of miles away.

Maybelle strummed her fingers through her hair. "You look just like your Mama right now."

Her words pulled Lena out of her thoughts. She glanced over at Maybelle and smiled. "Thank you. I wish I could've gotten to know her better before she left me."

"I wish you could have too."

"I guess that's why I try my best to be there for Nadia, you know? Because my mother wasn't there for me."

"That's a natural thing to want."

"And I'm so glad that you took me in. I don't know what I would have done if CPS would have gotten a hold of me."

"My greatest regret is not pushing your mama to get some help. I didn't know she was in it so bad."

"No one blames you, Big Mama." Lena hugged her tightly. "Mother was a difficult person to live with when she was high. And she was high all of the time! There are still many things she put me through that I will never speak of."

"I'm so sorry, Magdalena."

"Not your fault." She turned the burner down on the stove and covered the grits. She took note of all that she had made, and everything looked very good.

"I have groceries coming today with my medicine."

"Great. Any idea on dinner tonight?"

"Haven't gotten that far in the plan yet." Maybelle sat down and rocked herself slowly.

Lena could tell she was in pain. She wished she could take it all away from her. If she could, she'd do it in an instant.

She heard a bedroom door opening towards the back of the house and realized that the smells of her wonderful cooking had awakened everyone from sleep. She smiled and sat down opposite Maybelle and held her hand. "What time does the caretaker get here today?"

"Oh, about ten."

"All right. Maybe after breakfast, I can do some laundry for you."

"Sure. I'll see what I have."

They sat holding hands for a couple more minutes before Nadia came dragging into the room. She looked like she hadn't slept well. Her hair was disheveled, her pajamas on inside out. She dragged her feet over to the table and hugged Maybelle first and then Lena.

"Good morning," Nadia said.

"Good morning. You look rough," Lena said with a laugh.

"I couldn't sleep last night."

"Why?"

"These weird creatures were making noises outside my window."

Maybelle laughed. "What, you mean the tree frogs?"

"Tree frogs? That's what those were?"

"You mean to tell me you don't have tree frogs in Kansas?"

Nadia laughed. "Where we are located, we don't even have trees!"

They all shared a laugh while Nadia poured her a cup of coffee and sat at the table. There was room for one more person.

"Can I make myself something to eat? I'm starved," Nadia asked.

"In a minute, baby. We're gonna wait to see if Janine comes to eat."

Lena sighed. Maybelle glanced over at her and smiled. "It's a new day. Please try to be nice to your sister."

"She's not my sister."

"Maybe not by blood, but Big Mama knows you still love her like one."

Lena scoffed. She wasn't even going to entertain that statement. Her heart felt love only for Nadia & Maybelle. No one else. Lena had been lost in her thoughts when she looked up and saw Janine standing in the doorway. Unlike Nadia, Janine had made a silent entry, almost cautiously stepping into the kitchen. She was already fully dressed and looked as if she were about to go to work.

Last night when she arrived, Lena had been so angry and so disturbed that she really didn't get a good look at her. Janine's face showed signs of aging and a somewhat stressful life. She used to be extremely thin, but now she had filled out in all the important places. She had a physique like Nadia's. Her eyes were still a lighter shade of green, with hints of oranges and blues which made her eyes very mystifying.

Lena shook off her thoughts and focused on her cup of coffee once again.

"Come on in, baby." Maybelle said.

"Good morning everyone," Janine said.

Everyone but Lena said greetings. She just stared at her cup.

"Have a seat." Maybelle pointed to the chair opposite of Lena.

Janine sat down quietly and glanced at Lena. Finally, she looked up from her cup and locked gazes with her. Janine flashed a disarming smile her way and waited for her to reciprocate.

"Good morning, Jay." Lena's voice wasn't as cold as it was last night, but it lacked any recognizable emotion.

"Good morning."

"Do you drink coffee?"

Janine nodded.

Lena got up slowly and went and poured her a cup of coffee. "What do you want in it?"

"Two creams, two sugars, please."

Lena worked quietly and then a couple of minutes later, she came back with a cup and placed it in front of her.

"Thank you."

Lena just tipped her head and sat down.

Maybelle looked on with approval. Lena was trying. That's all that mattered. "Is everyone hungry?"

"Yes!" Nadia answered for the group.

Maybelle laughed lightly. "Let's thank the Good Lord for this meal?" Everyone joined hands except for Lena and Janine. Janine outstretched her hand and waited for Lena to take it.

"Hungryyy." Nadia sang lightly.

Lena sighed deeply and took Janine's hand. At first, she was hardly holding it, but as Maybelle said the prayer over the food, Janine tightened her grip. She reciprocated, but just barely.

"Dear Lord," Maybelle began, "Thank you so much for answering my prayers. I didn't think it would happen, but you showed me that I needed to have a little more faith..."

Lena gazed across the table and watched Janine as Maybelle prayed. She couldn't believe she was here. She couldn't believe that after all these years, they were sitting together in the same room. Her heart clenched inside of her chest.

"You gave me more than I asked for, Lord," Maybelle continued, "You didn't just bring them home, you brought them plus another baby for me to love. Thank you so much. Amen."

"Amen." The table said in unison.

Lena released everyone's hands and got up from the table. She began preparing the breakfast plates for everyone in silence. One by one, she placed the plates down in front of them.

"Oh my!" Maybelle said.

"I hope you all enjoy," Lena said as she made herself a plate and sat down. She avoided eye contact with Janine. She couldn't take her right now.

Everyone ate in silence. After about ten minutes, Maybelle pushed her plate away. She'd barely touched anything.

"You didn't like it?" Lena asked.

"It was very good, but my stomach can't take a lot."

She'd given her an extremely small portion of food and it was still hard for her to eat that. "What time does the pharmacy open?"

"About nine."

"I'll go then and get your medicine."

"Thank you, but it's being delivered by the grocery store. The pharmacy is inside of the store."

"When will that be here?"

"Yesterday, they told me around nine-thirty."

"I hate to see you in pain."

"The pain isn't that bad anymore. I told you, coffee is the cure all."

Lena sighed. "I'm sorry, Big Mama," she whispered.

"Now, now. All is well."

"But?"

"No buts. I know how long the doctors told me and I plan to use every minute all the way down to the end."

It was then that Lena glanced over at Janine. Her heart felt like it was being squeezed in a vise. It was all too overwhelming; the feelings that were running through her body at the moment. The main emotion she felt was fear.

Fear of the unknown.

Fear of seeing Maybelle die.

She squeezed her eyes and forced the thoughts out of her mind. Maybelle started coughing again. She'd coughed all night. Lena patted her gently on the back while Janine hopped out of her seat and ran towards her room. Lena only glanced briefly in her direction before turning back to Maybelle. Maybelle tried her best not to fall into a coughing fit, but it was difficult. The heat of the early morning didn't help either.

Janine reappeared a minute later with an inhaler. She placed her hand on Maybelle's shoulder and sat down in the chair beside her. "Have you used one of these before?" Janine asked.

Maybelle nodded and coughed again. She was wheezing now. Janine motioned for her to open her mouth. She placed it into her mouth and placed her hand on her back.

"Take a deep breath for me, Big Mama, okay?"

Maybelle inhaled deeply. Janine, at the same time, puffed a measure of Albuterol into her airways.

"Hold it as long as you can, okay?"

Maybelle nodded. She held the medicine in her lungs as long as possible before she had to exhale. She exhaled a long and raspy breath.

"That's great. Do it one more time. This time hold it a bit longer." Janine's voice was soft and reassuring.

Lena watched in amazement. She seemed to turn into a different person right before her eyes. Maybelle repeated the process, this time catching her breath fully.

She sat slouched over the table for about five minutes before she finally lifted her head and smiled. "Thank you, baby."

"No thanks needed." She reached behind her and pulled a stethoscope from her back pocket and put them in her ears. "I'm going to listen to your lungs for a moment, okay?"

"Yes."

Janine glanced over at Lena who was staring at her. She kept her eyes on her, only looking away when she placed the listening device over Maybelle's left lung, and then her right.

She listened for a minute straight, maybe even two before she looked back up at Lena. Lena frowned; Janine shook her head sadly. Her lungs did not sound good. Not good at all. She removed her stethoscope and slid it back into her pocket. She gave Maybelle a gentle squeeze on the arm. "I love you," she said.

Maybelle looked into her eyes and smiled. "And I love you, baby."

Janine got up and escaped into her room. Lena watched her run off, something deep inside of her wanted to go and see why she'd run off.

She didn't get a chance to progress further into those thoughts before the house phone rang loudly, startling everyone sitting in the room.

"Oh my God!" Lena yelped. "Big Mama, why does your phone ring so loud?"

"So, I can hear it. Why else?"

Lena laughed lightly and grabbed the phone from the wall. "Curtis residence."

She listened and said a few 'uh huhs' and 'okays' and then hung up the phone.

"Who was that?" Maybelle asked.

"Bailey's. They said the delivery boy is sick and they won't be able to deliver your groceries today."

"Oh dear," She said quietly. "We will have to go get it then."

"I'll go," Lena said.

"If you don't mind, could you send your baby to get it for me?"

Lena frowned and looked over at Nadia. Nadia had been occupying herself with her iPad during the ordeal with Maybelle. Nadia hated seeing people suffer. Especially people she cared about.

"I don't know about that, Big Mama."

"She will be okay. I need you here to help me with a few things."

Lena thought it over. She wasn't really concerned. But she was paranoid. Life had a way of dealing some pretty wicked cards to her.

"Okay. Hey sweet pea?"

"Yes?"

"Would you be able to run down to the town supermarket and pick up Big Mama's groceries?"

"Sure. When do I need to leave?"

Lena checked her watch. "Maybe in an hour or so."

"Okay. I'll just need the address for GPS."

"Your phone works okay out here?"

"Yes. I have four bars."

"Great."

Nadia collected the dishes from breakfast and started washing them in the sink. She worked quietly, not making a single fuss about it. Maybelle watched her and smiled.

"Don't even say it," Lena said.

"Say what?"

"I know what you're thinking. You're thinking if only I was that cooperative when asked to wash dishes."

Maybelle laughed and patted Lena on the hand.

"Yeah, that's what I thought."

Eventually Lena helped Maybelle to her chair in the living room and then set aside a breakfast plate for Uncle Zeke. Janine hadn't come out of her room yet so, after making sure Maybelle was comfy, she went to investigate.

She came to Janine's room and stood outside of the door for a moment. She couldn't believe her curiosity had led her here, but she wasn't going to turn back now. She knocked lightly and waited for a response. She knocked again more loudly.

"Come in."

She turned the knob and entered. Janine was sitting at the desk in the corner working on her laptop. Lena cleared her throat lightly. "Hey."

Janine spun around with a surprised expression on her face. She removed the earbud that was still stuck in her ear and stood up. "Oh, hi."

Lena nodded and released the death grip she had on the door. She stepped closer to her. "Um, thanks for what you did in there for Big Mama."

Janine approached her cautiously. "It was the least I could do."

"So, I see you made it. I mean, you're a doctor."

"Yes, technically."

"Technically?"

"I graduated from medical school, but I chose to pursue a career in dentistry."

"Dentistry?"

Janine laughed. "Yes."

"Wow, you rebel! You were supposed to be a doctor. I bet your parents had a cow over that."

Janine just shrugged and smiled. "Teeth are easier patients."

"Interesting." Lena glanced around the room. Janine's bags still sit where Nadia had put them. Only one was open and apparently being used. She walked over to the couch in the corner of the room and sat down.

Memories of yesteryear started flooding Lena's mind. This was basically Janine's room, the one she stayed in whenever they'd have sleepovers. She'd start out in Lena's room, but then something or the other would cause them to bicker and Janine would storm off through the connecting door. Then she'd sit on the other side and talk to Lena for the rest of the night. It made no sense whatsoever, but it was what made Janine unique.

"Did Big Mama ask you here because you are a doctor?"

Janine sat down at the desk. "I believe she asked me to come down so I could assist you, especially with the medical part of this process."

"What process?"

Janine glanced up from her laptop but didn't elaborate. She wasn't going to go into the details about Maybelle's requests.

"So, what are you working on?"

Janine shut the laptop cover. "Oh, I had to resign my position with my current practice in order to come here, so I was working on securing another position at a friend's private practice once I get back."

"Why did you have to resign?"

"I see you still carry on conversations by asking questions."

Lena shook her head. "Sorry. Just curious."

"The doctor who was over me, was a jerk. Hired only young women to work for him. You know the type."

"Yep, all too well."

"So, what do you do for a living?"

Lena clasped her hands together and wrung them slowly. "I'm a freelance photographer."

"Oh, that sounds exciting."

"Are you being sarcastic?"

"No, not at all." Janine leaned forward, "Do you get to travel a lot?"

"Yes, depends on the gig. I had a real big one coming up, but I had to back out of it."

"What was the job?"

"Capturing the essence of the Redwoods."

"That's amazing."

"Yeah, it was going to be really great, but this happened," Lena said sadly.

"Will you get another opportunity to do it?"

"Probably not in this lifetime."

Janine sighed. "Oh."

Lena hopped up from her seat. She was getting too comfortable. To her surprise it was quite easy to slip back into conversation with Janine, once she stopped being angry. But she couldn't let her guard down. Not ever again.

"So, yeah, I just wanted to say thanks for caring about Big Mama enough to stay and help."

Janine rose from her seat. "You don't need to thank me, but you're welcome. I love Big Mama too. Remember that."

Lena nodded. "All right." She walked towards the door. "I'm going to go."

"Okay." Janine walked her to the door. After she left, Janine shut the door behind her and pressed her head against it.

On the other side, Lena touched the door briefly before walking away.

Chapter 9

In addition to the groceries that Maybelle had already ordered, Lena sent for a few more items as well. Nadia pushed the grocery cart up and down the aisles in search of the things on Lena's list. Most were junk food items, and also some ingredients for meals that she planned to cook. From the looks of it, Lena planned to make her famous chicken parmesan meatballs with pasta.

She stood in front of the meat case searching for a package of ground chicken that looked good enough to buy. None of it looked good.

She made eye contact with the butcher behind the glass and waved him over. She could see he wasn't happy about being asked for assistance. He slammed his knife down and wiped his hands on his bloody apron. Then he walked over to her.

When he came to face her, she cringed a bit. His grey beard looked like he hadn't washed it in weeks, his eyes were bloodshot, and he looked just plain dirty.

"What you need help with?" His accent was thick, and his voice was low. Nadia had trouble understanding this simple question.

"I'm sorry?"

"I said what do you need help with, Miss?" He spoke slower and condescendingly.

Lena had warned her about these types that she might come in contact with while visiting Archer. The good ol' boy types who don't like change and who are intolerant of anyone who wasn't Caucasian.

The way he looked at her made her feel uncomfortable. Although his eyes traveled the length of her body in a fraction of a second, it was the way he smiled at her that made her stomach turn. His lips curled up into a crooked smile. He was missing several teeth and the ones he did have were yellowed and chipped. She glanced at his name badge.

"Yes, Dale. May I have some fresh ground chicken please?"

He glanced down at the three packs of chicken in the case in front of her. "Right there."

"Yes, I see those, but I would like fresh ones. Those don't look very fresh."

"It's all I got."

"What if I buy a pack of chicken breast and you ground it up for me?"

"Sorry, I don't do that."

"I don't understand."

"Look here, girl. I know things might be a little hard for you to understand, but this one here is simple. I only got three packs of ground chicken, and I ain't gonna ground up no more for you."

Nadia's eyes widened. The nerve of him speaking to a customer this way! "I want to speak to your manager, please."

"He's busy."

"Well, fine. I will go find him myself. Because you are being extremely rude and that's no way to treat a paying customer." Her voice elevated and she began grabbing the attention of other patrons walking by. "I demand to speak to your manager, right now."

"All right All right," he said walking over to the PA system and paging the manager to the back.

Nadia waited patiently. Five minutes had rolled by when a man who looked to be the same age as Dale showed up at the meat counter. He greeted her and then turned to Dale.

"How may I be of assistance?"

"This girl has a problem," he said.

The manager turned to her. "What seems to be the problem?"

She recounted the interaction with Dale to the manager and told him that all she did was ask for fresher meat, and she was denied. She pointed out that customer satisfaction was the key to a successful business. All the things he probably already knew but he listened anyway.

"I would just like to be treated with respect, but it's obvious that Mr. Dale here has a problem with serving me."

The manager's eyes narrowed at her. He gave her the quick up and down. "My apologies, ma'am." He turned to Dale. "Get rid of this old chicken, and please ground up ten pounds of chicken breast and give it to this young lady for $7.25."

"Ten pounds?"

"Yes."

"You might as well give it away."

The manager shot him a hot glare. "We will mark it as a loss for your department."

Dale's face tightened and he looked back at her. "Fine." He grabbed the old ground chicken and tossed it into the trash barrel. Then he stormed off into the back where he worked angrily at chopping and grinding up Nadia's chicken order.

While they were waiting for him to complete the task, the manager looked over at her and smiled.

"Was there anything else I could do for you?"

"No sir. Thank you for your assistance."

He nodded and watched Dale through the window.
"Are you from around here?"

"No. Visiting friends."

"Where are you from?"

She cut her eyes over at him. His expression had cooled to a more suspicious and callous one while he watched her from the corner of his eye.

"California," she replied.

"You've come a long way."

"Just stopping through." She kept her responses short and sweet.

He kept watching her from the corner of his eye, but she pretended not to notice. After several minutes, Dale reappeared from the cutting area and handed her two packages of meat.

"There you go. Ten pounds of fresh ground chicken. Have a nice day."

Nadia took the packages and placed them into her grocery basket. By then, a line had formed at the meat counter. She thanked the manager once more for his help and departed down another aisle. When she turned the corner, she glanced back and saw them staring at her. Dale had leaned over and said something to the manager, who in turn nodded and walked away.

She couldn't wait to tell Lena what happened at the meat counter. After she'd grabbed every item she could find on the list, she pushed her basket to checkout. She was greeted by a young high school aged girl. Jasmine was her name. She smiled brightly and asked her if she had a customer loyalty card to swipe.

"No, I don't. I'm not from around here." She glanced towards the front and saw the same manager duck into the customer service box. He watched her from over the top of the glass. She didn't know who he was, but he was seriously giving her the creeps.

The young cashier started checking Nadia's groceries. Her items were piling up at the bottom of the register, so Nadia began sacking the groceries herself.

"Leave them. We got someone coming to do it."

"Oh, okay. Where do I pick up the home delivery orders?"

"Customer service."

"Thanks."

Before she knew it, a tall man appeared at the end of the checkout table, seemingly out of nowhere. She jumped; her cheeks turned rosy red with embarrassment.

"Good morning," he tipped his hat and greeted her. His smile was warm and friendly.

"Hi."

"Would you like paper or plastic?"

"Paper, please."

"Good choice." He smiled and winked.

Nadia chuckled in response. She watched him sack her groceries. He packed them extremely fast. She picked a good station to come to. She got in and out in no time. By the time she was finished paying for her groceries, he had finished placing the last bag neatly into the grocery cart.

He walked around to the front of the cart and pushed it towards the entrance. "I will help you to your car."

"Thank you, but I need to pick up an order first."

"Okay." He rolled the cart over to the customer service desk and smiled. "They have the orders."

She waited for the manager to turn his attention to her. "Hi, I guess I do need something else from you."

"Sure, what is it?"

"I need to pick up a home delivery order. I was told to come here and pick it up."

"Yes. What's the name on the order?"

"Maybelle Curtis. She has groceries and prescription medicine."

"Maybelle Curtis?" He frowned at her. "You know Maybelle?"

"Yes. I do," she added nothing more to her answer.

He stared at her. The color gradually drained from his face, "Wait right here," he said. He placed his pen down and walked to the back of the customer service room.

He was gone for just a couple of minutes before he reappeared with Maybelle's delivery order. Five more bags of groceries.

"Thanks so much."

"No problem," he replied dryly. He tipped his head towards the sacking clerk. "Help this lady to her car, will you, Jack?"

"Yes sir," Jack said.

Nadia left quickly before the manager could ask her any more questions. Once they had exited the store, she sighed with relief. "Oh, shoot, I forgot to get his name. What's your manager's name?"

"That's Mr. Bailey. He kind of owns the store."

"Oh wow. I didn't realize he was the owner."

"Yeah. He walks around watching people all day. My dad says he's just an old coot."

Nadia laughed and continued to walk to her car. "This is me right here."

"Okay."

Nadia popped the trunk and waited patiently for Jack to place the groceries into the car. He was very careful not to crush delicate items.

"You're very good at that."

"Thank you, ma'am." After he was finished, he shut the trunk and tipped his hat to her.

It was then that she noticed his eyes. They were a lighter shade of blue and they sparkled when he smiled. They were so soothing. She also noticed a scar on his face, which was nearly covered by the beard he had. She reached into her purse and pulled out a couple of dollar bills and handed them to him.

"Thank you," he said, "But I can't take tips."

"Oh. Well you were very helpful. I would like to tip you."

"It's okay. I like helping."

"Okay then." She turned to get in her car, but he tapped her on the shoulder.

"Do you know Big Mama?" he asked.

"Yes. I do."

Jack rubbed his beard and shifted the weight on his feet. "Is she okay?"

Nadia sighed and shook her head slowly. "How do you know Big Mama?"

"She loves me. She calls me her baby." He glanced over his shoulder nervously. "But I'm not supposed to see her."

"Why not?" By now, Nadia recognized that Jack had some type of intellectual disability. She assumed it was a mild case because he functioned amazingly well and carried on the conversation without any problems.

Jack shrugged and rubbed his chin. "Because she loves me."

"She's a great lady."

"Is she sick?"

"Yes. I'm sorry to say, she's very sick."

"Oh." He lowered his head, "I want to see her."

"When did you see her last?"

"I can't remember. It was cold outside. She made me some awesome biscuits and gravy."

"Her biscuits are the best!"

"Yeah."

"If you are her friend and if she is yours, then I think you should come anytime and see her."

"I wish I could."

"Why can't you?"

"My dad. He says I need to stay away from those people."

"What people?"

"Niggers."

Nadia was confused, he didn't look like the type to use such a derogatory word. "I see," she said glancing down at his name badge, "Mr. Jack, to be honest, I'm offended by your use of that word."

"Offended?"

"Yes. You must know that it's a terrible word?"

He lowered his head, "I am so sorry. My family says it a lot and no one ever told me not to use it. I just thought that —"

"It's okay. But in my opinion, you look old enough to make your own decisions. Dude, you're sprouting greys!"

Jack chuckled and played with his greying sideburns.

"I don't think you should let your dad stop you from seeing Big Mama."

"You don't?"

"No. Big Mama is your friend. She loves you. And you love her, right?"

"Yeah. Her biscuits are great."

Nadia laughed. "Well then, by all means, take the time to come and see her. I'm sure she'd love to see you."

"I will."

Mr. Bailey called after Jack from the front door. "I gotta go," he said smiling at her. "It was nice to meet you."

"It was nice meeting you too, Jack."

He reached into his pocket and pulled out a card. "I like to text my new friends. Would you text me?"

She took the card and examined it. It had his name and his phone number, with several smiley face emojis all over.

"Thanks."

"I hope you don't think I'm too slow to text. Nobody ever texts me, but that's okay. One day someone will."

"Aww, Jack. Of course, I'll text you later." Her heart was touched by him. "Oh, by the way, my name is Nadia. I'll remind you who I am when I text later."

"Great, thanks!" Jack tipped his hat and ran back towards the entrance, grabbing stray shopping carts along the way.

Nadia watched him disappear into the grocery store. She'd made her first friend here in Archer. This may turn out to be a nice visit after all.

***

Lena kept looking out of the window and checking her watch.

"What's wrong, baby?" Maybelle asked.

"Nothing is actually wrong. I'm just stressed out."

"Why?"

"I'm just worried that Nadia's going to run into one of them, Big Mama. I'm not ready for that to happen. Everything is moving too fast for me."

"Come sit, Magdalena." Lena sat next to Maybelle. Maybelle sighed and caressed her hand. "She's bound to run into those same folks that you been running away from. Everything will be okay. You just gotta have faith."

"Faith in what?"

"Faith in the Good Lord."

"Well, this Good Lord you keep speaking of let some pretty terrible things happen to me, Big Mama. I'm not sure if I can have faith in someone who allowed me to suffer like that."

"I know you went through some pretty bad things. To go through so much at such a young age and still come out as strong as you are, shows me that He's been looking out for you all these years."

"I wish I believed that."

"You will. Before this is all over with. You will."

"I don't want you to go, Big Mama." She choked on her words. Her heart was in her throat.

"Now now, baby." She stroked Lena's hair softly. "I've lived a good long life. When it's time for me to leave this Earth, I can't stop it."

"I know, but you're all I have."

"No, I'm not. You have your baby. You have Janine."

"I don't have Janine, Big Mama. You have to understand that our friendship died twenty-four years ago, along with my hopes of ever living a normal life."

Maybelle gazed into her eyes. "Nothing in this world is normal. You have to make your own normal."

"Make my own normal?"

"Yes. The world will try to fit you into what they feel is normal. And if you don't fit the bill, then you'll be marked as different."

"I know all too well about that."

"And Janine does too." Maybelle nodded slowly. "Remember how she was treated because she loved you? She was marked as different. But did that matter to her?"

"No, I guess not."

"Then it shouldn't matter to you either. Make your own normal. You need to get your family back and make your own normal."

"My family?"

"I know you've lost your faith. But the Lord has not forgotten you or them."

"What do you mean?"

"My prayers weren't the only ones that brought you home, baby."

"I didn't pray for you to get sick!"

"Neither did I, but I am, and there's no getting around it. But sometimes good things come out of bad things happening."

"Who else has been praying for me to come back?"

Maybelle shrugged. "I don't know. But it seems to me that what's happening is something that cannot be fought against. It's the Lord's will for you to have your family back."

Lena shook her head slowly. "I don't know about that. It seems too far-fetched to me."

"Maybe to you. But nothing is impossible for the One up above. Especially when it comes to love."

Lena scoffed. "Love."

Maybelle smiled and patted her on the leg. "You were always the kindest and most loving one of all my grandbabies. And you know what?"

"What?"

"You haven't changed a bit."

Lena's lip trembled as she struggled to remain composed. "Thank you, Big Mama."

Maybelle caressed her face. "You have been strong for so long. I just need you to stay strong a little bit longer. They are gonna need you."

"I don't know if I can do this," she whispered. "I can't hold everybody."

"I'm not asking you to hold everybody, I'm just asking you to plant your feet and put your face to the wind. No more running."

"But I'm afraid."

"I know. But if you don't stop running, you're gonna miss out on the blessings that are right in front of you."

"What blessings?"

"The blessing of Nadia. She's your healing. She's the healing for everybody involved."

"I don't want her to get hurt."

"She won't. She's stronger than you think. Remember, it's a miracle she's alive. She lived so that you all can start living again through her."

Lena swiped the tears out of her eyes when Janine entered the room. Their eyes met, and in Janine's she saw the girl that she once loved and would do anything for. For the first time since she'd returned, she saw the girl she used to call Sis.

"I hope you're right," she whispered to Maybelle.

"I am." She dried Lena's tears with her apron and then patted her gently on the face. "How about you start that laundry for me? Big Mama needs some clean draws."

"Disgusting!" Lena laughed lightly and stood. "Thank you for the pep talk. I needed it."

Maybelle nodded in response and leaned back in her chair. "I'm going to take a nap, okay girls?"

"Yes, ma'am." They happened to answer in unison. They looked at each other and smirked before Lena disappeared out of the room.

***

Fred Bailey closed the door behind him and took his seat at his desk. He popped his knuckles and looked over at Roger Chamberlain standing by the window.

"Are you sure it wasn't her?" Roger asked, taking a long puff from his cigar.

"It definitely wasn't her. But she looked just like her."

"And she's staying with Maybelle?"

"I'm sure she is. She picked up her groceries for her a while ago."

Roger sucked on the end of the cigar and held the smoke in his lungs. A few seconds later, he blew it out slowly. "This is quite interesting."

"I'd say."

"What does your gut tell you?"

Fred pushed himself out of the chair and walked over to the window. "I think the girl is back in town. And I think the person I saw today is her kid."

"How old did she look?"

"I'm not good guessing ages."

"Try."

"I don't know. Between twenty and twenty-five."

"You better hope she's on the lower end of that or she's gonna be trouble."

"Trouble?"

"Yeah. Trouble."

A silence fell over them as they looked out the window. Roger took another puff of his cigar and blew the smoke into the air. Fred choked a little on it and turned away from him.

"Have you talked to Ty about her?" Roger asked.

"Not yet. I wanted to talk to you first."

Roger took a seat in the chair by the window. "I need you to get Ty on the phone and tell him about this girl. Make sure she's watched."

"Yes, sir."

"Also, I wanna know if Lena Pittman is back in town."

"And if she is?"

Roger's expression turned ice cold. "And if she is, I want eyes on her at all times. You understand?"

Fred nodded. "Yes, sir."

"Last thing we need is her coming back and causing trouble for me."

"You got that right. If she is here, she couldn't have picked a worse time, with elections coming up and everything."

"Exactly." Roger extinguished his cigar on the windowsill. "Keep an eye on my boy, too. Make sure you keep him busy so he will stay away from Maybelle's house."

"Yes, sir."

"I mean it. Work him longer hours and harder so when he's done, all he'll want to do is go home and go to bed."

"I get you."

"Lena Pittman is trouble. And so is that mystery woman who picked up Maybelle's stuff."

"What are you getting at?"

"Too soon to tell," Roger got up quickly and went to the door, "Just make sure you tell Ty to keep his eyes on them," he said walking out of the room.

Chapter 10

Jack looked down at his watch. He hurried to the breakroom to clock out for the evening. He was tired, and he was ready to go home. When he entered, he saw Mr. Bailey standing in his path to the time clock.

"Hey, Mr. Bailey." He tipped his hat and smiled.

Fred Bailey stepped closer. "Where do you think you're going?"

"Home."

"You're not done yet."

"But you said I get off at six."

"I said you get to go home when you finish working."

"But I did."

Fred grabbed Jack's arm and yanked him over towards the mirror. He pointed out towards the store. "I told you at noon, to straighten up those end caps, but you didn't do it."

"But I did everything else, Mr. Bailey. I even cleaned the bathrooms."

"If you don't finish everything I give you to do, you ain't going home."

Jack groaned. "I'll miss dinner."

"A big boy like you can afford to miss a meal or two. Now go straighten those end-caps."

Jack lowered his head. "Yes, sir."

Fred patted him on the arm. "Now, go on."

Jack walked quickly out of the breakroom and straightened the first end cap. A display of paper towels on sale for the week. Jack clenched his stomach. He was hungry and tired.

He glanced over his shoulder just as Fred Bailey was walking by. He turned back to the end cap and straightened the few paper towel rolls that were out of place.

His phone buzzed in his pocket. He jumped. He pulled it out and glanced down at it.

Nadia: Hi Jack. This is Nadia. We met this afternoon. You brought my groceries to the car.

Jack peeked around to see if Fred was looming anywhere nearby. Thankfully, he wasn't.

Jack: Hi.

Nadia: How are you?

Jack: Pissed off.

Jack stuffed his phone into his pocket and stomped over to the other end cap. This one was a display of cereal boxes. Jack sighed and straightened each box that was out of formation. His phone buzzed again.

He laughed. It excited him to get text messages from someone other than his parents. He glanced around for Fred and then darted off into the back storeroom. He had a secret hiding place, which he often used when Fred Bailey started hounding him. From his hiding place, he could see the whole storeroom and could see when anyone was approaching.

Nadia: Why are you pissed off? What happened?

Jack: Mr. Bailey said I can't go home.

Nadia: Why not?

Jack: Cause he said I didn't finish. But I did.

Nadia: I'm sorry.

Jack: I missed dinner. I'm hungry.

Nadia: I feel bad for you.

Jack: Thanks. What are you doing?

Nadia: Just finished dinner with my family.

Jack: I'm jealous

Nadia: Lol.

Jack: Gotta go. Boss coming.

Jack slipped his phone into his pocket just in time for Fred Bailey to come busting through the double doors. He looked around for Jack, knowing he was somewhere hiding.

"Where are you at, Jack?"

Jack appeared from behind the stack of dog food bags. "Here I am."

"Where you been? Did you finish the end caps?"

"I am finished."

"Okay." Fred glared at him. "You can go on home."

"Thank you, Mr. Bailey." Jack tipped his hat and skirted around him. Jack turned and looked at him. He was still glaring at him.

"Hey, one more thing."

"Yes, sir?"

"You remember that girl you sacked groceries for this morning?"

"Which one, sir?"

"The one who picked up Maybelle's groceries."

Jack nodded vacantly. His eyes drifted off to the left before coming back to meet Fred's.

"Yes. I remember her."

"Do you know her?"

"No, sir."

"She looked a lot like that girl we ran out of town twenty-five years ago, don't you think?"

Jack lowered his head and shrugged his shoulders. "Yes, sir."

Fred laughed at his demeanor. He enjoyed humiliating Jack. "Go home."

Jack nodded and ducked out of the storeroom. He sauntered to the front of the store. His head hung low.

Once outside, he unchained his bike from the rack and rode home. He entered his place, a quaint little in-law suite on the west wing of the estate and locked the door behind him. He walked over to the couch and collapsed on it.

He stared at the ceiling for a few minutes, doing nothing but gliding his thumb over the scar on his face. He squeezed his eyes tightly shut, forcing the tears out of them.

He felt his phone buzz in his pocket. He pulled it out and looked at the display. It was his father. He swiped and ignored the message before placing the phone down on the coffee table.

His stomach growled. It was too late to go to the main house and eat dinner. He didn't want to see them anyway. Thinking about them made him mad. He shuffled to his feet and went to the kitchen. He opened the fridge to see what he had.

Eggs. Milk. Bread. Jelly.

He shut the fridge and looked into the pantry. Peanut butter. Tuna. Nutella.

He grabbed the peanut butter, the bread, and jelly. It was quick. It was easy. It was going to have to do. After he was done making the sandwich, he sat at the table and ate quietly. Fred Bailey's words bounced around in his head like a bully taunting him.

He smacked his head repeatedly with his open palm, trying his best to force Fred's words out of his mind. When that didn't work, he did what he always did when he couldn't get thoughts out of his head. He sat down on the couch and played Bubble Pop on his phone.

He was well along in the game when another message popped up on his phone.

Nadia: Hi. I was texting to check on you. How are you?

Jack smiled. It was nice to have a new friend.

Jack: Okay. Finally got home.

Nadia: That's good. Did you have dinner?

Jack: Just a PBJ sandwich.

Nadia: Oh, those are my favorite!

Jack: What did you have?

Nadia: You don't want to know. LOL

Jack: Yes. I do. Tell me.

Nadia: My mother made us some Italian chicken meatballs with pasta.

Jack: Wow.

Nadia: I knew you didn't want to hear it.

Jack: How is Big Mama?

Nadia: She's tired today. She is getting ready for bed now.

Jack: I am coming to see her.

Nadia: When?

Jack: Tomorrow. I gotta go to bed. Sleepy.

Nadia: Goodnight, Jack.

Jack: Nite nite.

Jack got up from the couch and went to the bedroom. He stripped down to his underwear and climbed into bed before placing his phone on the nightstand. He laid on his back and gazed at the ceiling for an untold amount of time before finally drifting off to sleep.

***

Lena came outside and sat in the rocking chair next to Maybelle. She took her hand and kissed it softly. Maybelle smiled at her and nodded with approval.

"Did you like dinner, Big Mama?"

"I sure did, baby." She took in a deep and deliberate breath and then let it out. "The air is so fresh tonight."

"Yes. It is." She gazed across the open field in front of the house. It looked untouched by the years. Maybelle did an excellent job taking care of the property.

The screen door opened, and Nadia stepped out onto the porch. She was preoccupied with her phone as she took a seat on the steps in front of them. Lena and Maybelle watched her with amusement while she chuckled and smiled at her phone.

"Do you have a new sweetheart? Is that why you're giggling like so?" Maybelle asked.

Nadia glanced up and smiled at her. "Oh, no! Nothing like that!" She looked down at her phone and sent a quick text. "I made a new friend in town today."

"Oh, really?" Maybelle said. She glanced over at Lena whose face was void of expression.

"Yes, ma'am," Nadia said as she got up and took the stool sitting by the porch railing. "Just a friendly guy who sacked my groceries this morning."

"Oh my. That's so nice."

"Yeah, it is. He was friendlier than most of the people who worked there. Not a grumpy bone in his body." She looked up at Lena and smiled nervously. She wasn't sure how Lena was going to react to her making friends, let alone giving a guy from town her phone number.

Lena just nodded slowly and gazed across the field again. Nadia was looking for her approval, but she didn't immediately find it. Nadia sighed and fidgeted with her hands. An awkward silence filled the air. The only thing that could be heard was the sound of Maybelle's chair rocking.

After some time, Maybelle finally scooted to the edge of her chair. "It's time for Big Mama to turn in for the night."

Lena moved to get up, but Maybelle touched her arm gently. "Stay put. You and your baby enjoy the lightning bugs," she said tipping her head towards the field in front of them. As if on cue, the field lit up with intermittent displays of soft glowing lights.

Maybelle called for Janine. Janine appeared at the door less than a minute later.

"Come help me to bed, baby."

Janine quickly came to her side, wrapped her arm around her, and helped her inside of the house. She said nothing to Lena or Nadia during the short time she was in their presence. Her silence left Lena with a longing to speak to her again.

When the two of them disappeared into the house, Nadia took the seat next to Lena and copied her by staring out across the field. "That's beautiful," she said.

"Yes, it is."

Nadia glanced over at Lena. "Are you upset with me?"

"Why would I be upset?"

"I don't know."

"Sweet pea, listen. I can't stop you from making friends here. Not all people in Archer are bad. I just want you to be careful while we are here."

"I will."

Lena closed her eyes for a moment. It was quiet and peaceful. Nadia wasn't sure if she should take advantage of Lena's approachable demeanor.

"Mom?"

"Yes?"

"May I ask you a few questions about my father?"

She opened her eyes and looked over at her. "What would you like to know?"

In all the years that Nadia had tried to breach this subject, this seemed to be the most favorable. Lena was in a different mindset than she had been at home. She wasn't as guarded. Not as afraid. The look in her eyes gave Nadia the confidence to ask. She thought of all the questions she wanted to ask her. There were so many, but Lena wouldn't be this receptive for long. Eventually, she would close down again, her feelings and memories locking behind her vault.

"Did you love him?" Of all the questions, this one was the most important to ask.

"I loved him. And he loved me."

Nadia smiled. The answer to her question was so simple but so complicated at the same time. She forced her smile from widening, knowing that her mother's emotions were extremely unpredictable on this topic.

Lena held her gaze. Usually, Lena would have shut down her questioning by now, but here she was, inviting her to ask more of her.

"How did you meet?"

"We grew up here. Our families knew each other. We went to school together; you know how it goes in small towns."

"Is he still alive?"

"More than likely."

"Could you tell me what he was like?"

Lena crossed her arms and sighed again. Everything about her body language showed that she would soon shut down the questioning.

"Well, before everything happened, I had two best friends. Him and Janine. I was very picky with who I chose to hang around because I had trust issues." She laughed a little and glanced over at Nadia. Nadia was completely engrossed.

"Did they get along? You know, did they compete for your attention?"

"You better believe it."

Nadia laughed. "That's so cool."

"Yeah. I thought so too. Those two made me feel like the most important person in the world."

"Who was your favorite?"

"I didn't have a favorite. I loved them both. So very much. But I was conflicted when I fell in love with him."

"Why?"

"Janine got jealous. I started wanting to spend more time with him than with her, and I swore her to secrecy."

"Secrecy?"

Lena nodded. The conversation quickly turned in a direction she didn't want to go just yet. "Anyways, your father was a lovely and kind young man. He was gentle too."

"Really?"

"Um-hmm. You're a lot like him."

"What is his name?"

Lena sighed. "His name is Aidan."

"Aidan?"

"Yes."

Nadia sat quietly for a moment and gazed into her mother's eyes. Lena didn't budge. She just waited for her to process the information.

"That's my name spelled backward."

"Actually, your name is his spelled backward."

"Wow," Nadia said quietly.

Lena took a deep breath and closed her eyes again. She wanted so much to give Nadia what she wanted from her. The best gift she could ever give her was the gift of belonging.

"Before our lives fell apart, he wanted to move us away from here and away from the hate to somewhere safe. We had it all planned out. I mean, I had it all planned out, he kinda just went with whatever I wanted."

Nadia laughed with her. "What do you mean away from the hate?"

"His family hated me and anyone who looked like me." She ran her index finger up and down her forearm, indicating the reason why she was hated.

"Oh..." Nadia said vacantly. "My father is white?"

"As rice."

"Oh, dang!" Nadia ran her fingers through her hair and stood up from her chair. She walked back and forth on the porch before retaking her seat beside Lena. She didn't want to waste any time being shocked over her revelations. She wanted to get as much information as she could.

"Are you shocked?"

"I mean, I kinda figured my father wasn't black, but I had no clue he was white-white. I thought maybe he was Hispanic or something."

Lena laughed softly.

"He wanted to take us away from here and live a life together. He asked me to marry him when I told him I was pregnant with you."

"Really?"

"Yes. I said yes, of course. But it just wasn't in the cards for us." Her voice turned sad, and she fought back the tears. Her tears glistened in the glow of the porch light. "His father put an end to us."

Nadia opened her mouth to ask another question, but she recognized that Lena needed some time. So, she sat quietly and waited for her to either get up and walk away or continue. After a few minutes, Lena cleared her throat softly and continued.

"There's something I need you to know about him."

"Okay."

"Big Mama seems to think that you are destined to cross paths with him."

"Is that a bad thing?"

"No, it's just that so many things happened the last time I saw him. And then I left Archer, and he didn't know if you survived it. It's a miracle you lived through it."

Nadia stared at her. "Lived through what? I don't understand."

"The last time he and I were together, something terrible happened to me. His father did something very terrible to me. Because of Janine."

Lena spurted out incomplete sentences, her anxiety level skyrocketing as she anticipated sharing these details with Nadia. Hyperventilation followed, and then the shaking and sweats.

Nadia reached over and covered Lena's hand. "How was Janine involved in that?"

"She told them."

"Told them what?"

"Where to find us. I told her where I was going to be. And she went and told his father. They came after us. Barged in. Hurt me and made him watch."

"Oh my God," Nadia gasped.

"I couldn't fight them. All of the men in his family are big. Brutes." Lena trembled. "I'm sorry, I think I've said too much." She moved to get up, but Nadia stilled her escape.

"I need to know this, Mom. Please..."

After staring into her eyes for an untold amount of time, Lena finally nodded. "His father and uncle and two of his cousins busted into the barn where we were. It was our pretend home, you know. I mean, we were only kids using our imagination."

Nadia squeezed Lena's hand. "Okay."

"They just broke the door down. They dragged Janine in with them. It was then that I realized that she'd ratted us out. But I know she didn't know what they were going to do. She was jealous, but she wasn't evil like them."

"What did they do?"

Lena rolled her neck and cracked it. "Everything happened so fast. They came in, yanked him out of bed, and started beating him in front of me. I ran to defend him, and they turned their anger on me."

"Oh my God."

"His father pinned me to the ground with his hand around my throat. He was choking me. And he was telling Aidan how much he'd disgraced the family name by being with me."

Nadia sat quietly. Lena was outpouring, and she dared not stop her now.

"His uncle came over and held me down, and his father taught him a lesson about how to handle a black girl like me."

"What?" Nadia gasped. "What does that mean?"

Lena squeezed her eyes tightly shut. Tears streamed down the sides of her face. "They took turns with me. One after another. While they forced him to watch. One after another."

"Oh no."

"I was so damaged. So much blood. These were grown men, sweet pea. I was just fifteen years old. Your father was the only person I'd ever been with."

Nadia felt a wave of nausea rush over her. "How many of them were there?"

"Four. His father, uncle, and cousins."

"I'm so sorry."

Lena reached over and caressed Nadia's face. Her thumb swiped away the tears that streaked down her cheek. "The entire time it was happening, I could hear him screaming at them to stop. After it was over, I couldn't move. They had beaten and assaulted me so badly, I was certain that I was going to lose you."

Nadia swallowed hard.

"But I didn't. You lived through that ordeal and was born a healthy beautiful baby girl."

"I don't know what to say."

"I remember just lying there watching him fight his father. He was preventing Aidan from coming over to me. Everything seemed like a movie. The last thing I remember about that night is seeing his father take a knife and cut him." She made a slicing motion across her face. "He bled so much. From my vantage point, I thought he had slit his throat. I thought he had killed him because of me. I was so afraid."

"God, I'm so sorry."

"Me too, sweet pea. But we all survived it. They told me never to speak of it to anyone. But I told Big Mama, and Big Mama threatened to call the state police. So that's when they started terrorizing us. I had to leave. I didn't want them hurting Big Mama because of me."

"That's so sad..."

"Big Mama said that after I left, your father came looking for me almost every day for six months. And then he finally gave up."

Nadia clenched her chest. "It hurts so much to hear that."

"Life goes on. And you survived. That's all that matters to me."

"Do you want to see him again?"

"A part of me does. And a part of me wishes that we never cross paths ever again."

"Why not?"

Lena swallowed hard and gazed into her eyes. "Because I will always love him." She finally got up out of her chair and stretched. "I'm going to head to bed, okay?"

Nadia realized that the conversation had come to an abrupt end. She'd gotten so many answers in such a short period of time. She was so happy she decided to go and sit on the porch. "Thank you for sharing that with me."

"Janine probably thinks you belong to one of those men who hurt me, but you don't. You belong to your father, and only him. Do you understand that?"

"Yes."

"And even though he didn't get a chance to meet you, he loved you so very much. You were his future. Our future. He was nothing like them."

Nadia could hear how much love Lena had for Aidan in the way she expressed herself. She walked over and embraced Lena. She had always respected her mother, but knowing what she had gone through, made her have an entirely new appreciation for her.

"I love you so much, Mom."

"I love you too, sweet pea," Lena said guiding her towards the door. "Let's get some shut-eye so we can be alert to Big Mama's needs in the morning."

"Good idea."

Without saying another word, the two walked into the house and went off to their respective rooms. Nadia lay awake, replaying the words Lena told her over and over in her head. She waited years to get this information. To know what happened to her mother. But as she contemplated the events that happened, all she wanted to do was search out the men who were responsible for hurting her. She just wanted to see them and to understand how someone could hate so much that they would do something like that to Lena.

She would never understand hate on that level, but at that moment, she did feel hate. Hatred for the men who'd caused her parents the most significant pain that they'd ever felt. And sadly, those men just so happened to be her relatives. Namely, her grandfather.

***

Roger looked up from the newspaper and glanced at the clock. He grabbed his cigar and relit the flame. "Come in," he said.

The door opened just slightly, and Linda poked her head in. "Excuse me, Roger?"

"What?"

"Your brother is here."

"What does he want?"

"I don't know. He didn't say why he's here."

"All right. Send him in."

"Okay," she said. She turned to leave.

"Where are you going?" Roger asked.

"I was thinking about having a glass of wine and heading to bed."

His eyes narrowed as he looked her up and down. "You don't need any wine. Just go to bed."

"I would really like a glass."

"You would think by now, you'd know that drinking is not a good thing for you to do."

Linda crossed her arms and stood defiantly in the doorway. "I drink what I want to drink, Roger. I'm a grown woman."

Roger stood up from his seat. He stalked over and took her by the arms. "You do what I tell you to do. You understand that?"

She answered him with silence. Without warning, he drew back and struck her open-handed across the face. The force of his blow knocked her down on the floor. She cried out and held her face, cursing him under her breath.

"If you ever defy me like that again, you'll surely regret it." She lowered her head. "Do you understand?"

"Yes. I understand."

When he saw his brother appear from around the corner, he walked away from Linda. She pulled herself up from the floor and dusted off her clothing. She cleared her throat. "Goodnight, Tyson," she said quietly.

He tipped his campaign hat and moved out of her way. She disappeared quickly down the hallway. Roger waited for his brother to come in the room before closing the door behind him. "You want a smoke?"

"Sure." Ty said taking the cigar from Roger. Roger lit it and sat down at his desk. "Fred told me what's going on."

"What do you think about it?"

Ty shrugged and sat down in the visitor's chair. "I don't really know. I haven't seen this girl y'all are talking about, and I haven't seen Pittman either."

"I haven't either, but Maybelle is sick, and apparently she called Janine to come sit with her for a couple of months."

"And you think Maybelle called the other one too?"

"Yep."

"Hmm," Ty said, taking a puff on his cigar. "What do you need me to do?"

"Find out if they're staying there at Maybelle's."

"And if they are?"

"I don't want Lena Pittman in this town. So, you do whatever you have to do to make sure she isn't."

Ty sighed and inhaled long and hard on his cigar. "You know we can't force her out of town like we did before. Times have changed. The voices of the people have changed too."

"Times may have changed, but you're still the Chief of Police. And we still run this town, and the people of Archer still do what we say."

Ty put out his cigar and got up and walked to the door. "Fred said the girl at the grocery store may look like the Pittman girl, but she also looks like a Chamberlain too."

"Which is all the more reason why they can't be in this town."

"I agree."

"Do whatever you need to do. Just make them disappear."

"Yes, sir." Ty said. He tipped his hat and walked out of the room.

Roger stared at the door for a few minutes after Ty left before getting up from the desk. He walked over to the window and looked out. He'd spent the last two and a half decades making sure no one found out about what happened that night at the barn. He clenched his hand into a tight fist and put it through the window.

He glanced down at his hand. Blood dripped off the shards of glass sticking out of his knuckles. He tugged off his tie and wrapped it around his injured hand. Lena Pittman and that woman with her had to disappear.

And soon.

Chapter 11

When Janine entered the kitchen, Lena was standing by the stove frying bacon in the skillet. She looked around for Maybelle, but she was nowhere in sight. She peeked over Lena's shoulder.

"Something smells good," Janine said.

"Breakfast wouldn't be complete without bacon."

"Wow. Those look crispy."

"Because they are."

"Yum. I love crispy bacon."

Lena sighed and handed a piece to her. "Here. Stop begging."

"I wasn't begging."

"You certainly were."

"I was not."

"Whatever, Jay." Lena laughed while keeping her back turned to her. "Help yourself to some coffee."

"Thanks." Janine made herself a cup of coffee and then sat down at the table. "Where's Big Mama?"

Lena took the remaining pieces of bacon out of the skillet and turned off the burner. She came and sat down across from Janine at the table. "She went to church."

"Oh, okay." Janine sipped on her coffee. "Why didn't you go with her?"

"I don't do church. You know that."

"Still?"

"Still."

Janine nodded and sat back in her chair. She gazed across the table at Lena, who was staring at her in return. She didn't look so angry anymore.

"Big Mama asked me if I could drive down to Leyman today," Janine said.

"To do what?"

"She said she had bought a bunch of chicken feed, and she needed it picked up from the supplier."

Lena chuckled.

"What's so funny?"

"She asked me to do the same thing. That's why I finished up breakfast, so I could go and come back. It's two hours one way."

"Looks like we've been set up," Janine said softly.

"I agree." Lena toyed with the edges of her apron and stared at Janine.

"What?"

Lena just shook her head in response. She cleared her throat softly and then sighed. "Honestly, I don't want to ride down there with you."

Janine laughed. "Wow, I forgot how brutally honest you were."

Lena shrugged her shoulders and held her gaze. "Well, it's true."

"Fine. You can go alone. I'd much rather not anyway."

"Oh, really? Why not?"

"Because I don't want to be stuck in the car with someone who's going to be rude to me the entire time."

Lena got up from the table and grabbed the coffee pot. She came back and poured herself some coffee and topped off Janine's cup as well. Lena sat down roughly.

"You're such a drama queen, Jay."

Janine rolled her eyes at her comment and sipped on her coffee. Just then, Nadia appeared in the room. When she walked in, she probably could sense the tension in the air.

"Oh..." She said, looking from Janine to Lena. "Did I interrupt something?"

"Not at all," Janine said quickly. "Your mother was finished being a jerk to me."

"Whatever." Lena bit back.

Nadia approached Lena, "Good morning, Mom."

"Good morning, sweet pea." She motioned for her to sit next to her. Nadia took her seat. "How did you sleep?"

"Okay, I guess."

"You guess?" Lena reached over and caressed her face. "What's up?"

"Nothing. Just couldn't sleep very well."

"Okay." Lena frowned a bit and retracted her hand from Nadia's face.

Nadia turned to Janine and smiled. "How are you?"

"I'm doing well, sweetheart. Thanks for asking," Janine answered.

"What do you guys have planned for today?" Nadia asked.

"I'm supposed to drive down to Leyman and pick something up for Big Mama."

"And I'm supposed to do the same thing," Janine added.

"But we are not going together," Lena said.

"Why not?" Nadia asked.

Both Lena and Janine laughed. "Because Big Mama set us up!" Lena said.

"Then that's all the more reason to go together, don't you think?" Nadia asked. "I mean, we are here for her, right, Mom?" She turned to Janine. "We all are here because she wanted us here during this time, so it's only right that we give her what she wants."

Nadia got up from the table and stood over by the stove. She kept her back to them and held her head low. They were watching her quietly. She was right. They knew it.

Lena looked over at Janine and sighed lightly. Janine gave her a half of a smile and fidgeted with the napkin in her hand. "Sweet pea?" Lena called her softly. "Come here for a moment, okay?"

Nadia detached herself from the counter and walked back over to the table. She sat down with a heavy sigh.

"Baby, what's wrong?" Lena asked while caressing her cheek. Nadia's head hung low; her eyes hidden away from the two women.

"I'm not sure."

Janine reached over and touched her lightly on the forearm. Something that she wasn't intending on doing, but it was instinctive. Her touch pulled Nadia's eyes from her lap and to Janine's. Janine smiled warmly at her and caressed her arm. Nadia just stared at her without saying a word and without responding to Lena's saying her name.

Tears brimmed Nadia's eyes as she again lowered her head and sniffled.

"Did something happen?" Lena asked.

"No." Nadia grabbed a napkin from the table and wiped her nose. "I am just sleep-deprived and sad."

"About what?" Lena said.

When Nadia looked into her mother's concerned eyes, another set of tears welled up. "About Big Mama mostly." She blew her nose gently and cleared her throat. "And I was thinking about other things we discussed. I was thinking about my friend and how he's treated. I don't understand this town."

Lena sat and gently caressed her shoulder while she talked.

"I just met Big Mama, and I love her so much, you know."

Lena nodded and swiped a tear from Nadia's cheek.

"Outside of you, I've never had anyone love me as much as she does. I mean, I can truly feel how much she loves me, and she doesn't even know me."

"You're her first great-grandchild. You will always have a special place in her heart."

"I just wish I had more time with her. I wish I could've grown up with her, you know?" she whispered. "I am having a hard time accepting the fact that she's dying."

Lena sighed heavily and took her hand. "I am so sorry I kept you away from her for so long. I was trying to protect you."

"I know."

"And I guess, in my mind, I put off the idea of something like this happening to her. I thought I still had time too."

Nadia nodded briskly and raced her fingers through her hair. "I'm not blaming you at all, Mom. I know why you did it. I'm glad you stayed away from those awful people who hurt you."

Out of her peripheral, Lena could see Janine pull away from Nadia. She knew Nadia's words pained her. Lena glanced over at Janine and was surprised to see tears in her eyes.

Their exchange was short, but Lena saw the pain in her eyes as well. All these years she'd spent being angry with Janine for what had happened, but it wasn't until now that she saw the truth. The truth was in her eyes. The fact that she wasn't the only victim of that night. Janine had no choice. Her father was an abusive monster who wielded so much power that even grown men in places of authority yielded to his influence.

Lena sighed and squeezed Nadia's hand.

"All of that is in the past, sweet pea. Let's cherish the time we have with Big Mama now. All of us." She glanced over at Janine. Janine offered a weak smile.

"I plan to. I'm just scared."

"I know. Me too," Lena said softly. An awkward silence followed while Lena comforted Nadia. After she seemed to have calmed down, Lena patted her softly on the shoulder. "So, tell me about this new friend of yours."

Nadia chuckled and smiled. "It's nothing like that, Mom."

Lena shrugged and laughed softly. "Okay. Well, tell me about him. Where did you meet him?"

"At the supermarket."

"Oh, really?"

"Yes. He's a very friendly guy. Much older than me, from what I can tell."

"I thought you liked older men."

Nadia laughed out loud. "Mom, stop it!"

"Sorry, sorry."

"Like I said, I'm not interested in him romantically. I mean, I just met him. What kind of a woman do you think I am?"

"A very decent, beautiful, and brilliant woman."

"Oh, you only say that because you're my mother."

They shared a laugh while Janine looked on. She smiled at them. Lena was so motherly towards her, grooming her frequently during the conversation.

"But seriously. I'm just wondering. I don't want him to turn out to be a weirdo."

"He's not. He's not like other guys. He's so friendly. We've been texting a lot."

"About what?"

Nadia shrugged. "Stuff. We talk about his job. My job. Our hobbies. Food."

Lena laughed.

"He loves food apparently," Nadia said. "But he's a sad guy."

"Sad?"

"Yeah. I get the feeling he's not being treated right at home."

"What do you mean?"

"I mean. I think he lives with his parents and he's got to be over forty if not fifty. And he seems to be fearful of his father."

Lena frowned slightly and nodded her head. "What else can you tell me about him?"

"That's about it," Nadia said. "He's just nice, and I don't get the feeling he's trying to get into my pants. That's refreshing."

"Just be careful, sweet pea. I don't trust a guy who's too nice and not interested romantically."

Nadia laughed. "I know you don't. You don't trust anyone."

"Hey, it's kept me alive all these years."

Nadia pulled out her phone and showed her some of his text messages from earlier. They were talking about video gaming.

"He sounds like a kid. Are you sure you're texting the same guy?"

"Yes. I'm certain. He's kind of like a big kid. Like the big brother, I never had."

Lena stared at her for a moment. And then she looked over at Janine. Janine was watching them interact, not saying a word.

"What does he look like?"

"I think you might know him."

"How do you figure that?"

"He knows Big Mama."

Lena laughed. "Everyone in this town knows Big Mama, sweet pea."

"I get that, but this guy said that Big Mama called him her baby. Don't you have to be pretty special to be called that?"

Lena shuddered slightly and closed her eyes for a moment. She sighed deeply and tried her best to compose herself.

"Yes. You do have to be pretty special to be called that by Big Mama." Her voice cracked. Her heart rose into her throat and choked the words right out of her mouth. She cleared the emotion from her throat. "What did he look like?"

"I don't know. I guess he was a normal looking white guy. Big. Tall, I mean. He looks to be six something — dark hair with some grey. Clean low beard. Blue eyes. He looks like he could be scary, but he's not at all."

Lena nodded and sat back in her chair. "All right."

"Do you know him?"

"What's his name?"

"His name is Jack."

Lena sighed and wrung her hands. "Yes. I know him."

"So, then you know he's harmless, right?"

Lena nodded. She picked up her cup. Her hands trembled as she brought the cup up to her lips and sipped in silence. "Yes. He's harmless."

Nadia watched her curiously.

"Janine could tell you all about him."

Nadia glanced over at Janine and she smiled at her.

"He's my brother."

"Your brother?"

"Yes. He's my big brother."

"Wow. It's such a small world."

"That it is," Janine said. She stood from her seat and stretched. "What time do you want to be leaving for Leyman?" she asked Lena.

Lena glanced at the clock. "Big Mama will be in church until noon she said. If we leave within thirty minutes, we can get down there and back before three."

"Okay." Janine got up and went down the hallway to her bedroom.

When she had disappeared, Nadia turned to Lena and observed her closely.

"What?" Lena asked her.

"Are you okay?"

"Yes, I am."

"You're acting weird."

"Weird how?"

"I don't know. Just weird."

Lena shrugged and sipped again on her coffee. It was cold and it made her want to gag.

"I promise you, Mom, I am not interested in him. He's got an intellectual disability," she whispered.

Lena shot her an intensely hot glare. "What does that have to do with anything?"

Nadia was caught off guard by her mother's sudden mood change. "I mean, nothing really. I was just saying that I would never try to date a guy with an intellectual disability."

"Why not?"

"Because it's like something that most people wouldn't do. Because a person with an intellectual disability can't function in a normal relationship."

"That depends on the level of disability. A person with a mild case can actually function just fine. That kind of attitude about them is what you call prejudice."

"What?" Nadia gasped. "I wasn't being prejudicial. I really like him, but as a friend. I was just trying to explain why I wouldn't ever think of going there with anyone like him."

Lena scoffed and finished off the rest of her coffee. "I heard what you said." Her voice turned cold.

Nadia couldn't understand. "What did I say wrong?"

"You said nothing wrong."

"Then why do you have this attitude with me?"

"I'm just disappointed to hear you speak like this. I thought I raised you better than this. It sounds like you are prejudiced against people with a mental disability."

"That's not true! Oh my God."

Lena just stared at her.

"You misunderstood everything I just said." Nadia fidgeted with her hands and sighed heavily. "If I offended you, I am sorry. I didn't mean to. I was just trying to say that you don't need to worry about me falling for this guy because he's not someone I would want to date."

"Because he's disabled."

Nadia tossed her hands up in the air. It was no use going back and forth with Lena. Lena always won.

"No. Because he's old."

After a solid minute of staring at her, Lena finally laughed lightly. Nadia's attempt to diffuse her mother with humor worked.

"Let me tell you something, sweet pea." Lena leaned closer and stroked Nadia's forearm. "There are so many people out there in the world who are prejudiced against anyone who isn't like them. They'll hate someone just because of their race, skin color, nationality, level of intellect, you know this – It's got to stop."

"I don't hate anyone."

"I didn't say you did. I'm just asking you to be careful. You want a friendship with this guy, but you are sitting here saying that intellectually disabled people can't function in a normal relationship. While that may be true of those whose case is major to severe, someone like Jack can function pretty well."

Nadia nodded.

"How do you think he would feel if he heard you speak like that and you are trying to cultivate a friendship with him?"

Nadia thought on it for a few quiet moments. "He would be hurt."

"Yes. He would."

"I'm sorry. I didn't mean to sound hateful."

"I know. Plus, I saved you from the wrath of Janine. She's fiercely protective of her brother. If she heard you say that, she would chew you out for sure."

"Oh boy." Nadia chuckled a bit. "Thanks for the save."

Lena nodded and smiled. "I love you, sweet pea."

"I love you, too."

Lena stroked her face gently and then kissed her lightly on the forehead. When she pulled away from her, tears brimmed her eyes.

"What's wrong? Why are you crying?"

Lena shook her head slowly and swiped her tears away. "It's nothing." She rose from her seat. "I need to get ready for this trip with Janine, okay?"

"Oh... Okay."

"We will talk more when I get back."

"All right."

"When Big Mama gets home, please make sure she rests. I left her lunch in the fridge."

"Great. And I will do that. Enjoy your car trip."

"Thanks." Lena opened her mouth to say something else, but she thought better of it, and turned and walked out of the kitchen.

She left Nadia sitting there wondering about what just happened.

Chapter 12

Lena made the first stop for gas halfway, in the town of Calston. She was surprised by how much the once sleepy little town had changed. The landscape didn't even look the same. The people seemed different, more twenty-first century here. If only Archer was like this.

"Thanks for stopping," Janine said, "I shouldn't have drunk so much water."

Lena scrolled through her phone. "No problem."

"Do you want something from inside?"

"No."

"Are you sure? I could get you a coffee or a candy bar or maybe some—"

"I'm good, Jay. I just want to get to where we're going and back, okay?" Lena said with more than a hint of irritation as she glanced up at her.

Janine's smile disappeared from her face. "All right," she said while opening the door, "I'll be right back." Janine slammed the door shut and disappeared into the store.

Lena shook her head and scrolled through her phone. She hadn't checked her email or updated her Instagram since she'd been in Archer. She couldn't think about anything but Big Mama and helping her. She opened up Instagram and saw that she had ten new followers. That wasn't bad for a few inactive days.

She glanced up and saw Janine returning to the car. She put her phone down and started the ignition. Janine got in the car and slammed the door again.

"Must you slam the door like that?"

"Oh, I'm sorry. Does that irritate you?"

"Yes. As a matter of fact, it does."

"My apologies. It seems like everything I'm doing today is irritating you."

"Really?"

"Please tell me, Queen Lena. Does my breathing also irritate you?"

Lena laughed and threw the car into reverse. She backed out of the parking spot and made her way back to the freeway. She said nothing to her while she navigated her way through traffic.

"What's your problem?" She finally broke the awkward silence.

"I don't have a problem," Janine answered.

"Sounds like it to me."

"You're just being you."

"What does that mean? Me being me?"

"Anytime I open my mouth, you act as though I'm irritating you. I was just trying to be nice."

"Nice, huh?"

"Yes!"

The slight elevation in Janine's voice made her look over at her. Her eyes were wide and blazing with an emotion that was unique to her and only her. Lena hadn't seen it in over two decades, but the moment she saw it, she recognized it immediately.

Janine was upset and hurt by the way Lena was treating her. From the time they left Maybelle's house and stopped at the gas station, Lena hadn't said but three words to her, maybe four. It was one long hour of silence.

"I didn't want any coffee or candy. What's the problem?"

"The problem is you're being rude to me. Just like I thought you would."

"I am not rude."

"You've barely spoken to me this entire time. I would much rather walk than sit here with you like this."

Lena rolled her eyes and pulled the car over to the shoulder. She parked it and gestured towards the passenger door. "There you go."

"What?" Janine gasped.

"You said you'd much rather walk. So, walk."

"I am not walking the rest of the way there!"

"Then don't say stuff you don't mean." Lena threw the car into drive and pulled back onto the freeway.

The silence that followed was so profound that it made even Lena feel uncomfortable. She wanted to say something to fill the void in the air around them, but she couldn't think of anything. She used to know this person sitting beside her, but she knew the girl, not the woman.

So much had changed over the years. Even if she wanted to, it was impossible to recapture the love and friendship they had so long ago. She glanced over at Janine just as she was swiping a tear from her eye.

"Look, I'm sorry." Lena finally said. Her voice was warmer and apologetic.

Janine didn't respond, she just looked out the window. Lena tightened her grip on the steering wheel and sighed.

"I'm sorry," she said softer, and she meant it. She hoped that Janine could hear how genuine she was.

Janine turned her head towards her. "Okay."

Lena continued to drive in silence. She didn't want to come off as a jerk the entire time they were alone together, but it was hard. It was hard trying to act normal under these circumstances. Maybelle wished for them to reconcile their friendship, but it seemed near impossible.

"You look good," Lena said. Her statement floated through the air, only to be absorbed by the humming of the tires against the pavement.

"You do, too," Janine replied a few minutes later. She fidgeted with her hands resting in her lap. "This is all overwhelming for me as well, Lena. I hope you understand that."

"I do." She glanced over at her. "I mean, I know it must be difficult for you as well."

"It is," Janine said, "I never thought I'd see you again."

Lena swallowed hard. Janine always had a way of cutting straight to the chase. She was still the one to speak her mind and heart without hesitation.

"Well, here I am."

"Yeah, here you are. And you hate me."

Lena wanted to ignore her statement. But she couldn't allow it to go unacknowledged. "I don't hate you."

"Feels like it."

Lena reached into the middle console and searched for her pack of gum. She swerved a bit when her eyes left the road.

"Would you please keep your eyes on the road?" Janine said while placing her hand on Lena's. "I'll find it. What are you looking for?"

"My gum should be in there somewhere. Spearmint Extra."

Janine pushed her hand away and searched for it. She found it quickly. "Here."

Lena took it from her and shoved it into her mouth. Janine made her nervous. Every time she looked at her, she remembered.

"Thanks."

"You're welcome."

Lena felt the tremble in her hands. It started out dull, but then it increased in intensity. "Hey, would you mind looking in my purse and giving me some of my medicine, please?"

"Sure." Janine dug into Lena's purse and retrieved the pill bottle. She read the label before opening the bottle. "Are you okay?"

"Yeah. Some days I need a little help."

Janine handed her the pill. Lena popped it into her mouth and swallowed it down with the water.

"How long have you been on these?"

Lena shrugged. "Those, in particular, about six months now. I tried to manage all these years without medication, but I can't."

"I'm sorry," Janine said quietly.

"Yeah, well, it's not the end of the world."

Lena drove while Janine worked on her iPad. They seemed to be satisfied with the silence. It wasn't so uncomfortable anymore. Lena was good keeping to herself for the entirety of the trip down and back, but she knew Janine would make good use of this opportunity.

"Your daughter is beautiful," Janine said without looking up from her iPad.

"Thank you."

"She looks a lot like you."

"Yep, she does."

"And she also looks like a Chamberlain."

Lena's stomach churned inside. She glanced over to see Janine staring at her. Of course, Janine would recognize her as one of them. Nadia had some of the same features. Same mannerisms. Now that they were back in town, those similarities were extremely evident.

"What's your point, Jay?"

"How do I ask without offending you?"

"You can't, so just ask."

"She told me that her birthday is in February of ninety-five."

"Yes. That's true."

"The math doesn't add up."

"What math?"

Janine turned her body to face her. Lena cut her eyes over briefly. "Is she my sister?"

Just hearing Janine ask her that question, sent her mind traveling back to that night. Her heart clenched inside of her chest as images of what Roger Chamberlain did to her came rushing back.

"What kind of a question is that?"

"Is she my father's child, Lena?" Janine touched her gently on the arm. "Is she my sister?"

Lena swallowed hard. She could hear Roger's voice in her head now, calling her every sort of filthy name imaginable while he violated her in front of them. In front of Janine...

She wondered if she remembered that night like she did. If she still lived with the horror and the trauma of what happened. She wondered if from her vantage point, what Janine saw, what she felt, while her father was taking her best friend so violently.

"No, she is not his child," she forced out, "She's not your sister."

Janine let out the breath she'd been holding.

"How did it make you feel, Jay?"

"How did what make me feel?"

"Standing there and watching what he and your other family did to me?"

"Lena—"

"How did it make you feel when you heard me crying out for you, and you did nothing?"

"I couldn't do anything."

"You could've stopped them."

"I begged them to stop."

Lena forced her eyes to remain on the road instead of looking her way. "You saw it all, didn't you?"

Janine sighed and squeezed Lena's forearm.

"Didn't you, Jay?"

"Yes. I saw it all."

"How did it make you feel knowing that if you hadn't brought them there, none of it would have happened?"

Janine pulled away from Lena and looked out the window. "I felt terrible."

"The only thing that kept me going was knowing that Nadia was alive inside of me. If she weren't there, then I would have just died."

Janine turned back to her. "You were already pregnant?"

Lena nodded. "Yeah. I was."

Janine frowned, "But how? Who?"

Lena cut her eyes over, "Who else? I was only with one person. You knew that."

She saw the blood drain from Janine's face. Her mouth dropped open, but no words formed on her lips. "What?" she gasped.

"That's why when they were beating me the way they were, I did everything I could to protect her from being hurt. It's a miracle she survived the attack."

"Oh my God, Lena. Why didn't you tell me you were pregnant?"

"Because you were acting crazy! You see what you did. You would have told your parents the first chance you got."

"No, I wouldn't have!"

"Well, that stands to be unproven. All I know is you betrayed me and told them where to find me. I knew then I was right by not trusting you with the secret of my pregnancy."

"I was fifteen years old, Lena!"

"So was I!" she yelled. Her voice echoed around the small space of the car, her tears forced their way out as she continued driving and looking straight ahead. "I was fifteen too, Jay. I was just a kid. And you see what they did to me." She pulled the car over to the shoulder and parked it. She trembled as she struggled to compose herself.

Janine watched her, too afraid to touch her or comfort her. What Lena was experiencing right now was her fault. It was all her fault. "I am so sorry for what I did to you, Lena. I had no idea what they were going to do. He just told me he wanted to talk to you. I didn't know what happened was going to happen."

"It makes no difference now."

"I wish I could go back in time. But I can't."

"Neither one of us can."

"Please forgive me," Janine whispered. "Please."

Lena swiped the tears out of her eyes with her sleeve and took a deep breath. "I told myself all these years that if I ever saw you again, I would tell you to your face how much I hate you for what you did." Janine's eyes fell into her lap. "But I can't. I can't hate anybody. Especially not you."

"I am so sorry."

"I know."

Janine reached over and touched Lena again on the arm. "Does she know?"

Lena turned the car off and leaned back in her seat. "No, she doesn't."

"Are you planning to tell her about him?"

"I'm not sure how to."

Janine reached for Lena's hand and squeezed it gently. "He never forgot about you."

She laughed. "I was kind of hoping that he had."

"After you left, they told him things about you. Things that I knew were lies, but he started believing them."

"What things?"

"Dad told him that you had changed your mind about him, and you said you didn't want to be with him."

"Jesus."

"And he kept reminding him that no one would ever want to be with someone like him. He told him that you were just desperate for a boyfriend, and that's why you chose him."

"I hate your father so much."

"After a while, he stopped going over to Big Mama's looking for you. He stopped going down to the barn waiting for you to return."

"Okay, I don't want to hear anymore." Lena pulled her hand away and covered her face.

"But he never stopped believing that you'd come back home one day."

"Yeah."

"He needs to see you, Lena. You need to see him."

"If this is your way of somehow redeeming yourself, I don't want any part of it. I'm here for Big Mama."

"So am I. But she wants us to be together again."

"No."

"Yes, she does. You know it."

"There is no us, Jay! The three of us were us a long time ago!"

"I know," Janine said. "But this is what Big Mama wants, right?"

"Don't do this. Please."

"Nadia needs to know her father. He needs to know she exists. He needs it."

"What about what I need?" she yelled. Her entire body trembled on the edge of a panic attack. "What about what I need, huh?"

"I know you may never forgive me, and if that's the case, fine. But my brother needs you and Nadia in his life. He needs his family."

"Stop it!" She turned away from her and sobbed. "You can't just demand this of me after twenty-five years, Jay. How is this fair to me?"

"If it weren't for my family and me, you would be together now, right?"

Lena shrugged. "I don't know."

"I know what you were planning and how you guys were going to leave Archer. If I knew then what I know now, I would have helped you. I would have gone with you guys."

Lena peered into her eyes. There wasn't even a hint of deception in them. "I can't just pick up where I left off. Too much has happened. We are both grown people."

"I know you are, but can't you just start from here and keep going?"

"Why is this so important to you?"

"Because no matter how much I tried to deny it, I still love you, Lena."

"You still love me?"

"Yes, I do. And I have missed you so much. I missed our friendship and the closeness I felt with you." Janine paused briefly to collect her thoughts. "And I told myself, if I were ever allowed to see you again, I would do my best to show you how sorry I am for everything that happened. Including breaking up your family."

"Christ, Jay." Lena swiped the tears from Janine's cheek. "Don't start all that crying. Please."

Janine chuckled and smiled at her. "I can't help it. I'm forever grateful to be here with you, even under these circumstances."

Lena nodded.

"Please, can we move forward from here?"

"All right."

"Big Mama always knows what's right for us. Let's do this for her?"

Lena cursed under her breath as she tucked a stray hair behind Janine's ear. "I don't even know how to begin reconciling all of these years."

"Just start by talking to him. He will be delighted to know you're here. And even happier to know about Nadia."

"How can you be so sure that he'll be happy?"

"Because I know him."

Lena leaned back against her seat and closed her eyes. She took several deliberate quiet breaths. Janine kept holding her hand and squeezing it supportively. After what seemed like hours, she opened her eyes again. "All right. I'll talk to him."

Janine was very pleased. It showed in the way her face lit up the entire car. "Thank you so much, Lena."

"Yeah. I hope you and Big Mama are right."

Janine nodded in response and moved back into her seat. "Big Mama is never wrong."

Lena started the car and pulled back onto the highway. Janine's last words bounced around in her head. Maybelle had a knack for being right about things. Call it experience or good luck. She didn't know. But she did know that Janine was correct about that.

Big Mama was never wrong.

Chapter 13

Nadia was sitting at the kitchen table with Maybelle when there was a knock at the back door. Nadia glanced up at the clock. It was going on one o'clock.

"I wonder who that could be? Is it your Mama back already?" Maybelle asked.

"I'm not sure." Nadia got up and walked over to the door. She peeked out of the window, and a big smile raced across her face. "It's my new friend, Jack!" she said and opened the door.

"Oh, my heavens, my big baby has come!" Maybelle exclaimed.

Nadia glanced up at him and smiled. "Hi, Jack!"

He waved and laughed. "Hey, Nadine."

"Nadia."

"Oh, that's right. Sorry."

"Come on in." She ushered him inside and shut the door behind him.

When he saw Maybelle sitting at the table, he walked quickly over and knelt down in front of her. "My queen," he greeted her.

"Oh, Suga. Stop that. How many times have I told you to stop calling me queen?"

"But you are the queen, Big Mama." He smiled up at her. He bowed his head to her.

She sighed lightly and touched his head with her hand. "My sweet baby boy." She sniffled and kissed him tenderly on the top of his head. "Where you coming from, Suga?"

"Home. I was bored."

"Does your daddy know you're here?"

He looked up at her and smiled. "He asked me where I was going. I told him to shove it up his—"

"Jackson..." Maybelle kindly censored him, "You better not get yourself in trouble, young man."

"I don't care what he thinks. I wanted some biscuits."

"Is that the only reason you're here?"

"Oh yeah. And to see you."

Nadia chuckled and sat down at the table. Eventually, Jack got up from the floor and sat in the chair next to Maybelle.

"I like the beard," Maybelle said.

"Thank you. It's itchy." When Jack glanced over at Nadia, his smile faded from his face.

"What's wrong?" Nadia asked.

"Nothing. You're just pretty."

"Aww. Thanks, Jack."

"You look like a friend of mine."

"Oh, really?"

"Yeah, she left me a long time ago."

"I'm sorry."

"Yeah." He swiped his nose and looked around the kitchen. "Hey, do you have any biscuits, Big Mama?"

"I sure do. Nadia, baby, get him some biscuits from the breadbox."

"All right." She got up and fixed him a plate of the fresh biscuits Lena had made this morning. "Gravy, too?"

"Yes." He watched her perform the task. He rubbed his beard again, his thumb grazing down the length of his scar. After a few moments, he snapped out of his daze and cracked his neck.

"Where are you working these days?" Maybelle asked.

"Right now, with Mr. Bailey at the store."

"Oh, that's nice. Do you like it?"

"Yes, it's fun most days, but Mr. Bailey is rude."

"How so?"

"He calls me a dummy, and he thinks I can't understand people."

Nadia had returned and placed the plate in front of him. "There you go," she said softly.

"Thanks." He picked up the first biscuit with his bare hands and stuffed it into his mouth. The whole thing disappeared in an instant. Gravy dripped down the corner of his mouth while he licked his fingers. "Wow, these are good, Big Mama."

"Thank you, baby, but I didn't make them."

"Who did?"

Maybelle tipped her head towards Nadia. "Her mama made those this morning."

"Good stuff. Your mom cooks good, Natalie."

Nadia laughed. "My name is Nadia, Jack! Nadia."

"Oh. Sorry again. I'm bad with names."

"That's okay." Nadia watched him sink his teeth into the second biscuit. From the looks of it, she was probably going to have to make another plate for him in a few minutes.

"Anyways," he tapped his head with his index finger, "Mr. Bailey thinks I can't understand when people ask me for things. He thinks I can't understand when they talk about me, but I do."

"What do they say?" Nadia asked.

Jack looked over at Maybelle. "It's okay, you can trust her," Maybelle said.

He took another bite of the biscuit and licked the gravy from the sides of his mouth. "The workers call me Forrest Gump. But I'm no dummy."

"I know you're not," Nadia said.

"Since I was a kid, people always say the same thing. Say I'm slow and stupid. And dumb. Everybody but my sister and my friend. But she's gone now."

Nadia kept silent and listened to him.

"But I'm not dumb. I just can't do things fast, but that doesn't mean that I'm a retard like they call me."

"That's terrible." Nadia felt so bad for him. He had strong feelings about how he was treated.

Jack nodded and washed the biscuits down with a glass of water. "It's okay. I'm used to it, I guess."

Nadia was at a loss for words. She didn't really know what to say to him. Her conversation with Lena earlier came back to her mind.

Maybelle reached over the table and took Jack's hand. "When Jackson here was about four years old, he wandered outside when his mama was asleep. And he fell into the swimming pool. I was in the garden tending to it when I heard the splash. When I got to him, he wasn't breathing."

"Oh, how terrible," Nadia said.

"His daddy came a running, and his mama stumbled outside too." She made a motion with her hand, mimicking someone taking a drink from a wineglass. "His daddy gave him breath until he started breathing again. He was never the same. He did things a wee bit slower. Had to be taught things over again." She squeezed his hand. "But he was still my sweet baby boy."

Jack looked over at her and smiled.

"After that, Mayor Chamberlain told me to just watch him and Janine instead of housekeeping until their mama kicked her drinking habit."

"Wait, what? His father is the mayor?"

"Yep."

"Holy smokes," Nadia gasped. "That's awesome."

Maybelle gave her a sympathetic smile while wiping the sweat off her brow. "My Jackson is a smart and capable man with a beautiful spirit."

Nadia smiled. "Yeah, I believe it."

Maybelle pushed away from the table. "You wanna stay for dinner, baby?"

"Yes, ma'am!" He answered quickly. "What are you making?"

"I ain't making nothing. I have a new cook in the house."

"Doesn't matter. I love food."

Maybelle stood on shaky legs. "Help Big Mama to the living room please," she said holding her hand out to Jack. He stood and scooped her up into his arms.

"You are lighter now, Big Mama," he said. His voice was low and sad. "Are you okay?"

"Yes, I've lost some weight. I will be okay in time."

He frowned and pursed his mouth to say something else, but he didn't. He adjusted Maybelle in his arms and carried her to the living room. He placed her gently down in her favorite chair and knelt down beside her.

"Big Mama's a little tired, okay? I'm going to take a little nap before suppertime."

"Okay." He got up and sat on the couch. He saw Nadia approaching him. He scooted over on the couch and patted the spot next to him.

She sat down and gazed at Maybelle. She had closed her eyes and leaned back in the chair. She fell into an instant sleep. Her breaths came out stable, but wheezy.

"She sounds bad," Jack said as he fidgeted with his hands. "She's all I have."

"What about your parents?"

"They don't like me. I think they are ashamed because I'm like I am."

"I'm sorry."

"My dad always says he wishes he had another son. A normal one."

Nadia touched him lightly on the arm. "I am so sorry he treats you that way."

"It's okay. I deserve it."

"Why would you say that?"

"Because I do."

"What did you do to deserve that kind of treatment?"

Jack draped his arms over his knees. "It was a long time ago. I should forget it. Forget her. But I can't."

"Why can't you?"

"Because she was the only one who liked me. She was my friend. That's why I don't have friends now. Because I was a bad one."

"I'm sorry, but I don't understand."

"Friends are supposed to watch out for each other, right?"

"Yes."

"But I didn't. I let them hurt her." He lowered his head and sighed. "That's why I'm alone."

"I don't believe that anyone deserves to be alone. You have me, Jack."

He laughed a little and looked up at her. "You'll leave too. Everybody leaves me."

"I won't." She put her arm around him and gave him a gentle side hug.

He brought his trembling hand up and ran it through his hair. "Where do you live?"

"Kansas."

"Wow. That's a long way from here, right?"

"Yes."

"How can we be friends if you live far away?"

"The distance doesn't matter. You're a pretty cool guy. I like being your friend."

He smiled and nodded. Thankfully, he was pleased with that answer. He pulled out his phone. "Let me show you something." He opened up his favorite game and turned the phone towards her. "See level 67!"

"What? That's awesome, Jack. Let me show you something." She pulled out her own phone and opened up the same game. "Level 60. I'm right behind you."

"That's so cool."

"Are you on Instagram or Facebook?"

"No."

"Hey, is it cool being the Mayor's son?"

"No. It sucks."

Nadia laughed. "Besides your dad being a jerk, why else is it bad?"

"People are afraid of him. I don't like that. That's why my sister left me."

"Because of your dad?"

"Because of what he did."

"What did he do?"

"We don't talk about it." His voice got deeper and suddenly sterner as if warning her not to tread on the subject. He cut his eyes over to her. His eyes looked like a pair of blue flames as they peered into hers.

"I'm sorry, it's none of my business."

"My dad hurts many people. If he knew you were my friend, he'd make you leave me too."

"Because I'm black?"

"Yeah. He hates people like you."

"Wow." She couldn't bring herself to say anything else. "And he runs this town?"

Jack nodded.

"That's scary."

The conversation died momentarily when Jack got lost in playing his game.

"Hey, Jack?"

150

"Yeah?"

"How did you get that scar on your face?" She swallowed hard and hoped she wouldn't offend him with her bold question. He seemed open to discuss things, so hopefully, she didn't overstep.

He ran his thumb along the length of the scar. He avoided her eyes. He cleared his throat softly and scratched his chin. "I can't talk about it," he whispered.

"I'm sorry. I shouldn't have asked such a personal question."

"Okay." He slipped his phone into his back pocket and stood up.

"Are you leaving now? Did I offend you?"

"No. I gotta pee."

Nadia burst into laughter and punched him playfully on the arm. He laughed with her and rubbed his arm. "Oww, you punch like a boy."

"You better remember that."

He headed toward the bathroom, tiptoeing past Maybelle so he wouldn't wake her up. After he had disappeared into the bathroom, Nadia sat back down on the couch and scrolled through her phone. There was nothing of importance, just a message waiting from Richard. She didn't even bother reading it.

Now that she was back in her mother's hometown, there were many things to do to keep her busy. Especially uncover the mystery behind her father and his family. She was browsing through Instagram when she heard a car pull up outside. She went to the window to see it was Lena and Janine returning.

She went back over to the couch and sat down. She caressed Maybelle's hand gently and waited for them to come inside. They entered quietly about five minutes later. They must have known that Maybelle would be resting at this time of the day.

Nadia greeted them with a smile. "Hey. I'm glad to see you guys didn't kill each other." She whispered.

"Funny, funny," Lena said.

"Sorry, I couldn't resist."

Lena came over and took a seat next to Nadia. Janine sat on the ottoman and stroked Maybelle's leg.

"How is she?" Lena asked.

"She was exhausted after church. She barely ate her lunch. When she fell asleep, she was breathing heavily and wheezing, but she seems to be breathing normally now," Nadia reported.

"Did the caretaker come by?"

"Yes. And she administered some of her pain medication because she was in a lot of pain. It seems to be getting worse every day."

Lena was deeply concerned. "Oh, I forgot about Uncle Zeke."

"I took care of him. I gave him what Big Mama didn't eat."

"Thanks so much, sweet pea."

"You're welcome, Mom. I'm glad I could help."

The toilet in the hallway bathroom flushed. Lena and Janine both turned and looked towards the hallway. Jack had been in the bathroom so long Nadia had forgotten he was there.

"Who's in the bathroom?" Lena asked.

"Oh, that's just Jack. He came by earlier to see Big Mama, and they visited until she fell asleep."

"What?" She stood slowly.

Janine calmly got up and started toward the bathroom. Lena turned her back and cupped her mouth as Nadia came to her side.

"Mom, what's wrong?"

"Nothing, honey."

"Why did you react like that? Big Mama said he could come."

"It's not that, sweet pea. Just surprised. That's all."

"Are you sure?"

Lena kept her back towards the hallway. "Yes," she answered quickly.

Jack came down the hallway just as Janine was opening her arms and inviting him in for a tight hug.

"Hey, big brother. What are you doing here?" Janine asked, turning him away from Lena, "I thought you'd be working today."

"No, not today. I came to see Big Mama."

"Oh, that's nice."

"Yeah. I didn't know she was that sick. Why didn't you tell me?"

"I was going to tell you. But I hadn't had the chance yet."

He started to turn, but Janine pulled him back around. "Jack, I need to tell you something."

"Okay," he said, looking down at her.

She glanced past him and saw that Lena was now facing them. She sighed with relief. She motioned towards Lena. He turned around and saw her.

At first, he stood there motionless. Perhaps he wasn't sure if he was really seeing her. Lena looked the same, only older. He opened his mouth to speak, but nothing came out. He unglued himself and stepped closer. And she also took a step closer.

Janine placed a supportive hand on his back, encouraging him to move closer to Lena. He turned and looked at her. "She's come home," Janine said nudging him forward, "Lena's home."

He swallowed hard and gazed at Lena again. "It's really you?"

"Yes," Lena answered. "It's me."

He clenched his chest and groaned. "No. You're playing a trick on me." He backed slowly away only to bump into Janine's hand. "It can't be you."

Lena stepped closer to him, cautiously closing the distance between them. "This isn't a trick. It's really me." Her voice was soothing and calm. She offered her hand to him. It trembled. She was anxious and scared. "See?"

After a few moments of hesitation, he took her hand into his. He pulled it to his face. Her thumb swept over his cheek in her own unique way. By this, he knew it was really her. He smiled, gazing down into her eyes.

"It's me," she whispered.

"You came back?"

"Yes."

He wrapped her in a tight hug. He held her in that embrace for what seemed like hours before he finally pulled away. He couldn't stop staring at her. He was in a state of disbelief. He pulled her over to the couch and sat down. Nadia sat in the vacant chair next to the couch and watched them.

"I thought you were never coming back," he said.

"I thought so, too."

His brow furrowed; Lena could see the questions all over his face. "Where did you go?"

"Far away from here. I had to heal."

Jack glanced past her and noticed Nadia watching them. "Oh, this is Nikki."

Lena nodded. "Her name is Nadia. She's my daughter."

"Daughter?"

"Yes. She's my daughter."

Maybelle stirred in her chair. She looked over at them and smiled. "My babies," she said softly. She smiled at Janine standing by her chair. "All my babies are here." She reached out her arms towards Jack and Lena. They came to her. Lena on her right, Janine on her left, and Jack kneeling at her feet.

"We're all here, Big Mama," Lena said.

"I've waited so long to see this right here." She reached out for Nadia. "You too, come here." Nadia hesitated at first, but then she joined them, kneeling in the vacant spot next to Jack.

"The Good Lord brought all my babies home to me." Maybelle sat up in her chair and looked at each one of them. "You all are so special to me." She smiled. "I wish I had more time to enjoy this."

"You do, Big Mama. We still have time," Lena said.

She stroked Lena's face. "This old body is getting so tired. Tired of it hurting."

"Then rest a little bit more. I can start dinner later."

"No. That's not what I mean."

"What do you mean?"

Maybelle continued to caress Lena's face softly and smile into her eyes. "I don't feel like I have two months left in me."

Lena covered Maybelle's hand. "Please, don't say that."

"I need you all to be okay."

"No, we can't do this without you."

"I'm going to try my very best to give you the time you're expecting."

"I know it hurts, but you've got to fight this."

"I will try."

"Promise me," Lena whispered. She squeezed her eyes shut, forcing the tears to stay inside.

"I promise," Maybelle said. "Now, promise me something?"

"Anything, Big Mama." Lena tightened her grip on Maybelle's hand and looked into her eyes.

"Before I leave this Earth, let Nadia meet her daddy." Lena broke down. "Don't make me promise that."

"Promise me, Magdalena."

After a few long minutes, Lena finally pulled herself together. She dried her eyes with her shirt and sighed heavily. She glanced over at Nadia, whose face was shining bright with hope and anticipation.

"All right. I promise," she exhaled. "I promise I'll introduce Nadia to her father."

"Thank you," Maybelle said.

Lena rose from where she was kneeling and stretched out her back. All eyes were on her. She turned towards the kitchen. "I am going to go get dinner started." She shut the conversation down and disappeared out of sight.

Nadia got up to go after her, but Maybelle stopped her. "Give her the time she needs. She'll be okay." Nadia retook her seat on the couch and Jack sat next to her. Maybelle tapped Janine on the arm and tipped her head in the direction of the kitchen. "Go help your sister."

Janine stood slowly and took a deep breath. "Are you sure she needs my help?"

"She doesn't need anybody but you." She patted her hand. "Go on now."

Big Mama was never wrong, but at this moment, Janine questioned whether or not it was a good idea to go in and bother Lena. They'd come so far; she didn't want to ruin the progress they'd made.

She sighed again and forced her feet to move. She followed the same path Lena had taken and disappeared into the kitchen with her.

***

Lena was dry heaving when Janine walked into the kitchen. She cautiously approached Lena's side and placed a supportive hand on her back. Lena spun around and saw Janine's concerned eyes gazing at her. She fixed her mouth to say something, but the only thing that came out was a sob, followed by another dry heave over the sink.

Janine felt Lena's body trembling. She rubbed circles on her back, trying to soothe and comfort her agitated spirit the best way she possibly could. She was surprised that Lena had not pushed her away. She expected her to, but Lena seemed to want her close by.

She placed her head on Lena's shoulder and gave her a gentle squeeze of support. Lena groaned and swore under her breath.

"Do you need your medicine?" Janine asked.

"No," Lena answered, "I just need a few minutes."

"Do you want me to leave you alone?"

Lena inhaled deeply. "No," she whispered. "Stay."

Janine gave her another gentle squeeze. She remained silent while Lena allowed her emotions to run their course. Janine realized that she didn't really need to say anything. Her presence was enough. She was so glad that Lena was open to her at this moment. Just as Maybelle had planned, the car ride turned out to be good for them.

Eventually, Lena ran some water over her face and collected herself. She stepped away from the sink and leaned against the counter. She glanced over at Janine and held her gaze for a few long seconds. "Big Mama told you to come in here, didn't she?"

"You know it."

"She's giving me such a tall order to fill, Jay." She ran her trembling fingers through her hair. "I'm not sure if I can do it."

"You're doing fine so far. I mean, you haven't chewed me up and spit me out yet."

She laughed softly. "Well, that doesn't mean that I don't want to."

Janine stepped closer and touched her arm. "She wouldn't be asking you to do any of it if she didn't think you could."

"Yeah."

"You were always the stronger one."

"Yeah but being strong just got me hurt and alienated."

"You are still strong, Lena. Look at you now."

Lena scoffed and turned to look out the window. "I'm a mess."

"So am I."

"You seem to be doing pretty good, Doc."

"That's just my work. I worked so much because I was missing something in my life."

"That's hard to believe."

"Try walking in my shoes, Lena." Janine pulled her closer. "Try being me for one day and having to live every day with the guilt of what happened to you. Knowing that all of it happened because of me and my insecurities."

"You survived it. And so did I."

"You're right. And now it's our chance to heal. Big Mama brought us back together for this reason. We agreed to do this for her, so we should do it."

"I plan on it."

"It's hard to deny how things are turning out for us. I mean, we all ended up right here together."

"Because she called us."

"True, but it seems like something more is at work here."

"Oh, god. Not you too."

"I'm just saying how I feel."

"And you're entitled, but regardless of how great you and Big Mama think things are going, she's still dying. A little bit every day. And one day, whether you want to think about it or not, she will die and there's nothing we can do to stop it."

"I know," Janine whispered, "But what good is it to her if we just sit here and wait for it to happen? How is that fair to her if we stop living just to watch her pass away? She taught us better than that, Lena."

Lena turned toward the window and looked out. The sun was inching toward the horizon. Another day was ending and bringing them closer to the inevitable.

"She is the only mother that I've ever really known," Lena said.

"Same here."

Lena turned and frowned at her.

"I love my mother. She gave birth to me, but with her habit, she wasn't available to be my mother. That's why dad hired Big Mama."

Lena scoffed and forced her eyes from her. She couldn't bear the look in her eyes. She knew that look well. Every time she gazed into the mirror in the days following her own mother's abandonment, it was her constant companion.

"My earliest memories are of Big Mama holding me and singing to me and comforting me when I was sad."

"How is that even possible?"

"My mother drank terribly. You know the story. So, they had to make sure to keep the family looking good.

After the accident with Jack, dad made sure to have someone there full time so nothing like that would happen again."

Lena sighed.

"And there were times I remember being so hungry and my mother was passed out on the sofa. I would walk around the house looking for my dad, but he wasn't there. Just when I thought I was alone I'd find Big Mama in the garden." She laughed softly. "And Jack was always by her side."

Lena smiled at her.

"She would pick me up and hold me so tight in her arms," Janine hugged herself, "and she would say, 'What's the matter, baby?'"

Lena laughed at her impression of Maybelle. "Hey, you nailed that one."

Janine smiled. "I felt so safe with her. Because I knew she loved me. Loved us. And she cared about what happened to us."

"Yeah. She is good about showing how much she loves you."

"When I thought of a mother figure, she always came to mind first."

"Me, too." Lena admitted.

Silence fell over them. Lena tried her best not to give attention to the tears in Janine's eyes, but it was a losing battle. Seeing any sign of emotional pain caused her to react the same way she always reacted. She wanted to ease it. As quickly as possible.

She couldn't stop herself from taking Janine into her arms. She quickly pulled her in before she could protest and held her. Janine reacted instantly. She clenched the fabric of her shirt, hugging her tighter than Lena was holding her. She buried her face into the crook of Lena's neck and suppressed a cry.

"You're such a cry baby," Lena whispered, ignoring her own tears stinging the backs of her eyes.

Janine held her tighter. "I'm sorry."

Lena cleared the lump of emotion in her throat. "No, you're not."

"I've missed you so much."

Lena closed her eyes. This woman wasn't going to make her confess anything else today. She refused. But the longer she held her, and the more cherished memories of yesteryear flooded through her mind, the more she wanted to tell her how much she missed her too.

She couldn't bring her guard down. At least not yet. She pulled Janine away and looked at her. It seemed like time had been frozen in her eyes. She still looked at her like she was the most important person in the world to her. How was this possible? How could she still feel the same way after all these years and after everything that has happened?

"I'm afraid, too," Janine said, "That's why we need to do this together."

"I know." Lena pressed her lips against Janine's forehead and gave her a tender kiss. The last time she'd kissed her like this was the night before her life fell apart. It was the last thing she did before they parted ways.

When she pulled away, Janine's eyes were closed. Lena wondered if she remembered it as well. After a few quiet moments, she finally opened her eyes and gazed at Lena.

"Thank you."

Lena released her. It was too easy to be overwhelmed by Janine's personality. She once was her everything and could easily become that again if she wasn't careful.

"I need to start dinner." Lena put further distance between them. "Would you like to help?"

"Sure, but I can't cook as good as you can."

"Not asking you to cook. Just help."

"That sounds easy enough." Janine rolled up her sleeves and washed her hands in the sink. "Do you remember the first time we cooked together?"

"How could I forget? You almost burned down this kitchen."

"I know, I know. I read the instructions wrong."

"Which is why I cook, and you help."

They shared a meaningful laugh and smiled at each other. Lena tossed her an extra apron and started peeling the potatoes.

Chapter 14

Maybelle and Nadia were sitting around the tv watching an episode of Wheel of Fortune, when Lena came into the room. Lena looked around and down the hall. Jack was nowhere to be found.

"Where's Jack?"

"His daddy wanted him to come home, so he left." Maybelle said.

"Oh," she said vacantly, "Okay, well dinner is ready."

"Help Big Mama up, babies."

While Nadia helped her up from the chair, Lena came to her side and offered her arm. Maybelle groaned. Her frail body trembled as she attempted to pull herself out of the chair.

She winced and gasped. "Lord Jesus."

"What's wrong?" Lena asked.

"Something hurts."

"What hurts? Your chest?"

"No, something different. In my stomach."

"Show me."

Maybelle straightened up. Beads of sweat decorated her forehead. Her body trembled steadily. She placed two fingers right above her belly button near the center of her stomach.

"Here."

Lena placed her fingers there and pressed lightly. Maybelle retracted in pain. Lena didn't know what it was that she felt, but it was hard like a stone. She gently lowered Maybelle back into the chair and knelt down beside her.

Maybelle trembled. Her eyes clenched shut. She looked to be in extreme pain.

"Give me my phone." Lena pointed to her purse. Nadia fished the phone out of her purse and handed it to Lena. She was about to call an ambulance when Maybelle touched her lightly on the arm.

"I'm okay."

"You are not okay. We need to get you to a hospital."

"No hospitals. I've had enough of them."

"But something is wrong, and I don't know what it is."

"Get your sister. Let her."

"She's not practicing. I'm calling an ambulance."

"No!" Maybelle raised her voice as best as she could. "I don't want no hospitals. You understand?"

"But—"

"No hospitals, Magdalena." Maybelle reached and stroked Lena's cheek, softening the sting of her rebuke.

Lena covered her hand with her own. "All right." She lowered her eyes in defeat. "Please go get Janine, sweet pea."

Nadia disappeared quickly into the kitchen and reappeared less than a minute later with Janine. Janine rushed over to Maybelle. "What's wrong?"

"I don't know. We were helping her out of the chair and then she started feeling a lot of pain in her stomach. I touched the place where she was experiencing pain and it was hard."

"Hard?"

"Yes," Lena tried to keep the fear out of her voice. "Hard like there's a rock in it or something."

Janine sat on the ottoman and rolled it close to Maybelle. "Go to my room and get me the small black bag sitting on my desk." Lena ran down the hall and got the bag and came quickly to her side.

"Here."

"Thanks." Janine placed the bag on the floor beside her and unzipped it. She reached in and pulled out her stethoscope.

"What's going on with her?" Lena asked.

"I don't know yet. Please just give me a moment."

"We need to get her to the hospital. You're not a real doctor."

"I am a doctor and I know what I'm doing."

"This is insane, she's in pain and we have to get her to a hospital before she—"

Janine spun around. "Lena, that's enough!" She nodded her head, hoping that Lena would stand down. "It'll be okay. I promise." Lena stared at her, her gaze excruciatingly painful to hold, but it was important that she not upset Maybelle right now.

Lena stood on the verge of tears. Her hands trembled as she raced them through her hair. "We gotta do something, Jay."

"That's what I'm trying to do," Janine said calmly. "Please calm down." Janine flicked her attention over to Nadia and tipped her head towards Lena. Nadia walked over to her mother and put her arm around her, tugging her toward the couch.

Eventually, Lena gave up the fight and plopped down. When Janine was sure that Lena wasn't going to interrupt her, she turned her attention back to Maybelle.

"On a scale of one to ten, how bad is your pain?" she asked while taking Maybelle's hand.

"Fifteen."

She placed the stethoscope on the area of concern and listened. She glanced up at Maybelle. "Are you sure you don't want to go to the hospital?"

Maybelle nodded. "Nothing can be done anymore."

"Are you certain?"

She nodded again. "Not much time left for me."

It took everything for Janine not to react to her answer. It was too soon. She swallowed the lump in her throat. "I am going to give you some medicine for the pain, okay?"

"Okay."

Janine reached into her bag and pulled out a vial of pain medicine and a syringe. She placed them on the coffee table and squeezed Maybelle's hand. "This will make you comfortable so you can sleep. Do you want to go to your bed now?"

"No. I'll stay here. I'll just lean the chair back."

"Okay." She patted her hand and measured out a dose of medicine, knowing this particular pain medication would ease her pain and help her sleep. It was very strong, but it's exactly what she needed right now. After making sure she had the correct dosage, she administered the medicine to Maybelle.

It took a few minutes for Maybelle to relax and fall asleep. They all sat watching her, too afraid to move or leave her side. Eventually, Janine assured them that she was going to be okay for the moment. She was just resting. And she finally convinced them to go and eat their dinner. She stayed with her, making sure that her sleep was as peaceful as she'd hoped.

Janine laid her head down on Maybelle's shoulder and closed her eyes. Before long she, too, drifted off to sleep.

Chapter 15

"Have a seat, son." He gestured towards the chair opposite of him. He took a puff from his cigar and blew out a plume of smoke while he waited for Jack to sit.

Jack slowly sat down. He kept his eyes on the ground, just like he'd been taught. He was a good son.

"What took you so long to get home?" he asked.

Jack wrung his hands nervously before rubbing his beard. "I was on my bike."

"Where are you coming from?"

Jack glanced up at him. Roger's eyes narrowed in anticipation of Jack's answer. Jack could never lie to his face. In a text, yes. But never to his face. And Roger knew this.

"I said, where have you been, Jackson?"

"I was visiting a new friend." He wiped the sweat that beaded his brow and sighed heavily.

"Who's your new friend?"

"A girl."

"What girl?"

"I sacked her groceries at my job, and I gave her my number."

Roger chewed on the end of his cigar. His eyes watered from the smoke. "Is that right?"

"Yes, sir."

"It's funny you mention it because Old Fred told me something interesting about this girl."

"What did he say?"

Roger sat up in his chair and stared at him. Jack nearly caved. "He said the girl you gave your number to knows Maybelle Curtis."

"Yes, sir."

"And that she looked like that other girl we ran out of town a while back."

Jack lowered his eyes. "What girl?"

"I know you're a little on the dense side, but I know you ain't that dumb."

Jack grazed his trembling thumb across his cheek.

"Does this new girl look like the other one?"

"I don't remember."

"Look me in the eyes and say that again," Roger said.

Jack looked up at him. He clenched his jaw. His father hated him. He could tell. He knew his father was ashamed of him. "Maybe a little."

"You know what I have trouble understanding?"

"What?"

"I'm having trouble understanding why my children are keeping secrets from me."

"Secrets?"

Roger stood up slowly and walked over to him. Jack knew not to stand in the face of his father. The last time he tried to do it, he was beaten for it.

"I have eyes everywhere," Roger said. He stood ominously over Jack, eliminating what personal space was left between them.

"What do you mean?"

"Keep lying to me, and you'll regret it."

Jack wanted to stand up for himself. He felt courageous tonight. Perhaps it was knowing that Lena had come back home. After all of these years, she was finally back. And she was still the same.

"I don't know what you mean, Dad."

Roger chuckled under his breath. He walked back over to the fireplace and tossed his cigar into the fire. "I know your little friend, Lena, is back, and I know she's staying at Maybelle's." He stalked back over to Jack. "And I know you and your sister both have seen her. Seems like every time she's in the picture, you and Janine start lying and keeping secrets."

Jack swallowed hard. He wasn't going to lie. He didn't want to lie. He stood and faced Roger. Roger backed away as Jack stuffed his hands into his pockets. "I saw her," he confessed.

"Why is she back?"

"Big Mama is sick."

"Who is the girl with her?"

"She said her daughter."

"Her daughter, huh?" Roger nodded his head, his eyes narrowing to thin slits. "How old is this daughter of hers?"

"I don't know."

Roger sat down in his chair. He lit another cigar and puffed on it a few minutes in silence. "You know Maybelle ain't got long before she dies, right?"

"What do you mean?"

"Doc Murray told me the cancer's eating her up inside. She's got about a month. If that."

Tears welled up in Jack's eyes. He shuffled his weight on his feet and fidgeted with his hands. He knew what cancer was. He'd read about it in the health magazines that came to the house. He knew the stages and outcomes.

"How do you know?"

"Just told you how."

Jack lowered his head. "I didn't know she was that sick."

"You need to stay away from that Pittman girl."

"Why?"

"You know why. Don't act like you ain't got no sense in your head."

"She's my friend. I just want to talk to her."

Roger pushed out of the chair. "Remember, you're the reason for what happened." He walked over and poked his finger into Jack's chest. "You... are," he laughed. "You think after all this time, that girl wants anything to do with you? If you think that, you're dumber than I thought."

His father's words sliced through his heart. He tightened his fists in his pockets. "I am not dumb."

"You sure are. Had your Mama not been drunk as a skunk the day you fell into the pool, I would have a normal son now."

"I am normal. I just can't think fast. That's all." Jack straightened himself up. He'd learned over the years that if he stood taller, then Roger would lessen his verbal insults.

Roger dismissed Jack's comment with a wave of the hand. "There's nothing normal about having a slow kid. It's plain embarrassing. I'm the mayor, and I have a drunk for a wife and a retard for a son. The only hope I have is your sister, but she's even more dysfunctional than you and your mother."

"I am normal," he repeated. "I have feelings."

Roger laughed again. "I don't care nothing about your feelings. If you think you're so normal, then you need to start carrying your weight around here."

"What do you mean?"

"Get involved. Do something in this town like you're supposed to do."

"But I don't know how."

Roger grabbed Jack's shirt and yanked him towards him. "You are a disgrace! I'm done talking to you." He shoved him away.

Jack stumbled backwards and fell across the chair. He stayed in that position, hoping to avoid any more confrontation. "I'm sorry," Jack said. He looked up at his father and saw a look of disgust on his face. "I'm sorry I am like this."

Roger stared at him for a long time before flicking his cigar into the fireplace and walking out of the room. Jack's heart burned inside. This kind of treatment had been going on for too long. He needed to get away from him.

He pulled himself to his feet and checked his watch. It was nearly eight o'clock and he could only think of one place where he wanted to be right now; and it wasn't here.

Chapter 16

Lena, again, found herself outside on the porch. She reclined in the chair and rocked slowly back and forth. She closed her eyes, hoping for a quiet moment to calm the uneasy thoughts in her mind. She heard the door open. And then the sound of footsteps approaching her. She opened one eye and saw Nadia coming near.

"I thought you'd be sleeping by now," Nadia said while taking a seat next to her.

"Can't sleep."

"Me, either."

"What's your excuse?"

"I'm a little stressed out."

"Why?" Lena asked. She closed her eyes again and swallowed hard.

"Same reason why you're stressed, I assume. Big Mama's health."

"Yeah."

Nadia took Lena's hand and squeezed it. "She looks really bad, Mom."

"I know."

"Do you think she's getting sicker?"

"Yes. Of course, she is. And there's nothing I can do about it. Nothing any of us can do about it."

"Janine said that we need to start planning for—"

"I don't care what Janine said," she cut her off, "Planning for her to die makes no sense whatsoever."

Nadia sighed. "Mom?"

"What?"

"Please, look at me."

After a minute, Lena opened her eyes and looked over at her. "Yes?"

"I know you don't want to deal with this or even discuss it, but if you don't prepare, it will be harder."

Lena turned away from her. "Advanced preparation doesn't make it better."

"Maybe it makes it easier managing through it."

"How many people have you lost?"

"None."

"So, why do you feel comfortable approaching me like this?"

"Because I know you and I are just alike. And I know how I would feel if that was you in there. I would want to prepare myself, because if you died, I know my world would completely fall apart. And I want to be prepared for that."

Lena stared at her. There was no doubt in her mind whether or not Nadia loved her. "All right," Lena said. "I promise I'll talk to Janine in the morning about this."

"Thank you."

A sound from somewhere down the driveway caught their attention. Lena squinted down the drive but couldn't see anything or anyone through the darkness. It was the sound of something approaching. Slowly making its way up the gravel path.

In time, she made out the shadowy figure of a man approaching on a bike. It was Jack. They watched him draw closer to the house. When he finally came into view of the porch light, he hopped off his bike and laid it on the ground beside him.

He walked up to the porch steps. His hands were clasped tightly at his sides. He nodded at them. "Hi," he addressed Lena first.

Lena sat up in her chair. "Hey. What are you doing here so late?"

"I didn't get to say goodbye."

"That's nice of you to come back," Lena said. "Would you like to come and sit down?" She said, pointing to the chair beside her.

He nodded but took the top step instead. He rubbed his beard and glanced over at Nadia and smiled. "Hi, Nadia."

"Hey, you remembered my name!" she chuckled softly.

He tapped his head. "Your name is stuck in here now."

"That's awesome, Jack. I feel special."

"You are."

"Aww."

"I mean. You're special like you're really nice. And you're my friend."

"I know what you meant. And thanks. I'm glad to be your friend. How did it go with your dad?"

Jack looked up at Lena. "Pretty bad."

"Aww, why?" Nadia asked.

"He's mad at me because I am like I am."

"What do you mean?"

Jack lowered his head and toyed with the fabric of his shirt. "He said he's embarrassed to have a son like me."

"Oh my God!" Nadia gasped. "No offense, but your father is a jerk!" She slid out of her seat and sat next to him, putting her arm around him. "Don't let him bring you down, Jack. There are so many people in this world who just want to hurt other people. He seems to be one of them. Don't let him make you sad like this."

"Thanks," he said without looking up at her.

"Have you eaten dinner?"

"No."

"I'm going to go make you some of what we had."

"What did you make?" He looked up; his eyes were wide with excitement.

"Mom made some baked chicken, mashed potatoes, and green beans."

"That sounds good. I love food." He smiled.

"See, that's why we're friends. I love food too!" Nadia hopped up and walked to the door. She pointed to the chair beside Lena. "Tell my mom about your game," she said disappearing into the house.

Jack watched her walk inside before he got up and took her place in the chair. He stared off into the distance before shifting his gaze to Lena. She was smiling at him. Her smile was barely a smile, a slight crease at the edge of her mouth, but definitely a smile.

"I like the beard," Lena said. "It looks good on you."

"Thank you."

"What game is Nadia talking about?"

"Oh," he said. He reached into his pocket and pulled out his phone. He opened the game app and showed it to her.

"Oh, dear. You play that game too?"

"Yeah."

"Nadia plays it all the time."

Jack laughed and rubbed his chin. He reached back into his pocket and pulled out a contact card.

"What's this?" Lena asked.

"If you ever need something, just text."

Lena glanced down at the card and smiled. She memorized the number before sliding it into her pocket. "Thanks."

He glanced back over at her. His eyes scanned her from the top of her head to the tip of her toes in a matter of seconds. "You have grey hair."

Lena laughed out loud. "It looks like you have more than me."

Jack laughed and grazed his fingers through his hair. "Yeah, I do. Makes me look old," he said quietly, "You have grey hair, but yours makes you look very beautiful."

Lena smiled at him, "Thanks."

"You're welcome."

An awkward silence fell over them. Lena didn't know what to say or even where to begin talking to him. "Nadia is nice," he said.

"Yes, she is." Lena was relieved that he'd broken the extremely long silence.

He got up and walked over to the screen door and peered inside. He watched Nadia as she prepared his meal by the stove. He shoved his trembling hands into his pockets and continued watching her. "Is she our baby?" He turned and looked her way.

She nodded, "Yes."

"I didn't know. I thought they hurt you too bad," he whispered and looked back into the kitchen. He smiled before retaking his seat next to her. He sighed and fidgeted with his hands. "She's beautiful."

"Thank you. Yes, she is."

"Do you need some money?" he asked.

"Money?"

"Yeah?"

"No. Why would you ask me that?"

He rubbed the back of his neck. His hands were trembling even more now. "I can give you some if you need some."

"No, I don't need any money."

He pulled his wallet from his jacket and took out three twenty-dollar bills. "This is all I have, but I can get more," he said, handing her the cash.

She raised her hand in protest, preventing him from sliding the money into her hand.

"No, please. We don't need any money. We're okay."

Slowly, he slid the money back into his wallet and stuffed it into his pocket. "Okay."

She touched him lightly on the hand. "But thank you. I appreciate the gesture."

He nodded in silence.

He covered her hand with his. Lena's body stiffened on contact. He took a deep breath and squeezed it lightly. He glanced up to see Lena staring at him. She was frozen. Her eyes traveled down to their joined hands. His thumb lightly grazed across the top of her hand.

"What are you doing?"

Jack said nothing in response. He just looked down at their joined hands and smiled.

"Aidan?" she said with a little more force.

He snapped out of his daze. "Yeah?"

"We can't. So many years have passed."

"But you came back."

She pulled away from him. "I came back for Big Mama."

He looked down at the ground. "Okay," he sighed, "But can we be friends again?"

Lena squeezed her hands into tight fists. "As long as your father is still running things around here, we can never be friends like we were. I can't risk being hurt again. I can't risk Nadia being hurt."

"But—" His words were cut off by Nadia walking out onto the porch. He hopped up from his seat and met her by the door. "Thank you," he said, taking the plate of food from her and sitting on the porch step in front of Lena.

"You're welcome," Nadia said. She took her seat next to Lena and started scrolling through her phone. "Can you believe he's been trying to reach out to me?"

"Who, sweet pea?"

"Richard." Nadia groaned. She leaned over and showed Lena a message from him. "He's been texting and calling for days."

"What does he want?"

"He says he wants to talk to me."

"About?"

"Probably trying to get back together with me, but that's absolutely out of the question."

Jack looked up from his plate. "Why is that out of the question?"

"Well, because he cheated on me and left me for someone else."

"Oh," Jack answered vacantly. "But did he say he was sorry?"

"Yes, why?"

"Because sometimes, people do things they don't mean, but that doesn't mean they don't love you."

Nadia stared at him. And then she glanced over at her mother who avoided eye contact with her. "I've never looked at the situation like that."

"Do you like him?" he asked.

"I used to."

"You should talk to him. Because he's probably really sorry for making you upset."

"I don't know about that."

"At least give him a chance to say sorry to you, and not just on text. Big Mama always said that tomorrow is never promised. To anyone..."

It was then that Lena turned her attention toward them. After a few quiet moments of observing the two,

Lena sat forward in her chair. "Sweet pea," she exhaled. "I need to tell you something."

Nadia frowned and sat up. "Okay. What is it?"

Lena took Nadia's hand. "I don't even know how to begin to tell you this."

"What is it? Is it bad?"

"No, not at all," she caressed her cheek and smiled at her. "I've wanted to tell you this for so long, but it was never the right time for me."

Nadia remained silent.

"You've wanted to know for many years who your father was, and I told you I would tell you one day."

"Yeah?"

"Well, today is that day."

Nadia smiled and tightened her grip on her hand. "Really?"

"Yes." Lena closed her eyes momentarily and willed up enough courage to tell Nadia the truth about her father. She hoped Nadia's reaction wouldn't be as adverse as she imagined it would be. "The reason that I never told you about him was because I felt like if you knew, you'd try to seek him out, and then your life would be in danger."

"Danger from him? You think he would try to hurt me?"

"Not from him, but his father. Your grandfather."

"What do you mean?"

Over the years, Lena had thought about how she would tell her hundreds of times, but when the time finally came, she was at a loss. Too many words would lead to confusion, and too little words would lead to questions. And she didn't want either thing.

"Your grandfather is a dangerous man. He's hurt so many people, including me."

"I remember you told me that."

"And I was afraid that if he knew about you, he'd hurt you as well. And you're all I have."

"I understand that."

"I want you to forgive me for keeping you from your father for so long."

Nadia smiled and tugged on Lena's hand. "That's okay. I understand why you did it. I just want a chance to get to know him and talk to him, at least," she laughed a little. "I just want to be able to see him."

"You already have."

"I have what?"

"You've seen him. And you've spoken to him on numerous occasions since we've been here."

Lena would never forget the look of confusion that crossed Nadia's face. At that moment, the hundreds, if not thousands of questions Nadia had ever asked about her father paled in comparison to the one question that now lingered on her face.

"But how is that possible? I've only spoken to the rude meat clerk and—" Her words faded from her lips. Nadia glanced over at Jack who was engrossed in eating his meal. "No..."

Lena nodded. "Yes."

"But how is that possible, he's—"

"He's your father," Lena added before Nadia could finish her sentence. There was no other way of putting it. The truth was the plain simple truth.

Nadia dropped Lena's hand and sat back in her chair. "Are you serious?"

"Yes." Lena realized that Jack was purposely avoiding looking at them. He was nervous. He heard everything they said but kept his eyes on his plate.

Nadia shook her head slowly. "That's why you got angry with me for what I said earlier."

"I didn't get angry. I was just disappointed."

"Disappointed? How do you think I feel now?"

Lena expected this, but there was just no other way to tell her. "I thought you'd be happy to learn about him since you were already friends with him."

"No! You thought wrong!" Nadia snapped. She jumped up from her seat and stepped away from them. "You should've told me years ago when I asked, then maybe I would have been prepared for this. Maybe I would know how to handle this!"

"Handle what?"

"Handle knowing that he's my father," she yelled.

Jack looked up from his plate. When he made eye contact with Nadia, her eyes narrowed to thin slits as she stared at him. The Chamberlain temper was quickly overtaking her.

"Calm down, sweet pea."

"This is not cool at all, Mom. You know how many years I asked you just to tell me his name? And you wouldn't. Now when we get to Archer, you want to drop all these bombshells on me."

"Bombshells? This is what you wanted to know!"

"Yeah, it is!" she bit back, "But I didn't know he was going to be him!"

Lena got out of her chair and walked over to her. "Listen, I get that you're upset, but I don't understand why you're upset. I just told you who your father is."

Nadia glanced over at Jack and then backed away from Lena. "This is so crazy."

"What is?"

"You and him?" Nadia's face was distorted. It was part confusion and part disgust. Lena's heart broke inside. "I don't get it."

Lena sighed and took Nadia by the arms and pulled her closer. "Baby listen to me. It's important to me that you try and understand this news and accept him."

"Accept him?"

"Yes."

"I accept him just fine as my friend, but I cannot wrap my mind around how he could be my father, too."

Jack walked over to them and stood behind Lena. He reached out to touch Nadia, but she retracted. Everything about her behavior at the moment was very uncharacteristic. He turned away and walked towards the edge of the porch, leaving the two of them alone.

"Don't blame him, Nadia. This was all me."

"If he's my father, then that means Janine is my aunt?"

"Yes."

"Does she know that?"

"Now she does. I told her when we were in Leyman. I told her because she thought you belong to her father."

"You mean the mayor?"

Lena nodded.

Nadia whimpered, pulling away from Lena, "What kind of soap opera crap is this?" she laughed. "Here I am thinking that my father was some successful businessman, only to find out he's—" She bit down on her knuckles, as she started pacing in front of Lena.

"Nadia, please calm down," Lena said it as calmly as she could, "I understand you may have had your expectations of who he might be and what he might be like, but—"

"Save it!" She cut her off. "Save the speech."

Lena held her tongue. "All right. I won't say it, but you really need to stop before you say something you don't mean."

"Why don't you let me worry about me, okay? You've always wanted me to just worry about myself, so how about this, I'll start right now." She turned to walk away, but Lena caught her by her arm.

"Wait a minute!" She said spinning her around. "You can't just walk away from me like that."

"Why not? I'm an adult and I can do whatever I want."

"Oh my God, what is wrong with you?"

"What's wrong with me?"

"Yes!"

Nadia shrugged out of Lena's grip. "You lied to me for decades and then all of a sudden you want to be truthful with me?"

"I didn't lie to you."

"You refused to tell me about him!" She said pointing to Jack. He seemed to be on edge watching them argue in front of him. "You kept me in the dark about who I was for years. Every birthday, I asked you to please tell me who my daddy was, but you refused. And now you expect me to accept this?"

"Whether you choose to accept it or not, that's your decision, but it is the truth. He is your father."

"Oh, what do you know about truth?"

Lena's eyes widened. Nadia's tone was bitter and unforgiving. "Excuse me?" Her eyes betrayed the fact that Nadia's words had cut deeply into her.

"Thank you for divulging this deep secret to me, but I could've lived without knowing it." Nadia couldn't hold back her tears any longer. She'd worked herself up so much that now she needed to release the anger. "I need to go," she said backing away from her and dashing into the house. Before Lena could go after her, she had reemerged from inside and walked off the porch.

Lena went after her. "Wait, where are you going?" She caught up with her and retook her by the arms, pulling her close. "You don't know where you're going. You can't just run off like this!"

Lena attempted to hug her, but Nadia shoved her away. "Don't touch me!"

Lena lost her footing and stumbled onto the ground. She landed with a heavy thud. Seconds later, Jack was by her side, helping her to her feet.

Lena's elbow was scraped and bleeding. "What in the hell has gotten into you?"

Horrified at what she'd just done, Nadia backed away from her mother. "I... I'm so sorry. I just need some time." Without saying another word, she ran off down the driveway leading away from Maybelle's house.

Chapter 17

"Christ!" Lena yelled and ran back towards the house. She needed to find her before someone else did. Nadia had inherited her speed, so she needed wheels to overtake her. This was the first time in a few years that Nadia had taken flight on foot. It used to be a regular occurrence in her teen years. Lena spent hours searching for her on foot. This was just a sad reminder of those days.

She was met at the door by Janine. "Not now, Jay, I gotta go find Nadia," she said pushing past her. All she could think of was getting her keys and getting the heck out of there. She snatched her keys from the dresser by the door and turned to leave out.

"Big Mama's gotten worse," Janine said.

Lena stopped dead in her tracks. "What?"

"It seems that she's failing faster than we originally hoped."

"What does that mean?"

Janine took a hold on her arm. "We're losing her."

"What?" Lena gasped.

Janine nodded and turned back to where Maybelle was laying.

"But I don't understand. She was just fine this morning."

"I know, but with her being in stage four, she could go a lot sooner."

Lena's heart jumped into her throat. "But, I'm not ready," she whispered.

Janine squeezed her arm. "Please help me get her to her bed?"

"Okay," she said glancing back at the door, "All right." She tossed the keys to Jack. "Hold those for me, please."

Janine guided her into the living room where Maybelle was laying. "Her pulse is weaker," Janine said.

"Can't we do something?"

"No," Janine sighed, "She has an advanced directive."

"And?"

"She has specific wishes that have to be honored during this time."

"Who says we have to follow them? I mean, she's ill."

"I say we have to follow them."

Lena immediately went on the defensive. "What do you mean by that? Now's not the time to try and call the shots."

"I'm her health care agent."

"What does that mean?"

"It means that she appointed me to make decisions for her during this time and to make sure her wishes were honored."

Lena knew what this meant. Regardless of what she wanted, Janine would keep Maybelle's wishes all the way to the end. And that's what worried her. She nodded.

"All right."

Janine caressed her arm gently before nodding to Jack. "Jack, carry her to her bedroom, please."

He came forward and carefully scooped her up into his arms. He carried her to the bedroom, laid Maybelle in her bed, and pulled the covers over her. He knelt down beside the bed and took her hand.

"Big Mama? Are you okay?" he asked.

Maybelle tried to speak but she couldn't. She just nodded her head and turned away from him.

"What's wrong with her?" He turned towards Janine. His eyes were desperate and panicked. "What's happening?"

Janine came forward and put a hand on his shoulder. She looked over at Lena and shook her head. "I'm sorry, Jack."

"What's happening?"

Janine couldn't bring herself to say the words. She turned away from him, unable to bear the look in his eyes.

"Lena?" he said turning to her. "Is she going to be okay?"

Lena walked over and sat on the bed. When she sat down, the weight of the world came down with her. She couldn't breathe. She couldn't hear anything but the heartbeat in her ears.

She reached over and took Maybelle's other hand. Her heart seized up inside of her chest. "Big Mama?" she whispered. "You gotta hold on." Maybelle didn't respond to her. "Big Mama?" she called her again, but still no response. Lena choked on her tears as she turned to Janine in desperation.

When their eyes met, Janine came to her side. She touched her gently on the shoulder. After all this time, Janine could still read her mind. Janine squeezed her shoulder and sat down beside her.

Maybelle turned her head towards them. She squinted her eyes and sighed heavily. "My babies," she whispered.

"We're here," Lena said pulling Maybelle's hand to her lips and kissing it lightly, "We're here."

"I'm so tired, Magdalena."

"I know." She tightened her grip on Maybelle. "Just try to rest."

"Where's Nadia?"

Lena's heart twisted inside of her chest. "She's not here right now."

"Did you tell her?"

"Yes." Lena nodded. "I told her."

"Is she okay?"

"Yes." She didn't know where Nadia had gone. She was so upset when she left. She should've gone after her.

Lena felt Janine's hand slide down and rest on the small of her back. She turned. In Janine's eyes, she saw the reflection of her own sadness. She knew what it meant. She turned back to Maybelle.

"I love you so much," Lena said. She held back her tears and cursed inside when she recognized death staring back at her.

"I love you, too. I love you all," Maybelle said. Her voice was low and weak.

"We know."

"Where's your sister?"

"She's here next to me."

"Take care of each other." She took a deep breath and held it. It seemed like she'd held her breath for hours before she finally let it out. "You three. Stay together."

"Yes, ma'am," Lena said, "We will."

"Promise?" Maybelle whispered.

"We promise."

Maybelle groaned as her hand released her grip on Lena's. She gasped several times before her breaths gave way to moans of pain. She turned her head away from them, trying her best to protect them from watching her suffer. She cried out in pain and prayed to her God.

Lena couldn't handle watching her suffer. She needed to do something, anything to help her. She jumped up from the bed and turned her back. She couldn't watch her. She couldn't listen to her plead to a silent God who would never answer her prayers. But all she heard was Maybelle's sobs and her groans and her whimpers.

Her mind couldn't wrap around this moment. Her body felt numb. Maybelle's cries reverberated throughout her body, piercing through every layer of protection that surrounded her. She felt a pain she had not felt before, shredding its way through her heart.

She couldn't breathe. She couldn't think. She had to escape from this nightmare. Lena felt her legs move way before her brain understood that she was walking out. She was almost to the door when someone caught her by the arm, preventing her from leaving.

It was Janine. She turned Lena to face her. Lena stared into Janine's calming eyes. "Don't leave," she said cupping her face, "I can't do this by myself."

Lena's body trembled. She brought her hands up and gripped Janine by the wrists. "I can't watch her die."

"She wants to be home."

"I know, but—" Lena glanced over to see Maybelle struggling in the bed. "I can't watch her die," she repeated. "I need to find my daughter." She tried to pull away, but Janine held her tighter.

"She will be back."

Lena felt trapped. Her mind told her to stay, but her heart told her to run; to run away as far as possible. She needed to find safety in the distance.

"Let me go, Jay." She felt her tears building inside of her, just waiting for the perfect time to spew out. "Please."

Janine pulled her into her arms. At first, Lena resisted, but when she realized that Janine wasn't going to let go, she relaxed and returned the hug. She needed to be stronger, for Big Mama's sake.

Janine tightened her arms around her, "I love you," she whispered into her ear. She had said it before when they were on the way to Leyman, but tonight when she said it, it took Lena back to their last summer together. She said it the same way she always did. A way that left no doubt in Lena's mind of whether or not she meant it.

Lena's tears forced their way out. She buried her face in Janine's shoulder and cried. "I love you too, Jay." Lena allowed Janine to hold her for an untold amount of time, but then she pulled away from her.

She had to find Nadia. She felt torn. "I need to find my daughter." She knew she should stay, but she also had an obligation to Nadia. She was the one who dragged her into this. She should have told her a long time ago about Jack. But she was a coward.

And now Nadia was somewhere out there running around Archer confused, shocked, and upset. What did she expect her to do? What hurt most was knowing that Nadia felt betrayed. Lena knew that feeling all too well.

Janine nodded and squeezed her arm. "I understand. I am going to give Big Mama something for her pain and make her comfortable."

"Will she be able to sleep with the medicine?"

"Yes. I'm going to give her some morphine. She will be able to sleep while you go look for Nadia."

"Good. I'll be right back, Big Mama."

Maybelle nodded once and turned away.

Lena grabbed her coat and hurried towards the door. She didn't even know where to begin to look for Nadia. She just knew she had to find her. She was outside on the porch searching her pockets for the car keys when Jack stumbled out behind her. She spun around, surprised and a bit confused to see him outside with her.

"Hey."

He showed her the keys. "I'll go find her."

"What?"

"Let me go find her."

"But you don't know where to look for her. Where would you start?"

"I have an idea. Please. Let me go?"

Lena stared at him in disbelief. He was determined and apparently, he wasn't going to back down.

"You stay here. I'll go find our daughter."

His words tugged at her heart. "She's very angry right now. She may say things that'll hurt you."

He shrugged. "That's okay. I'll buy her some ice cream when I find her. Ice cream always makes me feel better."

Lena cleared the lump from her throat. "All right. Please bring her back as quickly as possible."

He clenched the keys in his hand, "Don't worry. I'll find her."

"Okay," Lena whispered and stepped away from him. She watched him run down the steps and hop into the Equinox. There was an urgency in his stride. It was an urgency to find something that belonged to him. He started the car and sped off down the drive. Lena hoped Nadia hadn't found trouble wherever she had gone.

Chapter 18

Nadia stirred her coffee slowly. Her mind raced with thoughts. Everything that she'd ever imagined about her father was dissolved in an instant. As an adolescent, she imagined him to be a brave firefighter or an astronaut. And in her teens, she dreamed of him being a successful tycoon who had enough money to buy anything she could ever want.

She sighed and took a sip of her coffee. He was nothing like she imagined he would be. Nothing at all. The waitress came to her booth and placed the plate of pie down in front of her.

"Thanks," Nadia muttered.

"You're welcome," the waitress said before going to the next table.

Nadia inspected the piece of pie. It looked kind of like her mother's sweet potato pie, but it lacked the same vibrant colors she was used to seeing. She took her fork and cut a small piece of it off the edges and slid it into her mouth. It didn't look the same as her mother's, but it sure tasted the same.

She noticed a uniformed officer sitting at the high bar. He was watching her in a creepy old guy kind of way. He didn't try to hide the fact that he was staring at her. She held eye contact with him. She wasn't intimidated by anyone. Especially not some small hicktown cop. Eventually, she got tired of it and rolled her eyes in disgust. The policeman laughed under his breath and turned his back to her.

She ignored him and nibbled on her pie. Her phone rang again. It was Richard. He must have heard the news about her going to Georgia with Lena. She didn't want to hear from him. At least not now. She just wanted to be alone.

She felt her chest tightening up again when thoughts of what she said to Lena came rushing back to her mind. She was so harsh. She couldn't understand why she reacted like that. Never in a million years did she think she would respond the way she did when Lena finally revealed the identity of her father.

She saw a shadow on her plate, and she looked up to see the same policeman standing at her booth. She frowned at him. "Can I help you, Officer?"

He smelled of Old Spice. She recognized it right away because it was the same cologne that Richard wore. It almost made her gag.

"What's your name?" he said leaning against her table. His voice was cold and emotionless.

"Why do you want to know?"

"What's your name?" he repeated.

Nadia glanced to her side and noticed the waitress and cook staring in her direction. She sat back in the booth and placed her fork down. "All right, I see how this is going to be. My name is Nadia Pittman."

"Pittman, huh?"

"Yes. Sir." She knew of his kind. Lena warned that trouble would find her.

"Do you have some ID?"

"Did I do something wrong, Officer?"

"I need to see some ID," he snapped. "Right now."

Nadia held her tongue. She was well aware of the kinds of things that could happen to people like her in small towns like this. So, she knew what she had to do. She had to comply and not show any signs of aggression, but something about this officer made her feel extremely aggressive.

It was the way he looked at her. The way he smelled. And the way his lips curled up at the end of his mouth. She could tell that the thoughts he had in his head were all evil. She reached into her jacket pocket and pulled out her wallet purse. She took out her driver's license and handed it to him.

He took it from her and eyed the card. "Kansas?"

"Yes, sir."

"What's your business in town?"

She remained silent. She stared up into his eyes and clenched her jaw tightly shut.

"I said, what's your business in this town?"

"I am visiting my family."

"What family?"

"Have I done something wrong? I'm just trying to eat my meal."

"I'm the one who asks the questions around here, girl."

"Girl?" Nadia felt her insides catch fire, but she still held her tongue. And stayed compliant. "Okay."

"Who is your family?"

She looked back in the direction of the waitress, but she had turned her back to them. A vivid picture of how this town operated was revealed to her. It wasn't very appealing.

"Big Mama Curtis."

"How are you related to her?"

"She's my great-grandmother."

His eyes narrowed, and he rubbed his stubbled chin. "You must be the girl I've heard so much about."

"I don't know what you're talking about."

He laughed, "You look just like her. Anybody ever told you that?"

"Like who?"

"That whore you call your mother," he laughed. He waited for Nadia to say something. It was clear that he was trying to provoke her.

Her face reddened, and her eyes lit up with an emotion that nearly consumed her. "My mother is no whore," she said calmly, "and I would appreciate it if you would leave me alone so I can eat my meal in peace, please."

Ty Chamberlain sat down across from her. "I'm not done yet."

"What do you want?"

"I want you and your mama to get the hell out of Archer. Tonight."

"We cannot leave. We came here to care for Big Mama. We will not leave."

"I'm warning you, girl."

"My name is Nadia."

"I'm warning you, Pittman. You need to leave Archer before I make you leave."

"Who are you that you can force people to leave town like this?" Suddenly her mind recalled Lena telling her that she had been run out of town after she was assaulted. Her heart nearly seized up inside of her when she realized that the man sitting across from her was likely one of the men who had raped her mother.

"If you must know, I'm Ty Chamberlain, Chief of Police."

"Chamberlain?" she gasped.

Ty reached over and picked up the remaining piece of her pie and stuffed it into his mouth. And then he took her glass of water and washed it down.

"Yep, Chamberlain. I'm the watchdog in this town. And my brother is the mayor. So, if we don't want you here, we will first ask you nicely, and then if you refuse to leave, we will force you out. Both you and your mama."

Nadia was shocked. Her mind replayed every detail Lena had told her. Every single detail. She knew he was one of them. He was Jack's uncle. She leaned back against the booth seat, trying her best to put as much distance between them as possible.

"And you don't want me to force you to leave, now do you?"

She shook her head. "No, I don't."

"So why don't you be a good girl and go back to your Big Mama's and pack up your stuff and leave town tonight."

Tears of anger stung her eyes. She wanted to punch him square in the face. This was the man who had brutalized her mother when she was just a young teen. He was a filthy disgusting pig.

"All right," she said quietly.

"I'm glad we have an understanding." He smiled, revealing his yellowed tobacco-stained teeth. "Tell your mama Chief Chamberlain said hello." He bellowed out a laugh that was both sickening and misplaced.

The bell on the front door chimed. She glanced up and saw Jack standing there at the door. Before she could hide her face behind the Chief's body, Jack spotted her. She expected him to stand there or go sit at the bar, but to her surprise, he walked straight over to her booth. She kept her eyes on him as he drew closer until he was standing right next to them.

Ty turned around and saw him standing there. "Well, if it isn't Jackson. What are you doing here?"

Jack swallowed hard and looked at him. "I came to talk to her."

Ty looked back at her and frowned. "What do you need to talk to her about?"

"That's none of your business."

Ty stood and squared up his body. He and Jack were the same height. He moved closer to him. "What did you say?"

"I said, it's none of your business what I gotta say to her." Jack didn't seem so nervous anymore like he had been when she first met him. He seemed different.

"What the hell's gotten into you?"

"Nothing," Jack answered.

Ty stared him in the eyes in an attempt to intimidate him, but Jack wouldn't budge. He stood between Nadia and the Chief and refused to move. When Ty pressed against him, Jack took a step back, making sure his body was securely in front of Nadia.

"Your father will hear about this," Ty whispered. "You'd think you'd learned your lesson by now."

Jack gripped the side of the table and held his ground. His nails dug in as he held tightly onto it.

"Bye, Uncle Ty."

"Remember what happened last time when you tried to interfere." He reached up and swiped his finger across Jack's chin. "It'll be a shame if the same thing happened again with that whore's daughter here."

"She isn't a whore."

"She always has been and always will be," Ty whispered loud enough for Nadia to hear it.

"Shut up," Jack hissed.

Ty chuckled and then stepped away from Jack. He tipped his hat at Nadia. "I hope your stay was nice," he said before turning and walking out of the diner.

Jack stood, watching and making sure he didn't return. Eventually, he slid down into the seat across from her. He let out a heavy sigh and gazed at her. A smile creased his face.

"Hi."

"Hi." She didn't want to admit it, but she was happy to see him come through that door and even happier to see him stand up to the Chief. She felt shame because of her behavior earlier, and the fact that she had disrespected Lena in front of him.

"Are you still mad?"

She sighed. "I don't know."

"Don't be mad at your mom."

Nadia wanted to feed her sorrows with sweets tonight, but the jerk ate her pie.

"Was the pie good?" Jack asked.

"What I had of it. He ate the rest of it."

He waved the waitress over. "Can I have two pieces of pie?" he asked. "My favorites."

"Sure, Jack." The waitress shot Nadia a strange and unpleasant look before disappearing from the table. She reappeared with two large slices of sweet potato pie. She placed them down and left Jack and Nadia sitting at the table.

"Thank you," Nadia said.

"You're welcome." Jack grabbed a fork and went in on his pie. He ate it extremely fast, periodically looking up at her and smiling. "This is so good."

Nadia watched him. Just yesterday she called him a friend and today, he was her father. She tried to see past his disability, but it was hard. He wasn't who she imagined.

He realized she was staring at him, so he slowed down a bit. "Sorry. I eat fast when it's good."

"That's okay. I'm not bothered by that."

"What is bothering you?"

He stared at her with eyes as innocent as a child's. A smile started on the corner of his mouth.

"Nothing."

"Oh. I think I know." He stuffed the last morsel of pie into his mouth. "You wish I was someone else, don't you?"

Her heart ached inside. It hurt her earlier when he told her that his father wished he was someone else, and here he was saying the same thing of her. And it was true.

"No." She wanted to say more in defense of herself, but it would have been a lie. "I mean, I'm just in shock. I don't understand how you could be my father."

Jack frowned at her. "What do you mean?"

"I just don't get it. I thought you'd be like a normal guy!"

Jack sighed heavily and sat back in his seat. His eyes fell away from hers. "Your mom was the only person who treated me like I was normal."

Nadia felt terrible about how she expressed herself when she saw tears forming in his eyes.

"Kids always picked on me. Kids younger than me. But not your mom. She told me that I was her King."

"Really?"

He nodded. "She was my best friend. She beat up anybody who picked on me. And I would buy her things."

Nadia chuckled.

"Yeah. She never wanted the things I bought for her. She said she only wanted me, and to be around me. To her I was normal."

"I'm sorry, I didn't mean to say it that way. I didn't mean to hurt your feelings."

Jack took Nadia's hand. "I can't help who I am. But I'm your dad."

There was something about the way Jack said what he said that made Nadia feel a surge of emotions rushing to the surface.

"You are so pretty, Nadia."

"Thank you."

Jack smiled. "I am so happy. I'm not alone now."

She whimpered. She tried to hold in the tears, but it was a losing battle. Jack tugged a napkin from the dispenser and dabbed her eyes dry.

"I am so happy right now."

"You are?"

"Yep, I am." He caressed her cheek; she leaned into his hand and sighed.

"I'm sorry I hurt your feelings, Jack."

"It's okay. I know you didn't mean it."

"No, I didn't. This is all overwhelming for me."

Jack nodded. "Do you want some ice cream?"

"What?"

"Ice cream? It always makes me feel better. It'll probably make you feel better too."

She smiled, "Sure. Ice cream sounds good."

He waved the waitress back over and ordered two bowls of butter pecan ice cream. She returned to their table five minutes later with the ice cream and check. Jack pulled out the money and paid before Nadia had a chance to grab her purse.

It was then when she realized that the Chief had kept her driver's license. She felt the blood drain out of her face. Panicked thoughts rushed through her mind, thoughts about what the Chief would do to them if they didn't leave town.

"You don't like it?" Jack asked.

She'd been staring at her bowl for an untold amount of time. Long enough for some of it to start melting. "Oh. Yes, I do. My mind kind of wandered."

"Yeah, mine does that a lot, too."

Nadia laughed lightly and scooped a spoonful of ice cream into her mouth. She had just faced one of the demons her mother had spent nearly a quarter of a century running from.

She glanced across the table and saw Jack smiling at her. He showed courage earlier and stood up to Ty. It made her feel strangely connected to him. She smiled back at him and continued to eat her ice cream in silence.

Chapter 19

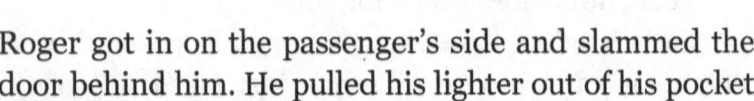

Roger got in on the passenger's side and slammed the door behind him. He pulled his lighter out of his pocket and lit his cigar. "So? What did you find out?"

Ty gripped the steering wheel. "It's true. That is Pittman's kid."

"And you know this for sure how?"

"She looks like her, and she looks like you too. I think you knocked her up that night."

Roger took a long puff from his cigar. "It very well could be you who did it too or one of your boys."

"All I know is she looks like us. Got the same eyes."

"That don't mean nothing," Roger said. He blew out a plume of smoke that filled the small space between them. Ty coughed and rolled the window down. "Did you tell her she needs to leave town?"

"Yep. I think I scared her enough. Then your boy showed up."

"Jackson?"

"How many boys do you have?"

Roger chuckled and chewed on his cigar. "Wish I had more than the dunce I got at home." He leaned his head back against the headrest. "Anyways, what happened when Jackson showed up?"

"Get this. He came there looking for her."

"That's no surprise. Nothing will be normal in this town until both that Pittman girl and the woman with her is gone."

"I tried to scare him, but he wouldn't back down."

Roger glanced over at him and frowned. "Really, now?"

"Yeah. I've never seen him like that. Well, once. You know when."

"Yeah, yeah. What did he say?"

"I asked him what his business was with her and he told me it was none of mine."

"He said it was none of your business?"

"Yep. And when I threatened to tell you, he didn't care."

"Damn it." Roger sighed. "I knew this would happen one day. That girl is back and got his mind all twisted up again."

"You think he'll start telling people about what happened?"

"He knows better. He knows he's not supposed to talk about it."

"Yeah, but he isn't a kid no more, Rog. He's obviously got a mind of his own that he's kept hidden."

Roger grumbled something under his breath but didn't address Ty's statement. "He won't say a word."

"But what about her?"

"Ha! You think anybody would believe her? Everyone knows what kind of girl she was. Like mother like daughter. Even if she does start running her mouth about what happened at the barn, we'll just deny it."

"What if DNA gets involved?"

"DNA?"

"Yeah, Rog. DNA. It's not the nineties anymore. They can prove that the girl is yours."

"Would you stop saying she's mine? She could be any one of ours, and you know it!"

"Well, she ain't mine. I know that's for sure. She looks more like you than me."

"Whatever. I don't want to discuss who she belongs to. I just want her gone."

"I don't think they're gonna leave voluntarily."

"Then we make them leave! Immediately!"

"Hey, calm down, Rog. I'll take care of it."

"We can't have that Pittman girl going around town telling people anything. It's enough having Maybelle and Jackson knowing. Now Pittman and Janine are here. That's too many people."

"True."

Roger reached into his pocket and pulled out a business card. "This is a friend of mine. Make Pittman and her bastard kid disappear," he said handing him the card.

"Disappear?"

"Yes."

"What about Janine?"

"She doesn't need to know what happens to them. You just call that number and set it up."

"Are you sure about this? Are you sure it won't get back to you? If the town finds out, you'll be removed from office."

"Then you best make sure nobody finds out, right bro?"

Ty gazed at the card before he slipped it into his shirt pocket. "Right." He started the car. "I hope you're right about this. I don't have a good feeling about any of it."

"Your gut feelings are of no concern to me. I want them both gone, so you better make it happen or I'll make sure Archer will be calling someone else Chief before long."

Ty narrowed his eyes. "Fine."

Roger hopped out of the car and slipped away under the cover of darkness.

***

Janine pulled the covers over Maybelle. "She should sleep comfortably for a few hours." She slowly cleaned up the used medical supplies on the nightstand. She worked in silence, although she could see Lena watching her from the corner of her eye.

She knew Lena was upset. She knew that if anything, Lena was aware that she would follow Maybelle's wishes to a T. That's how she was. She wasn't a rule breaker; she always stuck to the rules, even if it meant crossing others. That's how she got herself into this whole mess with Lena in the first place.

She switched off the light on the nightstand and sat down at the foot of the bed next to Lena. She sighed and looked over at her, facing her scrutinizing eyes head on. Janine touched Lena's hand, but she retracted and scooted away from her.

"What else am I supposed to do?" Janine asked.

Lena clenched her jaw. Her face quivered with tension. "The right thing," she said.

"I am. I am doing what she wishes."

"This isn't what's best for her."

"It's what she has determined is best for her. If I had it my way, I would take her to the hospital."

"Then why don't you do it?" Lena's voice was hoarse and heavy with emotion. "Right now, she needs to be in the hospital so someone can save her if she slips."

"That's not what she wants, Lena."

"I don't care!" she snapped.

"Big Mama wants to go in peace, while she's at home. She doesn't want to die in a hospital. You know this."

Lena covered her face with her hands, "What if she slips away? I don't know how to bring her back."

"She has a DNR in place." Reality suddenly hit her that once Maybelle's life slipped away, although she had the skills, she could not resuscitate her. "Per her wishes, we cannot resuscitate her."

"That's insane!"

"Shh..." Janine scooted closer and touched her on the leg. "Keep your voice down, please," she whispered. She glanced over at Maybelle and was relieved to see that Lena's short outburst hadn't awakened her.

Lena covered her face again, but this time she started sobbing. Even as a younger child, Lena was always the stronger one, hardly ever shedding a tear. Janine had only seen her cry a handful of times. The first time was when Lena's mother abandoned her. Lena completely broke down. And the last time Janine saw her cry was the night Roger and the gang attacked her.

Janine forced those memories to the back of her mind. She wasn't back there anymore. She was here with her. So much time had passed between them, but here they were; together because of Maybelle.

Janine approached her cautiously, touching her gently on the leg. "Lena?" She didn't respond. Janine moved closer. "Hey," she said.

Lena looked up at her as Janine swiped the tears from her cheeks. In times past, they could communicate without even saying a word. Their connection was special, one that was unusually strong for two people who were not bound by blood. Janine smiled at her, trying her best to diffuse any aggression that still might linger inside of her friend.

She knew one day Lena would forgive her for what she had done, but she also knew that it would take time. She didn't want to press her luck. But she felt something, something familiar while she gazed into Lena's eyes. Familiar thoughts, feelings, and memories.

Lena reached for the hand that was caressing her face and leaned into Janine's touch. She remained silent, allowing herself to be comforted for a brief moment. For the first time in over two decades, Janine felt the connection they'd always shared.

"I'm so scared." Lena whispered.

"I know."

"First Mama left me. Now she's going to leave me too." Lena glanced over at Maybelle laying peacefully in bed. She gave way to another set of tears. "My heart can't take this."

"It can. And it will. You're one of the strongest persons I know."

"I'm not that strong."

"Yes, you are. Nadia needs you. I need you." Janine pulled her into her arms and held her. Lena relaxed in her embrace. She could tell that Lena had allowed her back into her heart. This knowledge overwhelmed her. She'd been given a second chance.

At that moment, she vowed never to screw up what they had. Not ever again.

Chapter 20

Jack was opening the door for Nadia when Roger's car pulled into the parking space next to them. The driver's side door swung open and Roger stepped out of the car. His eyes were narrowed, and his hand clenched into a fist as he approached Jack. When Jack saw him coming, he stepped between him and Nadia.

"Who's this?" Roger asked. His tone was cold, judgmental.

Jack glanced back at Nadia and then at his father. He placed his arm across the door and nudged her into the passenger seat.

Roger stepped closer and looked Jack up and down. "I said who is this girl?"

Jack straightened up taller. "She's my friend."

"Hmm," Roger mused. When he laid eyes on Nadia, they burned with hatred. "Well, rumor is right."

"What rumor?" Jack asked.

"That this mystery woman looks just like the Pittman girl."

Nadia pushed her way out of the car. She squinted, trying her best to see this bastard's face, but it was cloaked in darkness. Jack nudged her slightly behind him again.

"She's her daughter," Jack offered.

"From who?"

Jack shrugged, "I don't know."

Roger glared at her again. "Do you know who I am, girl?"

Nadia stepped in front of Jack, "Honestly, I don't care who you are, especially if you speak to me that way."

Roger chuckled. "You're definitely a feisty one. Just like your mother."

"Don't say anything about my mother." By now, Nadia had already figured out who this character was, and the role he played.

He stepped closer, "Is that any way to treat a mayor?"

"Mayor? No way?" She faked surprise.

"Yes. I'm the mayor of Archer and you will show me proper respect or—"

"Or what?"

Roger smiled at her and stepped closer. When he did, she saw his face more clearly. She couldn't help but notice how much Jack looked like him. It was freaky and frightening at the same time. If he wasn't such an evil man, he'd be handsome. His ice blue eyes sent chills running up and down her spine.

She shivered under his scrutiny. As his eyes traveled up and down the length of her body, a sickening smile played on the edge of his mouth. Suddenly, she felt exposed. Knowing that this was the man who'd violated her mother caused her to feel a feeling she'd never felt before. It was all-consuming; boiling like molten lava and directed at him.

He shook his head, "Man, I bet you're just as good as Pittman," he whispered to her. His breath was foul-smelling; a mixture of tobacco, alcohol, and something else unrecognizable to her senses.

Her stomach lurched. "Back away from me," she warned.

"Do me a favor, will ya?"

"What?"

"Tell Lena she should stop by my house so we can catch up on old times."

On reflex, she shoved him away. He stumbled but recovered instantly and pimp slapped her across the face. The force of the blow shot her backwards against the Equinox. Her ears rung; she literally saw stars in front of her eyes. She'd never been hit so hard in her entire life. The only thing that felt remotely close to this blow was when she accidentally got hit in the head by a box at work. But this felt even harder, more punishing.

She wiped the blood from her lip. She sucked the rest of the salty liquid from her mouth and spat it on the ground beside his feet. She glared at him. How dare he lay his hands on her! She attempted to stand taller, but her head spun out of control.

Jack jumped in front of her again and shoved his father back. "Don't you ever do that again," Jack said. His voice was deeper, heavier, and full of emotion. "If you ever touch her like that again, I'll—"

Roger shoved him back, "You'll what? Huh? Tell me, son. What will you do?"

Jack clenched his fist and stiffened his jaw. "You'll be sorry if you hurt her again."

"How noble of you. You must think you can redeem yourself now." Roger poked his finger into Jack's chest. "Newsflash, you don't get redemption. No matter how much you try to protect this one," he said pointing at Nadia, "It won't ever make the Pittman girl want you again. You know why?"

Jack clenched his jaw, "Why?"

"Because you're nothing but a dummy. Nobody wants a dummy like you."

"I am not a dummy."

"Keep telling yourself that. But I'm your father. I know who you are. The only thing you have going for you is your inheritance. And money is the only reason why anyone would want to be with you."

"That's not true."

Roger shrugged. "Believe what you want, but that's the truth about that whore. All she wanted you for was money."

"Take it back," Jack said.

"It's the truth. Females only want you for the money. You can't do anything for them, and everybody knows it. You're nothing but a dummy."

Jack's jaw clenched tighter as he stared down his father. After what seemed like hours, he finally turned and faced Nadia. He helped her into the vehicle and shut the door behind her. He touched her lip. It was swollen and bruised.

"Seat belt," he said softly and waited for her to buckle up. After she was secured in the car, he turned to Roger. "Bye, Dad."

"Where are you going?"

Jack didn't give him the satisfaction of a reply. They needed to get back to Maybelle's house and quickly. "See you later, Dad." Jack walked around and hopped into the driver's seat.

Roger came around and stood by the window. "You will regret this choice of yours."

Jack nodded. "I regret a lot of things. But sticking up for my friend isn't one."

Roger grinned and stepped away from the car. He watched as Jack pulled out of the parking lot and drove off into the direction of Maybelle's house.

Chapter 21

Lena laid her head down next to Maybelle and sighed heavily. She felt like her heart was about to implode. It clenched inside of her chest. Every time she breathed, it quivered. She wasn't sure if she was experiencing cardiac arrest or what. She'd never experienced this type of pain before.

Tears rolled out of the corner of her eye and onto the bed. She thought of how cliché this moment was. She'd seen it a million times in movies, a person lying next to a dying loved one and their tears flowing out and all over everything. She'd often thought it was ridiculous, that tears don't flow like that, but here she was, in a scene of her own, shedding the same type of tears she didn't think possible.

She heard Janine shift in her seat beside her, but she paid her no mind. All she wanted to do was hold on to the last few minutes that Maybelle had.

"Big Mama?" She squeezed Maybelle's hand a little. She couldn't understand why it had happened so quickly. She seemed just fine yesterday. But Maybelle didn't respond. Lena wasn't exactly sure if she could hear her at all, but she just wanted to make sure she knew she was there for her. Just like she'd promised.

"I think they're back," Janine said.

Lena hoped they would be back in time. Maybelle seemed to have given up. "Okay." She swiped her tears out of her eyes and straightened up in her chair. She scooted closer to the bed and stroked Maybelle's hair.

A couple of minutes later, Lena heard the hurried footsteps of Nadia racing through the house, coming to a stop at the door. She looked up and saw Nadia standing there, eyes wide and shocked. Nadia approached her cautiously and knelt down beside Lena.

"I'm so sorry I ran off."

"Are you good now?"

"I'm not sure," Nadia said.

Lena nodded slowly. "We can discuss it later, but right now, we all need to be here for Big Mama."

"What's happening?"

"We're losing her." She caught a glimpse of Jack coming into the room. She could tell he didn't want to see Maybelle like this. "So, it's best if we all stay here tonight."

Nadia's eyes instantly filled with tears. "But it's too soon. I thought we had more time?"

"I know, sweet pea." She caressed her cheek. It was then that she noticed her swollen lip. "What happened to you?" Nadia lowered her eyes and turned her head. Lena let go of Maybelle's hand, cupping Nadia's face gently. "I said, what happened to you?"

"Mayor Chamberlain did it."

"What?" Nadia continued to avoid her eyes, so Lena tipped her gaze so she could see her face. "Tell me what happened."

By now, her heart had switched over and now spewed out feelings of hate. For Roger. She didn't know how much more it could take. From the sadness of watching Maybelle slip away, to the hate radiating from the very core of her being. Roger Chamberlain had laid his hands on her child and injured her. She couldn't breathe. She forced the overwhelming feelings inside for now, but she'd determined in her heart that she wasn't going to allow him to get away with this.

"He showed up at the diner when me and Jack were leaving. I guess the cop told him I was there."

"The cop?"

"Yeah. He said he was the Chief of Police."

Lena's eyes fluttered shut momentarily. "Did he touch you?"

"No. Not the cop. But the Mayor got in my face and you know how much I hate it when people get in my face."

"I know, baby." She grazed her finger over Nadia's busted lip. Nadia winced. "What did he say to you?"

"That's not important. He just made me mad and I shoved him away from my face. And he came back and slapped me."

Lena glanced up at Jack and frowned.

"Jack made sure he didn't do it again." Nadia added quickly. "He ran interference."

Lena sighed heavily. The stress was mounting. She glanced back over at Maybelle and reached for her hand. "I don't want you going around him ever again."

"Trust me, I won't."

"Thanks." Lena stroked Maybelle's hair and started humming softly. It was a hymn, one that she couldn't remember name or lyrics to, just the melody. It was one that Maybelle used to sing while she cooked and one that always made Lena feel safe inside. The longer she hummed it, the tighter her chest got. She could barely breathe but she was determined to sing this tune for Maybelle.

To her surprise, Maybelle opened her eyes. She moved closer so Maybelle could focus on her. "Hey Big Mama," she whispered.

"My baby."

"I love you." Lena squeezed her hand gently.

"I love you, too." Her voice was weaker than before.

"Don't try to talk."

"Keep singing to me."

"But I don't know the words."

"That's okay."

Lena nodded and swiped her tears with her shoulder. "Okay." She continued to hum the tune of the hymn that was close to Maybelle's heart and hers. She closed her eyes, trying her best to remember the words, but nothing came. She couldn't see anything through her present grief. Janine came and sat on the opposite side of the bed. Maybelle was surrounded by those who loved her most.

"I'm so tired, Magdalena."

"I know, Big Mama, I know." She swiped her finger across Maybelle's cheek and dried the tear that had fallen, "It's okay to go to sleep now."

"I want my babies to be okay."

"We are." Lena blinked the tears out of her eyes. "We are okay. I promise."

Maybelle smiled and turned her head towards Janine. She gazed at her with sleepy eyes. "Forgive yourself," she told her.

Janine nodded and mouthed the words, "I love you so much."

Maybelle turned her head back to Lena. "Tell Jackson I'm so proud of him. Nadia, too."

Lena looked up at him. "He knows. And so does Nadia."

Maybelle smiled. "She knows her daddy?"

"Yes, ma'am."

Maybelle took a deep breath and then released it. A smile rested on her face. She gazed sleepily into Lena's eyes while Lena caressed her face. She closed her eyes and then opened them. And then she closed them again.

"It's okay to go to sleep, Big Mama," Lena said. "I will do everything you ask of me. I promise."

Maybelle nodded and closed her eyes. Her eyes stayed closed longer this time than before, but she opened them again.

"Goodnight, Mama," Lena whispered, "Thank you so much for loving me."

Maybelle inhaled deeply. Her breath seemed to be caught somewhere in her body. "Goodnight, baby." She exhaled.

"Shh..." Lena smiled. "You can go to sleep now, okay?"

Maybelle's eyes glazed over. She stared past Lena's shoulder. Her breaths came in slower and longer intervals until she let out her last and final breath. To Lena, it sounded like a huge sigh of relief. She sat watching her, hoping that she'd start breathing again, but nothing happened. Maybelle lied there motionless, lifeless.

Lena felt her heart tightening. She looked up and saw Janine rising from her seat with her stethoscope in hand. She came to Maybelle's side and listened. And she listened. And listened.

Lena prayed again for the first time in years. This couldn't be it. This couldn't be the final day of Maybelle's life. It was too soon. She sat still, afraid to move. Maybelle's hand was heavy in hers, lifeless, but still so warm. She kept watching and waiting, but another breath would never come again.

"We gotta do something, Jay." She was afraid to look at Janine. Afraid to see the truth in her eyes. "Please, do something."

Janine answered her with silence. Lena found the strength to look up at her. Janine shook her head slowly and pulled the stethoscope from her ears.

"No... Please no." Lena pleaded for her to do something, to act and bring Maybelle back to them. It was too soon. She hadn't had enough time to reconcile all the years she'd been gone. "We can't just let her go like this." Lena felt her heart rising in her throat. She tried to swallow, but the lump got bigger. Choking her. "Please, Jay."

She was helpless. Impotent.

Janine knelt down in front of Lena and caressed her cheek, "She's gone."

Lena glanced back at Maybelle, her tears blurring her vision. "No." She couldn't even recognize her own voice. It sounded strangely alien to her. Like someone else had taken over her body. "Please don't go... Don't leave me." She continued humming Maybelle's tune, while nuzzling her hand.

Janine got up and came to Lena's side. Nadia allowed her to take her spot and she went over and stood next to Jack. Janine put her arm around Lena and squeezed her.

"Lena?" Lena didn't respond, she just sobbed. Janine squeezed her again in an attempt to sever her from her overwhelming grief. "Sis?" she said. "Listen to me."

Lena turned her way. She blinked the tears out of her eyes. "Yeah?"

"She's gone."

Lena stared at her; her mouth opened slightly but no words formed on her lips. "Gone?"

Janine nodded, "Yes."

"Oh god." Lena clenched her chest; agony distorted her face. Her body shook uncontrollably as she struggled to hold on to this painful reality that had become her own. Janine sprung to her feet and pulled Lena out of the chair. It was difficult for Lena to stand with the burden of grief holding her down. Her knees were too wobbly and too weak to hold her weight.

"I've got you," Janine said, tossing Lena's left arm over her shoulder and stabilizing her with a warm embrace. She held her tight, allowing Lena's full weight to rest on her. "I've got you," she repeated.

Lena broke down and sobbed uncontrollably. She'd been so strong for so long and now she couldn't do it anymore. Janine held her securely in her arms. Just like she had always done in the past when Lena needed her. She held her, whispering comforting words of encouragement into her ear.

Lena's legs gave out and they both sunk down onto the floor next to Maybelle's bed. Janine pulled away from her and caressed her face gently. Lena didn't want to be in this place. The pain was too great. She needed to get away from here. It was a mistake coming back. Archer only caused her pain. Her thoughts raced, quickly flickering images of her life with Maybelle through her mind.

"Please bring her back, Jay. I know you can."

Janine shook her head. "I can't."

"Yes, you can. You're trained."

"I can't bring her back. She is gone." The words finally sunk in.

Maybelle was gone. Gone.

Lena started pulling away from Janine, but she held her tighter. "Let me go!" She pushed against her. She needed to get away. She couldn't breathe. Couldn't think. She forcefully disconnected herself, causing Janine to fall backwards.

Janine quickly recovered and took her by the arms, "I will never let you go again. Do you hear me?"

"What?"

"I let you go once and I'm not going to let you go again." She pulled Lena back into her arms and held her even tighter than before. Lena struggled against her, but eventually she gave up and relaxed in her arms. "Shh..." Janine consoled her. "I love you so much."

"I love you, too." Lena squeezed her eyes shut, forcing the image of Maybelle's lifeless body out of her tortured mind. She didn't want this to be her last memory of her. Janine turned her away from Maybelle's bed so her face would be to the door instead. When Lena opened her eyes, she saw Jack standing by the door, with his arm protectively around Nadia, comforting her also as she wept.

Lena had kept her word to Maybelle. She'd made peace with Janine and she'd told Nadia about her father. Lena didn't know how this would end. All she knew was that she had to keep moving.

Her heart was broken. The pain was too much. She couldn't catch her breath. The room spun around her. She couldn't feel the ground beneath her feet. The last thing she remembered was Janine reaching out for her before her head hit the cold floor.

Chapter 22

The past three days were a blur. Lena worked on autopilot, preparing for Maybelle's funeral service. She felt numb. There were times when she'd break down and sob until she didn't have any more tears to cry, but she tried to make sure those times were few. Over the past few days, she and Janine worked closely together while making the preparations for the services.

Maybelle wanted a normal service at the church where she'd been a member for nearly seventy years. She had planned it all out beforehand. It made things easier for Lena. She had a hard time dealing with the fact that Maybelle was gone. She had an even harder time thinking about what would have happened had she not come back home. Or better yet, what wouldn't have happened.

She glanced over at Janine who was doing something on her laptop and smiled. One thing that wouldn't have happened was this... Her and Janine in the same room and actually wanting to be in the same room together. Janine looked up and caught her staring at her.

"You okay?" Janine asked.

"Yes."

"Why are you looking at me like that?"

"Just thinking, Jay. That's all."

Janine nodded, "Have you eaten?"

"Not really hungry."

"You mean to tell me you made breakfast for everyone, but you didn't make yourself anything to eat?"

"I guess so, yeah."

Janine scoffed and pushed herself out of the chair. "I'll make you something."

"That's not necessary. I don't think I can eat anything until after this is all over." Lena felt the emotion rising inside of her again. She really had to get a grip, or she'd never make it through the funeral. She glanced down at her watch. Just a few hours more.

"I don't remember seeing you eat anything yesterday either."

Lena shrugged.

Janine grabbed a plate from the cupboard and placed a few pieces of bacon on it, along with a pancake. "This should help." She handed Lena the plate.

Lena looked at it with disgust. She really didn't have an appetite. The thought of eating right now repulsed her. "No, I'm good."

"No, you're not."

Lena sighed heavily and crossed her arms.

"You can be stubborn all you want. But I really need for you to eat this food, so you won't pass out on me again. I need you."

Janine's words were kind and gentle. They were exactly what Lena needed at the moment. She realized that Janine needed her to be physically stronger. She'd already passed out on her at least twice over the past three days. Lena was certain that her passing out put an additional strain on Janine.

"All right. Fine, I'll eat." She took the plate and sat down at the table. "I was planning on pigging out during the repass." Her lame attempt at humor was met with a sympathetic smile.

Janine sat down across from her and sighed. "Lena?"

"Yeah?" Lena already knew from the tone of her voice that she was about to get serious. She cut into her pancake and shoved a piece into her mouth.

"Would you be offended if I skip the repass?"

Lena frowned and placed her fork down. "Why would you skip it?"

Janine fidgeted with her hands. "Mostly because all of your family is going to be there."

"And?"

"You know how your family feels about mine."

"What are you getting at?"

"I just think it may be a good idea if I don't attend the repass."

Lena leaned back in her chair and crossed her arms. "The whole purpose of the repass is for everyone who loved her to get together and remember her and celebrate her life."

"I know."

"Then what's the problem?"

"I just told you."

"That's not a good enough answer for me."

"It may not be good enough for you, but that's all I have."

"All you have is a poor excuse for wanting to skip out on me like this."

Janine raised her hands, trembling palms facing Lena. "Please, calm down."

"I am calm!" Lena shouted. She grabbed her fork and angrily stabbed at her pancake.

"Listen, I'm not trying to skip out on you."

Lena cut her eyes over at her. She tried to calm herself down, because she knew she was over-reacting, but this felt so much like a rejection. She'd told herself time and time again, not to get too attached to Janine. It was just too easy to do so.

She didn't want to trust her again. She didn't want to get hurt. "That's fine. You don't have to come."

"Don't be this way."

"Don't be what way? You said you don't want to come, and I said fine."

"You have an attitude."

"I don't know what you're talking about. I'm good, Jay."

Janine stared at her for what seemed like minutes. She slowly shook her head and sighed lightly. "I'm sorry, I just feel that it's going to be uncomfortable for me."

"No problem." Lena got up and brought her plate to the sink. She looked out the window and took a deep and cleansing breath. "I'm going to go help Uncle Zeke get dressed for the service and then I'm gonna get dressed too."

"Okay."

"Is your brother coming?"

"Yes, he texted me about a half hour ago saying he was getting ready and he'd see us there."

"All right, thanks." Lena unplanted herself from her spot. "I'll be leaving for the church at eleven."

"I'll be ready."

Lena tipped her head and left the kitchen in a hurry.

***

Jack knocked lightly on his mother's door. After a few minutes, Linda appeared from behind the door. She squinted, the light from the hallway punished her hungover eyes. She looked up at him and frowned.

"Jackson, what are you doing here so early?"

Jack looked down at his watch. "It's after eleven."

"Oh. Okay. What do you need?"

He pushed inside the room and looked around. Linda had every curtain drawn. It was dark and depressing. Jack hated dark and depressing. He went over to the window and yanked open the curtains. When he did, he found his mother's personal room in a disarray. It looked like she'd been drinking all night. Her favorite brand of scotch lay empty by her bedside.

"Are you drunk?" he asked.

"That's not a very nice question to ask your mother, now is it?"

"Are you drunk?"

"No, I'm not! I was last night, now all I am is hungover." She laughed, but Jack didn't think it was very funny. "What do you need?"

"Can you help me tie my tie?"

"I thought I already taught you how to do that?"

"I forgot."

"Okay. Come over here." She pulled him closer and started tying the tie for him. "Where are you going all dressed up?"

"You don't remember?"

"Remember what?"

"Big Mama died."

Linda's face fell slightly. "Oh, that's right. I'm sorry, I did forget."

"I'm going to her funeral. It's at twelve-thirty."

"Okay."

"Do you want to come too? You have time."

"Oh, I don't know about that, Jackson."

"Why not? She loved you, too, and I know you loved her."

"Yes, I did care about her. She took care of my babies for me."

"So why don't you come with me?"

"Your father would never allow me to go. You know that."

"He's not here."

"I don't know, honey." Linda finished tying Jack's tie and moved away from him. She walked over to her bar and gazed at her collection of liquors.

"Please, for me?"

"Is Janine going to be there?"

"Yes."

"Then you have support. I'm sorry but I cannot go." Linda poured her a glass of brandy and brought the cup to her lips.

"Lena's back."

She paused before she took a sip. "I heard. Have you spoken to her?"

"Yes."

"And?"

"I have a daughter."

Linda spun around; her face looked horrified. "What did you say?"

"I met her at the grocery store first, but then I found out she's my daughter."

Linda slammed her cup down. She raced over to the door and shut it. She took Jack by the arms. "How do you know she's yours?"

"Because Lena told me."

"But how do you know it's true? How do you know she's not lying to you?"

"Because I know for sure."

"Oh my God." She cupped her mouth and paced the floor. "Does your father know about this child?"

"He doesn't know I'm her dad. I told him she was my friend."

225

She took him by the arms again and pulled him close. "Whatever you do, do not let your father know the truth about her."

Jack nodded.

"I mean it, Jackson."

"I know."

Linda hugged him and then glanced at the clock. "I'll go with you."

"Really?"

"Yes." She walked over to her vanity and examined her face. I just need to put a couple of layers of concealer on my face, so I won't draw any attention."

"What happened to your face?"

"I fell."

Jack frowned at her. He knew she was lying about how she got the bruise on her face, but there wasn't anything he could do to make her tell him the truth about it.

"Where's dad?"

"Working all day on his re-election campaign."

"So, you can be with me all day?"

"Yes, son. I'll tag along with you all day." She hurried him towards the door. "I need to get dressed and make up my face. Wait in the foyer. I'll be ready in twenty minutes." She shut the door quickly behind him.

He did as he was told and made his way to the foyer. When he passed Roger's office, he tried the doorknob. It was unlocked. He glanced down the hallway in both directions and stepped into his office. Roger's office was off limits at all times. His newfound courage had him venturing into places he'd never thought of going before. The Mayor's home office was one of them.

He was just curious. Wondering what was so secretive about a smelly old office, anyway. Not much caught his eye, so he turned to walk back out. As he was turning, he caught a glimpse of a green folder sticking out from underneath Roger's cigar box on the desk.

He opened the folder and immediately wished he hadn't. No amount of hypnotizing could ever help him unsee the images that he'd just seen. He shut the folder, replaced it under the box, and ran out of the door. He made sure no one saw him leaving Roger's office. One of the help may have seen him, but she probably wouldn't tell anyone.

He hurried into the foyer and sat down by the door and waited for Linda to join him. As he sat there waiting for her, the images he'd just seen haunted him. His father was a monster. A horrible monster.

He couldn't allow him to hurt Nadia like he'd hurt Lena. He had to be stopped.

***

Lena looked out across the auditorium and saw many familiar faces. Some of them she hadn't seen since the day she left home and some even longer. She glanced over at Maybelle laying peacefully in the casket. She knew she was no longer suffering. She was thankful for that, but the selfish side of her wished that she was here with her and alive. She and Janine had followed every final wish of Maybelle's completely.

They'd even contacted the state police to have two mounted troopers lead the procession of the horse drawn carriage through town, down Main Street and to the cemetery. Maybelle had touched so many lives. Fulfilling her last wishes was simple, because everyone wanted to contribute to her funeral arrangements. The two troopers provided by the State Police were brothers, both of whom Maybelle babysat when they were little. She taught them how to be good and considerate men.

She looked down at the paper in her hand. Maybelle had written out a few words that she wanted Lena to say to those in attendance. She never ceased to amaze Lena with her level of love and thoughtfulness. She could only hope to be a fraction of the woman that Maybelle was.

She skimmed over the note briefly, making sure that she could read all of it in front of this crowd of onlookers. Maybelle had so much faith in her. Lena glanced up and found Janine in the crowd. She cleared her throat again and took a deep and cleansing breath:

I thank you all for coming today to celebrate my life. I don't want you to be sad, but please rejoice in the fact that I have lived a long and happy life. If I've done everything right, only good things lie ahead for me. I hope that you remember me with fondness in your heart. I have loved each and every one of you. I've offered up a lot of prayers in my life, but the most important prayer was answered when the Good Lord brought my baby home to me. Love is what brought my sweet Magdalena back home to me.

Love is the most powerful thing in the universe. Without it, a person can't really live. Please continue loving each other. Please love her. There's someone sitting out there listening who proves that love really does conquer all. Please family, stick together. Be strong. And never let anything tear you apart. Although I may not be there with you in person, know that my love will continue with you until we see each other again. But I'm in no hurry to see you. Take your time. Live your lives. And be free.

Love, Big Mama.

She finished reading Maybelle's last words and took her seat next to Nadia. She felt everyone's eyes on her, many of which she would see at the repass following the graveside service. She felt like they were judging her. She'd been gone for so long only to come back weeks before Maybelle died. Seemed like cruel joke.

She looked over her shoulder to see Jack sitting three rows behind her. He made eye contact with her and smiled nervously. She smiled back. "Thank you." She mouthed to him. Today was her first time seeing Linda since before she left. She looked so old. Older than most people her age. Linda gave her a knowing nod and turned her attention back to the preacher.

Lena reached for Nadia's hand and held it throughout the duration of the service. After it ended, family and friends gathered outside and waited for Maybelle's casket to be loaded onto the carriage. Her casket was covered in a large uncut piece of royal purple cashmere fabric and topped with a beautiful spray of white and yellow roses. It was befitting of royalty.

The procession took forty-five long minutes to make its way to the cemetery. As Maybelle's casket was carried through town, residents stopped and stood respectfully as she passed by. Maybelle had touched so many lives. If only she could've seen this. The amount of respect paid to her was absolutely beautiful.

Lena gave way to tears when she saw the carriage being pulled into the entrance of the cemetery. It was almost time to say her final goodbyes. Her heart seized up so tight, she thought she was having a heart attack.

Nadia handed her a bottle of water and two of her anxiety pills. In all the preparation, she'd forgotten to take them. Thank god for Nadia.

"Thanks, sweet pea."

"You're welcome."

Lena leaned back against the seat and realized that Janine's arm was around her. She looked over at her and smiled.

"Are you okay?" Janine asked softly.

Lena nodded. "Feels like my heart is giving out on me."

"I know how you feel."

Lena frowned at her. It just dawned on her that she hadn't see Janine shed not one single tear since Maybelle died. "I saw your mom at the funeral."

"Yes, I did too."

"Is she healthy? She looks so different."

"She's married to my dad," Janine laughed softly.

"No need to elaborate."

Janine sighed and gazed out of her window. She kept her arm around Lena, giving her the support she needed. "I'm sure Jack wants to be here with you during this time." She continued looking out the window.

"He might. I don't know."

"If he does, you should let him." She turned towards Lena. "He needs you."

"He's done fine all these years without me."

"He's existed." Janine cleared her throat and removed her arm from around Lena. "I just want you to be happy. I want you all to be happy."

The limo came to a stop. Lena couldn't understand why Janine picked now of all times to start a serious conversation. She hadn't changed at all. "Thanks for caring about my happiness, Jay. I really do appreciate it, but I can't stay in Archer. After I finish here, I need to go back home."

"This is your home, Lena."

Lena started to reply but the limo driver came to her side and opened the door for her. She stared at Janine, uncertain of why she chose now to delve into this subject. She touched her lightly on the arm. "Can we talk about this later?"

"Sure."

"Are you coming to the gravesite?"

"Yes, but I'll probably get a lift back to town and hang out until the repass is over."

Lena nodded and hopped out of the car. Janine climbed out after her and stood close to her side. Even though she was going to abandon her during the repass, she seemed to be trying to make up for it now. Everywhere Lena went, Janine went.

It felt like old times.

The graveside service lasted about thirty minutes. Lena didn't hear any of it. Her mind was in a fog the entire time. She just stood there staring at the coffin, unable to wrap her mind around the fact that Maybelle was in it and she was saying goodbye to her for the very last time.

Slowly but surely, attendees started breaking away from the gravesite and leaving. Soon, only Lena, Janine and Nadia were left standing by the casket. Silent tears streaked down Lena's face. Nadia had her hand looped through Lena's left arm and Janine through her right. Lena was sure they were holding her like this because of her propensity of fainting.

"Are you ready to go, Mom?" Nadia asked.

"In a minute." Lena looked up and saw Jack and Linda approaching. She took a deep breath. She didn't know how much more her heart could take.

Jack came up to the casket and placed a single rose on top before walking over to Lena. She glanced at him briefly before gluing her eyes back on the casket. She didn't want to look at him. She didn't want to peer into his eyes and be reminded of the love that she'd only felt once in her entire life. She swallowed hard. The lump in her throat was persistent.

Out of her peripheral she saw Linda coming closer as well. She tried her best to keep her feet planted where they were, but it was hard. Anywhere Linda was, Roger wasn't too far behind. Finally, she found it inside of her to turn in their direction. She met Linda's gaze first. It was the lesser intimidating of the two. She smiled.

"Mrs. Chamberlain." She greeted her.

Linda cautiously approached her. The last time Lena saw her, Linda told her that she was a filthy human being and she would burn in hell for falling in love with her son. Lena didn't believe in hell, but as she gazed upon Linda's face, she knew that she'd been living her own personal hell as Roger's wife.

Linda's eyes cut over to Nadia and instantly filled with tears. She held her composure though, although seemingly hard, and stood taller in front of Lena. "Hello Lena."

Lena was on guard, uncertain of why this woman was here in front of her. Uncertain of why she wanted to speak to her, when years ago she made it abundantly clear that she hoped that Lena would disappear off the face of the earth.

"Thanks for coming." Lena's responses were quick and dry. She didn't want to disrespect Maybelle in any way, shape or form. Especially not now. She smiled at her.

Linda glanced back at Nadia. "Is this my son's daughter?"

Lena inhaled deeply. "Yes, she is."

More tears filled Linda's eyes. This emotional display confused Lena. Janine came over to her mother and put her arm around her.

"She's absolutely beautiful." Linda said.

"Thank you."

"What's your name, honey?" Linda asked, turning towards Nadia.

"Nadia."

"It nice to meet you, Nadia. I'm Linda, I'm Jackson's mother."

"It's very nice to meet you as well, Mrs. Chamberlain."

Linda blinked tears out of her eyes and smiled. She turned back to Lena. "I wanted to tell you how sorry I am for the horrible things I said to you when we last spoke."

Lena slowly nodded and swallowed her heart back down into her chest. She didn't know what to say. She definitely wasn't going to say that it was okay, because it wasn't. Linda's words had cut her deeper than Roger's, but she dared not let anyone know. Above anything else, she used to want Linda Chamberlain's approval. She used to have a semi-decent relationship with her because she was Janine's best friend. But that all changed the day she found out that Jack had lost his virginity to her.

"Thanks."

"I'm sorry about Maybelle. If there's anything you need, please let us know."

"Us?" Lena shot a glare her way. She didn't need anything from Roger Chamberlain. It would be a cold day in the Sahara when she'd ever accept anything from him.

"I mean, let me know. Just me."

Lena narrowed her eyes at her. She didn't recognize this person standing in front of her. "I appreciate the gesture, but I'm not staying long."

"Oh..." Linda glanced back over at Nadia. "I thought you'd be in town longer."

"I was only here for Big Mama. No one else. I'll be leaving soon."

"If you don't mind, please," Linda said stepping closer, "I would like to spend some time with my granddaughter."

"No." Lena didn't have to think about the request. It was an automatic no. She didn't trust her. She was Roger's wife. "And I'd appreciate it if you speak nothing of this to your husband, please. All of you," she said addressing all of the Chamberlains.

"But she's family."

"That may be, but as long as your husband is the monster that he is, you will not have a relationship with her." Her words were cold and biting. She hadn't intended on being that sharp with her, it just happened.

Linda stepped back, shocked. "I didn't do anything to deserve this."

"It's not what you didn't do. It's what you did!" Lena snapped. "You kept silent when I needed someone to back me up. You knew what they did to me and you said nothing. All of you said nothing!"

"I'm so sorry, Lena." Linda stepped away from her and looked from Jack to Janine. "What I did was wrong. I should've come forward when I had the opportunity, but I was afraid."

"What do you think I was? I was just a kid and the Chamberlains turned this whole town against me."

Linda lowered her head.

"I was afraid to come back, but I came back for Big Mama. Now she's gone so I am going to go too. And never return."

Linda shook her head and backed further away from her. It wasn't worth the fight. Lena was right about everything. The Chamberlains were powerful people, but cowards when it came to doing what was right.

"It was nice seeing you again, Lena. And it was nice meeting you, Nadia. Please, if you change your mind, I would love to get to know Nadia better."

"I won't," Lena had had enough. She couldn't take anymore drama. She turned and walked away from the gravesite, leaving the rest of them standing there. She wanted to punch something, she wanted to scream, she wanted to cry. She walked blindly down the long path leading back to the cars and had just made it to the limo when someone grabbed her by the arm.

She spun around, ready to punch whoever it was that had thwarted her escape. To her surprise it was Jack. She shoved him away from her. "What are you doing?"

He stumbled backwards and recovered. "Wait."

"Why?"

"I want to talk to you."

"I don't want to talk."

"Please."

Her heart was threatening to explode. This was the icing on the cake. She didn't want to face him right now. "What do you want, huh?"

"I just want to talk to you."

"There's nothing to talk about. I need to go. Right now."

He took her by the arms, something he always did in the past when she'd temporarily lose her mind to madness. He pulled her closer and peered deep into her eyes. His touch stabilized her.

"Let me go."

"No," he said, pulling her into an embrace.

This was the moment she'd feared most. Being in his arms again and feeling the resurgence of every single emotion that she'd spent years burying. They were still there, and they resurfaced with an intensity she wasn't ready for. Her heart seized up inside of her chest and she choked on her tears.

"Don't cry." He pulled her in tighter, her face pressed firmly against his chest. She felt it more than she heard it as his heart beat wildly inside of his chest. She still had the same effect on him that he had on her.

"Damn you, Aidan." She gave up the fight and hugged him back. She exhaled and allowed him to hold her close to his heart. She always felt so safe and secure when she was in his arms like this.

He kissed her on the top of her head. And then on her forehead. She pulled away from him and looked into his eyes. He seemed taller. Either that or she'd shrunken over the years. His eyes were still as blue as the ocean and as innocent as a lamb. He smiled at her while he caressed her face.

Her heart beat extremely fast now. She felt like she might faint.

"Please, Lena."

"Please what?"

"Don't go."

She choked on another set of tears. She looked away, but he tipped her chin back towards him. He still treated her with the same gentleness he did when they were teens, just with more wisdom. He knew what she needed.

He leaned in quickly and pressed his trembling lips against hers. It happened so fast that she thought she was imagining it, but when her mind understood what was happening, she gasped and detached.

He stared at her and she at him. Their lips were mere inches apart. There was absolutely nothing she could do once the magnetism of their hearts took over. It was exactly what she feared and what she wanted at the same time. She couldn't stop herself from leaning forward and taking his lips again with a kiss. He held her protectively in his arms, while they got reacquainted with each other. Her heart raced, her head spun, her legs felt weak.

She found the will to break away from the kiss. After all these years, he still felt the same. She gazed at him in disbelief. She stepped away from him and cleared her throat.

"I need to get back to Big Mama's now. The guests will be arriving soon."

He smiled, "Okay."

Lena opened the door of the car and turned towards him. He was still smiling at her. She shook her head in disbelief. Behind Jack, she caught a glimpse of Janine standing in the distance. When they made eye contact, Janine turned and walked out of sight.

Chapter 23

Janine's conscience wouldn't allow her to abandon Lena for too long during the repass. She tried though. But she'd grown so accustomed to helping Lena, that bailing on her now seemed so wrong. When she pulled up to Maybelle's house, she saw the yard was full of cars. Who knows who'd be hanging around inside. She got out of the car and made her way up to the house.

Nadia was sitting outside on the porch. As Janine approached, she saw that she was preoccupied with her cell phone. "Hey, sweetheart," Janine greeted her.

Nadia jumped with a start and looked up from her phone. "Oh. Hi."

"What's up? You look a little flustered."

"Um," Nadia glanced back down at her phone, "yeah, I'm fine. I just got a weird text just now."

"From who?"

"I don't recognize the number. It's a 478 number."

Janine frowned. "That's the area code around here. What did they say?"

Nadia swallowed hard and glanced up at her. "I'm not sure I should say."

"What do you mean?"

"It's about Mom."

Janine reached for the phone. "Let me see it, please." Nadia handed it to her. When Janine read the text message, her heart sunk. She yanked her phone from her pocket and quickly dialed the number that had been texting Nadia. She wasn't too surprised when no one picked up on the other line. "Who have you given your number to?"

"No one but Jack."

"Is there anyone else who could've gotten a hold of your personal information?"

Nadia groaned and facepalmed herself. "With everything that's been going on I completely forgot about the cop."

"What cop?"

"The Chief of Police."

"What about him?"

"The night I ran off, he approached me at the diner in town. He asked for my ID, so I gave it to him. Then he starts threatening me, telling me that my mom and I better leave town or else. Then Jack came in and they had a confrontation and the cop left. And he took my ID with him."

Janine sighed heavily.

"What? Do you think he's texting me?"

"I think it's a possibility he's got someone to do it for him. These are extremely hurtful things in this text. Your mother doesn't need this added stress."

"I agree."

Janine stared at her. She'd grown accustomed to having her around, she dreaded the day when Nadia and Lena would leave Archer. "Do me a favor and do not go anywhere alone for the entire time that you're here, okay?"

"Yeah. Why?"

"Honestly, because I'm afraid for your safety."

"Someone is out to get me?"

"It's very complicated, but I don't think you're safe here. I assume that Lena didn't want to bring you back here, right?"

She nodded.

"That's because the people who run this place – my family, are very powerful and influential people."

"Okay."

"And if they aren't happy about something or someone, they will do terrible things." Thoughts about Lena's past sufferings flooded her mind. Janine could never erase those images. At one point, she thought she had, but then they resurfaced in her dreams. She became an insomniac because of it. Because of the guilt of what she'd done and how badly Lena suffered because of it.

"Are you talking about your dad?"

"Yes. His hate is deeply entrenched."

"You don't seem that way. I don't understand. How can you have a father so hateful, but not pick any of it up?"

Janine smiled. "Because my brother and I had Big Mama. Her love was stronger than the hate. Her love constantly overpowered my father's racism, so much so that Big Mama's love was all we knew and all we longed for." Janine lowered her eyes. "God, I miss her so much."

She smiled and nodded at Janine's touching statement. "I know you must."

"She saved us from going down the same path as our cousins. Jack and I are the only Chamberlains who are not racists."

"That's unbelievable."

"I'm so happy to have met you, sweetheart. And I'm extremely happy to be your aunt."

Nadia hugged her, "That's so sweet. Thank you."

Janine held on tighter. Nadia was the product of a very special love, a love that defied all odds. The fact that she was a little bitty embryo and survived that vicious attack on her mother, proved that miracles do happen. And she was holding a miracle in her arms right now.

She pulled away and cupped Nadia's face. "I know you guys will be leaving soon, but will you keep in contact with me to let me know how you two are doing from time to time?"

"Yes."

"Thank you. That would mean so much to me." Janine didn't want to see them go. The past few weeks she'd been here with them at Maybelle's were the best few weeks she'd ever had. She'd gotten to apologize to Lena for her part in her violation and Lena forgave her and welcomed her back into her heart. And now she was going to leave her again.

"What's wrong?" Nadia asked as she pulled away from Janine.

Janine struggled. She felt the darkness of her life closing in around her. Lena and Nadia had brought new light into her life. "I'm just going to miss you and your mother, that's all."

Nadia handed Janine her cell phone. "Lock your number in my phone and I promise to keep in touch. Do you text?"

"Yes, I do."

"Great. I'll text you every day if you want."

"That's so thoughtful," she said programming her number and address into Nadia's phone. She snapped a selfie and saved it. "Just in case you forget what I look like."

Nadia laughed and took her phone. "I highly doubt I'll forget what you look like."

Janine caressed her face. "Listen, I'm going to go help your mom."

"All right."

"Remember what I said, please. Don't find yourself alone anywhere."

"Gotcha."

Janine rose from her seat and stretched. "Enjoy your quiet time." Reluctantly, she disappeared into the house.

***

She found Lena in the kitchen brewing a fresh pot of coffee. She had her back to the door, with her head hung low, watching the coffee drip into the decanter. As soon as Janine smelled the aroma filling the air, thoughts of Big Mama filled her mind.

"Coffee makes everything better," Janine said.

Lena spun around. A slight smile played on the corner of her mouth. It disappeared quickly, but Janine saw it.

"I thought you weren't coming."

Janine shrugged and walked over to her. "I figured the food would be better here. And the coffee."

"Hmm." Lena turned back to the coffee maker.

Janine retrieved two cups from the cupboard and placed them on the counter in front of Lena. "I hope you made it strong."

Lena glanced over at her. "I'm glad to see you."

Janine smiled and joined Lena in watching the coffee brew. Once it was done, Lena made two cups and brought them to the table. The two women sat and sipped together in peace, while the family and friends gathered in the front rooms.

Lena nursed her coffee, too far away in her own thoughts to notice Janine watching her. She finally looked up from her cup, "Oh. I'm sorry, did you say something to me?"

"No. I was just looking at you."

Lena laughed and sipped her coffee.

"When are you planning to leave?" Janine asked.

Lena shrugged. "I don't know. A couple of days maybe. I gotta make sure Uncle Zeke is squared away before I go."

"So soon?"

"Now you're sounding like your mother," she said glancing over the rim of her cup.

Janine stirred her coffee. "I asked Nadia to text me from time to time. I hope that was okay."

"Nadia is grown. She doesn't need my permission to communicate with you."

"I thought because earlier you said—"

"I know what I said," she interrupted, "but I don't mind her communicating with you."

"I really like her. She's like you all over again."

"She seems to like you too."

Silence settled between them while they stared at their cups. "Do you have an idea of where you'll be placing your Uncle?"

"My cousin, Gale, agreed to take him in. I just have to help pack his things and move him over there."

"Oh, okay." Janine could sense Lena's unease. She felt it strongly. She inhaled deeply and took another sip of her coffee to force her heart back down into her chest. Lena watched her with curious eyes. She felt openly exposed under the scrutiny of Lena's gaze.

"Jay?" Lena's voice was softer than usual, "What's going on with you right now?"

Janine wanted to tell her how much she enjoyed the last few weeks with her, how much she absolutely loved having the opportunity to get reacquainted with her, and how much she was dreading her departure. But no words formed on her lips. Emotion was the only thing that registered with her mind.

Lena waited, watching and carefully reading her every move. Janine promised herself that she wouldn't cry and so far, she'd kept that promise. She remained strong during the whole process of Maybelle's passing, in the days following, and at the funeral today. But as she processed the fact that Lena was about to leave out of her life again, and this time perhaps for good, her heart couldn't accept it.

Losing her once was bad enough but losing her again brought forth feelings she couldn't understand or easily explain. Lena reached over and took her hand.

"Talk to me, Jay."

Janine took a deep breath. "I am going to miss you," she confessed. "And I don't know how to deal with this."

"Deal with what?"

"Everything." She peered into her caring eyes. She could tell the person looking back at her now was genuine. Lena didn't look at her the same way she did when they were first reunited. Her guard was down, and Janine could see warmth and love in her eyes. And she was about to take it all away from her.

"We did what we were asked to do, Jay. There's no further obligation."

"I know."

"Big Mama wanted us to talk again. We did. We are. So, we can go our separate ways now."

Janine's heart lurched inside of her. "Is that what you truly want?"

"What? To go our separate ways?"

"Yes, Lena. Is that what you want?" The sudden rush of emotions made it extremely difficult for her to get the words out. "You came home with a child, who is my niece. She's my family and you're going to just leave? Just like that?"

"You said that you and her were keeping in touch."

"I know what I said, but I want more than that. I want to be able to get to know her and you."

"You already know me."

"I know the girl you used to be!" Janine shouted, "Not this remarkable, strong woman sitting in front of me."

Lena sat back, stunned. "Why are you yelling?"

"I didn't mean to yell, I'm just—" Janine tightened her grip on Lena's hand, "I'm just upset." She searched her mind for the right words to convey her feelings in a way for Lena to understand them, at least by a little. "I guess what I'm trying to say is that after being reunited with you, speaking with you, and being friends again, I don't want that to end, Lena."

Janine felt the tears rising in her eyes. Instead of forcing them to stay inside, she allowed them to come out. At least by this, Lena would see just how much she meant to her.

"God, Jay, don't do this."

"How do I get you to see how much I need you in my life?"

"You seem to be doing fine without me."

Janine laughed. "You don't know that." She snatched a napkin from the table and wiped the tears out of her eyes. Her reddened eyeballs made her green eyes blaze with emotion. "I've never told anyone this, but..." she smiled and fidgeted with her hands, "The night Big Mama called me and asked me to come and help her, I was contemplating suicide."

Lena frowned. "What?"

"Yeah. I was so close to ending my life, but her phone call stopped me."

"Why would you commit suicide? You're successful, filthy rich, and who knows whatever else."

"None of that matters to me, Lena, don't you get it?" She sighed and sat back in her chair. "I may have all of those things that make me look like I have it made, but I don't have the one thing that I truly need in my life."

"What's that?"

"You."

"Oh, come on Jay. You think I'm going to buy that? I can't add anything to your life."

"Yes, you can."

"No, I can't! Why would you think that I can?"

"Because you're my sister."

"No, I'm not and you know it." Lena pushed herself out of the chair and walked over to the sink. "That's just the line Big Mama fed us when we were little. It's not true."

Janine stomped over and spun her around. "How dare you disrespect her like that!"

Lena pushed her away, "Excuse me? I am not disrespecting Big Mama; I'm only telling you the truth!"

"The truth is she taught both of us how to love. When our own mothers didn't and couldn't love us, she gave us what we needed. And that was each other."

"I don't want to talk about this right now."

"You were all I had, Lena. You were the only person who understood me, you know?"

"Everything could've stayed the way it was, if you hadn't—" Lena cupped her mouth and turned away. "I can't do this with you right now."

"I know I messed everything up. Every day, I have to live with what I did. Every day I have to live with the reality of the hurt I caused our family."

Lena turned around. Her face was twisted with anguish. "The hurt you caused *our* family?"

"Yes. Jack, you and me. I shouldn't have told them where you were. But I didn't know what they were going to do."

"I know you didn't."

"I was just scared. I was afraid that I was going to lose you. I feel the same way now, only worse." Janine hoped that comparing the feelings that prompted her to betray Lena and the feelings she felt now wouldn't be taken the wrong way.

She waited. She watched her for her reaction. Lena stared at her; her eyebrows furrowed into a deep frown. "What are you trying to say?"

"We just lost Big Mama and I'm scared to death of losing you again, Lena."

Lena stepped away from her, but Janine reached out and took her by the arms, "Please, don't..." She pulled her closer. "If you must leave me again, then please just do this one thing for me."

"What?"

"Prove to me that we aren't still connected like we used to be, and I will walk away and never look back."

"Are you insane? That was child's play."

"It was real because I felt it."

"Christ, Jay!" Lena lamented.

"Please? Just this one time?"

Lena sighed deeply, "Fine."

Without wasting another second, Janine cupped Lena's face and pressed their foreheads together. Just like they'd done as children and just like they'd done as teens. They used to feel each other's emotions. Maybelle believed in their connection, even advocated the strengthening of it.

Janine felt her heart tightening inside of her chest. The emotions she felt being this close to her beloved friend after all of these years was nearly overwhelming. Lena reached up and clenched her wrists. Lena used to love this so much; the way Janine caressed her face. After Lena's mother abandoned her, she longed for tender affections like this. And Janine was always there when she needed it.

"You're not making this easy for me." Lena said.

"I am so sorry I hurt you."

Lena nodded briskly and sniffled. "I know."

Janine opened her eyes and saw tears streaming down Lena's face. Lena struggled to hold back the emotions threatening to overtake her.

Janine got her answer. She had her proof. Slowly, she pulled away, drying Lena's tears with her thumbs. Lena opened her eyes and looked straight into her heart. Janine knew she felt the same connection they'd always shared, but she wasn't going to press the issue any further. Just knowing that Lena was still connected to her was enough to strengthen and prepare for a life without her. At least she had her forgiveness. And that was all she could ever ask for.

Janine jumped when her phone buzzed in her pocket. She reached for it and glanced down at the display. She sighed heavily, "I'm sorry, but my mother needs me for a little bit."

"No problem, I probably should go and check on the family out there anyway," Lena said pointing towards the living room.

"I promise I'll be back as soon as I can."

"All right. Hey, fix a plate for Aidan. Okay? Just in case he's hungry?"

"Sure. I'll do that." She prepared a take-away plate for Jack and wrapped it in foil. She hugged Lena tightly. "Thank you so much." She didn't wait for a response and darted out the back door, avoiding the inquisitive eyes of Lena's family in the next room.

She felt a renewed hope in her and Lena's friendship. It may take a while, but she was determined to build something stronger than what they had before.

Chapter 24

The last of the guests had just left when Nadia finally came back inside. Lena was relieved to have some alone time with her so they could talk. She sat down next to her on the couch and laid across her lap. Lena strummed her fingers through her hair and sighed contently.

"I'm sorry for the way I behaved when you told me about my father."

"You had every right to be upset. I shouldn't have broken the news to you like that."

Nadia turned over onto her back so she could look into her mother's eyes. "I didn't mean to say the things I said the way I did. I can't get it off my mind."

"It's okay, sweet pea."

"Actually, it's not. Regardless of how upset I was, I should've tried harder to calm down. It was just hard."

"With the exception of Aidan, almost every Chamberlain has a temper like that."

Nadia groaned and put her hand over her face. "That's comforting," she chuckled. "Hey, why do you call him Aidan when everyone else calls him Jack?"

"His full name is Jackson Aidan Chamberlain. I've always liked being different than everyone else. So, I started calling him by his middle name and I guess it kind of stuck."

"I think that's cute."

Lena laughed softly. "Yeah."

"Big Mama told me how he got like that."

"Yeah. How do you feel about that?"

"It's tragic. I mean, if Big Mama hadn't been where she was at that moment, then he would have died."

"That's so true."

"Does his mom still have the drinking problem?"

"Yes, I'm sure she does."

"That's sad. Jack and Janine have a monster for a father and an alcoholic for a mother."

"I guess that's why Big Mama took them under her wing. They were always here with her. After I moved in with Big Mama, Janine and I were best friends by then and she tried to move in too."

Nadia laughed.

"Yeah, she was so crazy. Like in a geeky kind of way."

"What was Janine like back then?"

Lena shrugged and continued to stroke Nadia's hair. "I don't know, she was different from the rest of the girls."

"How?"

"For instance, she was extremely smart, like genius level smart. But the other girls didn't really like her because she saw life differently. She liked to mix with the blacks on this side of Archer. She'd come down to the baseball field behind Leroy's junkyard and play ball with us."

"Wow, that's awesome."

"She was amazing, I have to admit. My cousins were always trying to get with her, but she wasn't interested in anything but school and books. A total Einstein. But she also had a tough side. She fought anyone who made fun of Aidan. And she usually won."

They shared a laugh together.

"She was my shadow. I often felt unworthy of her friendship."

"I'm sure you were just as good a friend to her as she was to you."

"Hmm, perhaps."

"So, she became like family?"

"Yes."

"Have you two made up, like genuinely made up?"

Lena let out a deep sigh, "I think so."

"She asked me to keep in touch with her."

"Yes, she told me. Are you going to?"

"I would like to. She seems pretty cool, although mysterious at the same time. I feel like she cares about me."

"She does."

Nadia's phone buzzed in her pocket. She fished it out and checked the message. She sighed heavily.

"What's wrong?"

"I can't tell you."

"Sure, you can."

Nadia sat up on the couch and glanced back down at her phone. Her frown deepened as she read the text message. "I don't want to add anything more on you right now."

"I'm fine. You know me. I can handle whatever it is that's bothering you."

Nadia looked up from her phone. "Okay. Well, I've been getting these weird text messages from a number I don't recognize."

"What kind of messages? Do you think it's Richard?"

"No, it's definitely not Richard. The messages are about you."

"Me?"

Nadia glanced down as another incoming message popped up on the display. "Earlier when Janine came by, she was just walking up when I got one. I showed her."

"What are these messages saying?"

Nadia shook her head slowly. "Terrible stuff about you. Disrespectful stuff. Janine told me not to tell you and then she said something that kind of scared me."

"What did she say?"

"She told me for the rest of the time that I'm here in Archer, not to go anywhere alone."

"Christ!" Lena scooted to the edge of the couch. "Who has your number?"

"Just Jack."

"Well, I know he isn't doing it."

"I know, but Mom there's something you need to know."

Lena braced herself for the worst. She had this nagging feeling inside of her. One that she hasn't been able to shake since she set foot back in Archer. Things with Janine went better than expected and seeing Jack again after so long went well also. It couldn't remain this smooth. Her demons still lurked outside those doors, waiting to catch up with her.

"What is it?"

"When I was at the diner, before Jack found me, the cop took my ID."

"What?" Lena's heart sunk into her stomach. Ty had her address. He knew where she lived. And if he knew then Roger knew also. "Oh my God. How did he get your license?"

"He ordered me to show it to him. He started questioning me for no reason, and when he ordered me to give him my ID, I couldn't refuse."

"Like hell you couldn't!" Lena stood and paced the floor. She had to relocate. And find another place to stay. Immediately. "He was one of them, Nadia, and now he knows where I live. Where we live!"

"I know, and I'm sorry. I would have gotten it back but then Jack came in and he stood up for me."

Lena stopped in her tracks. "He did?"

253

"Yes. He stood between the cop and me and he wouldn't let the cop get anywhere near me. The cop looked like he was afraid of him."

"Wow."

"And he did the same when his dad approached us outside when we were getting in the car."

"How did all that go down?"

"It was really weird. The way his dad was looking at me gave me the serious creeps. It made me feel extremely uncomfortable especially knowing that he was my grandfather."

"I can imagine."

"He tried to get close to me, but Jack wouldn't let him. He asked Jack who I was, and Jack said that I was his friend. Why didn't he tell him I was his daughter?"

Lena sat down on the edge of the coffee table. "Because he was protecting you from his father. Roger is evil."

"I noticed." She ran her fingers along the healing cut on her lip. "If I hadn't shoved him, I wouldn't have gotten hit."

"We need to start packing our things. We need to get home and make some changes."

"What kind of changes?"

"We have to move."

"Why?"

"Because they know where I am now!" Lena tried to keep the fear out of her voice, but she was too afraid. Too afraid of what they would do to her if they found her, and too afraid of what they would do to Nadia. She couldn't risk it.

"Mom, I highly doubt they'll come all the way to Kansas to do anything."

"You don't know them!" Lena felt her anxiety boiling beneath her skin. She looked at her watch. It was nearly seven o'clock. "If we get packed up tonight, we can be on the road by morning."

"What? Wait."

"No, Nadia. I'm leaving in the morning, with or without you." She started pacing the floor again, anxiously looking from her watch to the clock on the wall.

"Just wait a minute!" Nadia grabbed Lena's arm. Lena spun around, her eyes burning hot with displeasure as she glanced down at the hand gripping her arm. Nadia instantly released her.

"You don't know the kind of people we're dealing with and I don't want to be here any longer than I have to."

"I get that, but we can't just leave without saying goodbye."

There was a knock at the door. Lena was relieved, because she really didn't want to get into a long and drawn out discussion about why they had to leave Archer as soon as possible. It was best just to leave and explain later.

"Go let Janine in," she picked up the stray paper plates left behind by relatives and tossed them into the wastebasket. She wanted to avoid a confrontation with Nadia as long as she possibly could, because Nadia was stubborn like a Chamberlain and it plain exhausted her.

Nadia mumbled something under her breath and walked over to the door. "I thought Janine had a key," she said turning the knob and opening the door, "Did you forget your—" Her words died on her lips. "Mom!" Nadia tripped over her own feet as she stumbled away from the door.

The sound of sheer panic in her voice sent Lena straight into panic mode. When she looked up and saw Ty standing in the doorway, her heart seized up inside her chest. She didn't even recall racing to Nadia's side and yanking her to her feet. "What do you want?" she half yelled; half snarled at him.

Ty stepped over the threshold and shut the door behind him. "I came to pay my respects to Maybelle of course." He walked towards her, his hand resting on his side arm.

Lena glanced down at it. Her stomach turned as the memories of him came rushing back. He still sounded the same and smelled the same.

"Don't get any ideas, Pittman." He smiled, baring his chipped teeth. Ty looked nothing like the other Chamberlains. He was the ugly duckling of the family, the black sheep. He was nothing but a weak link, a pawn in Roger's hand.

"I don't want any trouble." Lena backed further away from him. "I'd appreciate it if you left us alone."

"Now, why would I do that?" He glanced over at Nadia, his eyes traveling the length of her before he smiled. "Man, she looks just like you did back in the day, Pittman."

Lena had backed up against the wall dividing the rooms. To her left was the hallway leading to the back rooms, to her right was the living room. When Nadia groaned, she realized that she was trapped between the wall and her. It may have been uncomfortable, but at least she was protected from Ty.

"Stay away from her!"

Ty chuckled under his breath. He reeked of Roger's signature Cohiba cigars and booze. "We've already met, but why don't you formally introduce me to your girl here?"

"Stay back!" Her second warning came with more force.

He paused his advance and stroked his side arm. He flicked the latch that held the piece in its holster. "Is that aggression I detect?"

Lena drew back. She knew the rules of the game. Any slightest hint of aggression gave them the right to neutralize. And she was almost certain that Ty would neutralize her by shooting her dead on the spot.

"What do you want?"

Ty reached into his jacket pocket and pulled out a small card. He glanced down at it, "I'm sure you know it's illegal to drive without a license right, Miss Nadia Salome Pittman?"

Lena reached for it, but he pulled it back.

"Not so fast." He looked at Nadia's license again. "So, tell me about this little town you live in. Seems pretty remote."

Lena's stomach lurched inside. She felt like she was going to vomit. She kept silent.

"I have a vacation coming up, I should come up and let you ladies show me around."

Lena snatched the license from his hand and slid it in her back pocket. "If you come anywhere near me or my daughter, I'll kill you." And she meant it.

"That seems like a threat to me, seeing that I'm near you right now." Before she could react, he grabbed her by the throat and pinned her against the wall. Nadia pulled herself from behind Lena and readied herself to fight him, but Lena waved her off.

He lifted her off the ground and smiled into her eyes. She grasped his wrist with her hands, hoping to release some of the pressure on her neck. She glanced over at Nadia and saw panic on her face. Nadia moved to intervene, but Lena again waved her off.

"Don't touch him." Lena choked out. If Nadia touched him, he'd use that as an excuse to harm her. "It's okay." When she gasped for air, he released the grip a little. At least she could breathe, but the pressure in her head was slowly building.

"You better listen to your mama, little girl." He cut his eyes over at her. "Or I'll have to teach you the same lesson I taught her."

Nadia seemed to be at a loss. She stood there, helpless.

"You will not touch her!" Lena said.

Ty laughed and leaned in closer, "Who's gonna stop me?" His breath was so rancid, it stung her eyes.

She hadn't been this close to him since the night he violated her. His trademark Chamberlain blue eyes that haunted her dreams were staring straight into hers. She felt sick. She felt dizzy.

He leaned in to kiss her, but as he was about to press his foul lips against hers, his cell phone rang. He paused and fished his phone out of his pocket. Lena glanced down and saw Roger's contact picture on the screen.

He cursed under his breath.

"Better not make him wait," she forced out. Her head throbbed. She felt like she was going to pass out. He squeezed her throat tighter and answered the phone.

"Yep?" His cold eyes stared into hers. Lena could see the hate in them. "Yeah, I got 'em right here."

Panic streaked through her body. She made eye contact with Nadia and motioned for her to leave, but she refused to. She cursed her stubbornness and in the same thought she was amazed at how good she'd turned out. She saw a look in Nadia's eyes, one that she recognized all too well. She forced herself to pull her eyes away from her and not draw attention to her.

Ty hung up the phone and slid it back into his pocket. He released Lena and grabbed his weapon. Lena dropped to the floor gasping for air, trying her best to replenish her lungs of much needed oxygen. He turned towards Nadia, daring her to do what she was probably thinking of doing.

"You must think I'm dumb, huh, Pittman Jr?" He pointed the gun at her. "Get over there with your mama."

Nadia side-stepped over to Lena and crouched down next to her. She put her arm around her and apologized.

"Why are you here, Tyson?" Lena still felt dizzy, but she stood on her feet. She would not submit to him ever again. "What do you want from me?"

"I'm just here to make sure you don't leave just yet without your parting gift."

"Parting gift?"

Ty laughed and motioned for them to sit on the couch. "You gotta wait and see."

None of this sounded good. She should have left town right after the funeral. If she had, then this wouldn't be happening, and Nadia wouldn't be at risk. She sat down on the couch, keeping her eyes on him the entire time. The way he looked at her made her sick to her stomach, but at least he didn't have his eyes on Nadia. Perhaps he thought she belonged to him, who knows.

"You too," he said to Nadia. "Not sure what kind of tricks you got up your sleeve, but you ain't gonna be pulling 'em on me."

Nadia sat beside her. Everything about her body language told Lena that she was teetering on the edge of fight or flight mode. Nadia ran to avoid hurting people. The way she glared at him now, reminded Lena of a lioness waiting for an opportunity to pounce.

"Nadia?" Lena wanted to snap her out of it, but her voice couldn't reach her side of reason. Nadia was angry. Slowly, she turned and met her mother's eyes. Lena nodded at her. "It's going to be okay." She sought only to calm Nadia's spirit enough to prevent anything terrible from happening.

"Man, if looks could kill." Ty teased. "You definitely are a Chamberlain, wow!" He walked over to Nadia and cupped her chin. He smiled down at her. "You could be my kid, you know that?"

Nadia jerked her face out of his hands. "Get your hands off me."

"Now, now. Is that a way to talk to your daddy?"

"You are not my father!"

"How do you know that? You're at just the right age to be mine, ain't that right, Pittman?"

Lena remained silent. She just stared at the floor hoping this would all end soon. It had to end soon, and when it did, she'd take Nadia and leave and never come back.

"I know who my father is, and he certainly isn't you."

Ty walked over to the window and glanced out. "It's about time."

Lena took Nadia's hand and squeezed it. She'd dreaded this moment since the day she left Archer. Her mind came alive with ways to escape the inevitable, but every scenario came to the same tragic end. Either she was going to be hurt, or Nadia. And neither was acceptable. She didn't need to ask who was outside. She knew.

Ty opened the door and let him in. Lena's heart raced inside of her chest as she watched Roger step into Maybelle's house. He set his eyes immediately on her. She forced her heart down into her chest and said a silent prayer to whomever may be listening. There he was. The man who'd stolen her dignity, her innocence, and her future from her.

Roger peeked outside before closing the door behind himself. He stood at the door staring at her, his eyes narrowing as he scanned the length of her. "You've grown up nicely."

Lena felt sick again, but this time in a different way. She held his gaze, as he slowly walked towards her. She knew this day would come, but she didn't realize it would be today. He sat down opposite of her in the chair.

"Nice to see you again, Miss Pittman."

"Save your pleasantries." Lena mustered up as much boldness as she could, but his presence made her feel weakened, like that fifteen-year-old girl she used to be. "You have no right to be here in my grandmother's house."

"I'm the Mayor."

"And?"

"I can do whatever I want in this town."

In her peripheral, Lena could see Nadia stiffening up. "What do you want from us?"

"I want to know who she is." He pointed towards Nadia.

"She's my daughter."

"Is that so? Who's her father?"

She looked over at Nadia. "I don't know who her father is."

Roger laughed. "That's no surprise coming from a whore like you."

The memory of when he first called her that name set fire to her insides. She clenched her jaw. "He was just some guy I met who was on shore leave."

"Is that right, huh?" He narrowed his eyes at her, occasionally glancing over at Nadia, "It's funny you say that because I heard something totally different."

"I don't know what you're talking about."

He pulled a cigar from his pocket and put it in his mouth. He eyed her before he lit it. He took a long puff off the cigar and blew a plume of smoke into the air. A smile creased his face, showing his tobacco tinted teeth. His icy cold eyes glistened.

"A little birdie told me that this is my granddaughter."

She knew she couldn't trust Linda Chamberlain to keep her mouth shut. Lena's heart felt like it had stopped for a second. Her body numbed of all feeling by the rush of adrenaline pushing through her body. She clenched Nadia's hand.

"I don't know what you're talking about."

"So, you deny it?"

"I suggest you leave. Right now."

Roger laughed. "Okay, I'll leave, but you and my granddaughter here are coming with me."

"What!" Lena jumped up from her seat. Ty grabbed Nadia first, and then Roger laid hands on Lena, putting her in a chokehold. Unlike Ty, Roger squeezed her so tightly she thought she was going to pass out on the spot.

"Easy, easy girl. Let's not get out of control here."

Lena swatted at his arms, but all that did was make him squeeze tighter. She could smell his cologne, mixed with the cigar smoke as he breathed on her. He still smelled the same too. The last thing she saw was Nadia fighting with Ty as he tried to hold her in place.

Her world faded to black and her knees gave out, but before she went out completely, she heard Roger tell Ty, "Let's take them to the barn."

***

Something didn't feel right. Linda stood in front of her, nervous and distracted. She wouldn't look her straight in the eyes either. Janine placed the remaining seasoning into the pot and covered it with the top.

"I'm surprised you wanted my help with your chicken alfredo. You never need help."

Linda laughed softly. "Oh, honey, I just want to spend a little time with you. That's all." Linda continued to avoid her eyes as she worked around her at the island.

"Mother?"

"Yes?"

"What's wrong?"

Linda placed the rest of the food scraps into the wastebasket and turned to face her. "Nothing is wrong. Why do you ask?"

"Because you've been acting strange ever since I got here."

"No, I haven't."

"Actually, you have."

Linda reached into the cupboard and pulled out a wineglass. She stepped into the wine cellar and came out with a twenty-year-old bottle of red. She popped the top and poured the glass full. She drank it down with nearly one gulp.

"What in the hell is going on?" Janine snatched the bottle out of her hand and slammed it down on the counter. "Why are you drinking right now? I thought you wanted to spend time together."

"I do, but I need a drink."

"Why? Am I not good enough company?"

"No, it's not that."

Jack came into the kitchen and walked straight over to the stove and peeked inside of the pot. Janine took her mother's arm and pulled her closer.

"What is it then?" She didn't want Jack to hear, but she knew eventually he would detect that something was going on.

Linda's bottom lip quivered as her eyes filled with tears. "I'm sorry, Janine, I know I shouldn't have, but your father insisted and he—"

Janine's heart dropped. "You know you shouldn't have what?"

Linda lowered her head.

"What did you do, Mother?" The panic in her voice drew Jack's attention away from the chicken alfredo on the stove. "Tell me what you did!"

"I told him about Jackson's daughter."

Janine gasped, she spun around to see an equally stunned expression on Jack's face. He dropped the top and raced over to them.

"You did what? Why would you tell him about her?" Janine couldn't understand for the life of her why Linda would do such a thing.

"He asked if I knew who she was. I told him that I didn't know at first. I couldn't lie to him."

"Oh, my god."

"I told him that Lena didn't want me to have a relationship with her and he said he would talk to her."

"She has every right to forbid us from seeing her! You know what dad did to her. Why would you tell him?"

"I'm sorry. I just thought—I don't know what I thought, honestly." Linda poured herself another glass and took it back in one gulp. She coughed through the afterbite. "What have I done?" She cupped her mouth, stifling a sob from escaping.

"Where is he? Where's dad?" Janine asked. She glanced over a Jack to see the red in his face deepening with anger.

Linda ignored her questions, so Janine took her by the arms and shook her. "My god, Mother! Please! Where is he?"

"He said he was going to go talk to Lena. That's why he wanted me to ask you to come here."

"What?"

"He didn't want you or Jackson interfering, so he told me to invite you two over."

Janine released her. Her mind flooded with memories of what she saw that night. Of how she stood there, paralyzed with fear and watched helplessly while her relatives stripped her best friend of her innocence and dignity. She stood there and did nothing.

She squeezed her eyes shut and hit her head with her open palm, "Stop, stop..." When the train of thoughts subsiding, she turned to Jack. Without saying a word to her, he turned and ran out of the kitchen. Janine followed behind him. She'd deal with Linda's betrayal at a later time.

***

Janine had barely pulled the car to a stop before Jack jumped out of the passenger's side. She parked the car and followed in his footsteps inside. He was just coming from the back of the house when she came in. He went into the kitchen and quickly came out. He paced back and forth, running his trembling hands through his hair.

"They're not here."

"Are you sure?"

"Yes. Not back there. Not in the kitchen. They're gone."

"Where could they be?" Janine looked around the room. She saw evidence of a struggle. She smelled her father's cigars and cologne. "Dad was here."

"I know." She could hear the stress in his voice. "Where are they?"

"I don't know." Janine felt helpless. She knew they were with Roger, she could feel it, but where? "Do you know where they could've gone, Jack?"

Jack paced the floor. The more he paced the more anxious he became. He wrung his hands nervously. About his fifth or sixth pass by Janine, he stopped in his tracks. He stared at the ground; his face crinkled with an emotion that Janine couldn't quite place. He ran his thumb along his cheek, his face blazed as he looked up at her.

"The barn."

"What? How do you know?"

"Dad goes there still. I saw pictures in his office."

"You were in his office? What pictures?"

"I saw this folder. Green. Pictures of a lady and him."

"Who was in the picture?"

"I don't know. But he was in the barn."

"How do you know?"

"Because I never forgot it."

"But you think he's there?"

"Let's go check." Jack didn't wait for her to agree. He ran out and jumped in the car. Janine was right behind him. She started the ignition, the entire time hoping and praying that Jack was wrong about the location. If he'd taken her back to the same place, she knew she would lose Lena forever. Lena would never recover from a second round with him.

As she looked over at Jack and saw the panic on his face as well, she realized that they all had a personal stake in this. They all had been changed that night. They had to stop the madness. Roger's reign of terror had to end.

Chapter 25

Lena couldn't breathe. The air inside the barn was so thick that it suffocated her. Her lungs felt like they were giving out. After all these years, she ended up in the same place where her spirit had been broken. She smelled the scent of old blood. Her mind flickered with the memories of that night. She shook off her thoughts and readjusted herself in the chair. She looked over at Nadia. Ty held his gun against Nadia's temple.

She glanced up to see Roger standing over her like a statue, his eyes slowly traveling the length of her body. She felt violated, violated by the memories racing back and forth through her mind. She squeezed her eyes shut, but she still saw her younger self in front of her and still heard her own screams in her ears.

"If you so much as move one muscle, Ty will put a bullet in her." Roger said.

As much as Lena wanted to jump out of the chair, she couldn't. Doing so would put Nadia's life in danger. She nodded and lowered her head. This barn was the last place she wanted to be, especially after burying Maybelle today. She wanted to do something, but she didn't want to put Nadia at risk. Roger chuckled and walked over to Nadia.

Nadia stared defiantly into Roger's eyes. He moved closer to her. Eventually, she broke eye contact with him, looking down at the smartwatch on her wrist. She fidgeted with it, a sure sign of her unease.

Roger laughed. "That's what I thought. Show proper respect for your ol' grandpa, will ya?" He reached for Nadia's face.

"Don't touch her, Roger!" Lena yelled.

"You aren't the one giving orders around here. I am." He touched Nadia's chin and tipped it towards him. "This is an interesting creature you made here. She looks so much like you, but at the same time, she looks like her imbecile father, too."

"How could you talk about your own son like that?"

"Jackson stopped being my son the day he started fooling around with you."

Lena knew better than to engage him, but she couldn't help herself. She couldn't understand how someone could be so evil. "I did nothing but love him and care for him."

"I don't care anything about that."

"Why bring me back here?"

"Just wanted to give my granddaughter here a grand tour of where it all began."

"You're crazy!"

"I was crazy to think that this kid was actually mine. What a relief it was to find out she wasn't."

"Stop touching my daughter!" Lena's stomach turned.

Roger smiled into Nadia's eyes as he stroked her chin. Nadia stared at him; her eyes turned to ice as her body tensed up. Her hands had clenched into tight fists, trembling with restraint. Nadia wanted to fight.

"This is insane!" Lena said.

Roger came over and took Lena's face. "Yeah, you're right about that, but there's nothing wrong with traveling down memory lane, now is there?" He dug his nails into her face. The pain that streaked through her cheeks as his nails cut into her flesh, sent her mind flying back to that night. The memories assaulted her mind. Every inch of this barn space held a terrible memory.

Lena whimpered, baring her teeth as she felt her blood trickle down the sides of her face. "What do you want from me?" She held back her tears, because the day she allowed him to see her cry again, would be the day he did it over her dead body.

He released her, wiping his bloodied fingernails off with his handkerchief. He walked back over to Nadia. Nadia glared at him. He smiled. "The only thing I want is to make you disappear forever."

"What did I ever do to you?" She yelled.

"You're defiant, just like your mother. And it looks like you passed that gene down to her too."

"What are you talking about? You knew my mother?"

He laughed. "All of Archer knew your mother. If you know what I mean. You know she got around."

His words tore through Lena's heart. "I see."

"I'll have to admit, your mother, although she had the sad misfortune of being a nigger, was one of my favorites." He shrugged and bounced his brows, daring her to say something in response.

Lena stared at him; her blood boiled inside of her. "You're a sick liar."

"There's one thing your crackhead mother failed to understand, Lena. Would you like to know what that one thing was?"

"I don't care."

He leaned closer. "You see, she failed to understand that you don't say no to a Chamberlain, because bad things happen when you do." He smiled.

Lena wanted to punch him square in his mouth. "Did you do something to my mother?"

Roger shrugged. "Maybe. Maybe not."

Lena's stomach churned into knots. Memories of the day she came home and realized that her mother was gone rushed back. And along with the memories came also the feelings of abandonment, despair and heartache. She groaned as images of her mother's face flashed through her mind.

"Do you know where she went?"

"Nope."

Lena lowered her head. The pain was too much for her at the moment. The little girl inside of her, the one who misses her mother every day, started grieving all over again.

"So, you see, if your mother didn't even want you, what makes you think that my boy wanted you?"

"He did."

"He's slow as molasses. He didn't know any better!"

"He is not as slow as you all make him out to be. Aidan knows how to love, and he knows how to care for someone. He loves me."

Roger laughed. "Sure, he does."

"I don't need to explain anything to you."

Ty came over and whispered something into Roger's ear. Roger pointed to the back of the barn and then Ty grabbed Nadia and dragged her like a ragdoll towards the entryway of the next room.

Nadia fought wildly, kicking and punching at him. Her punches connected, but they didn't faze him at all.

Lena sprung to her feet and went after them, but Roger caught her by the arm. "Not so fast."

"Let me go!"

He yanked her back, slamming her forcefully against the wall. "You see, I'm not touching her, because that would just be wrong, but there's nothing stopping me from getting with you. Nobody's gonna stop me. Just like nobody stopped me the last time we were here."

Lena scratched at his face, clawing him with so much force that she broke off two nails in his flesh. He yelled and pulled back, grabbing at his face. He picked her nails out of his face and flicked them away.

He took her by the throat and almost struck her, but a light from outside the barn distracted him. "Someone's outside," he called to Ty. Ty put Nadia into a chokehold and dragged her over to the boarded-up window.

"I can't tell who it is." He squinted through the opening in the boards. He swore under his breath. "Rog, your boy's coming." Ty backed away from the window.

"Son of a —"

Before he could say or do anything else, Jack crashed through the door. It appeared as if he ran straight through it. The entire door splintered as he busted through. When he stumbled inside, he took in the scene in front of him. Ty holding his daughter in a chokehold. And there was Roger, holding the mother of his child against her will.

"What are you doing here, Jackson?" Roger asked.

Jack walked towards Ty. "Get your hands off her."

Ty tightened his grip around Nadia's neck and dragged her towards Roger and Lena. Jack rushed him, grabbing his arm in an attempt to pry it from around her neck. But all that did was make him tighten his grip. Nadia choked as they fought over her.

"Stop it!" Lena yelled. "You're going to kill her!" She struggled to free herself from Roger, but he held her in place as they watched Jack and Ty struggle over Nadia.

When his other attempts to free her failed, Jack swung at Ty as hard as he could. His fist connected with a sickening thud. To the left temple. Ty dropped to the ground, pulling Nadia down with him. Jack knocked him out cold. Jack pried Nadia from him and scooped her into his arms.

"You're gonna regret doing that, Jackson." Roger said calmly.

Jack hurried and placed Nadia into a secure corner and then approached his father. "Let her go," he said.

"I don't know what you're trying to prove, but being all hero right now isn't going to change the past."

"I'm not trying to." Jack stepped closer, cautiously closing the distance between them. "I just want you to stop hurting my family."

"Your family?" Roger laughed. "You mean this girl and that mulatto?"

Jack clenched his fists. "They are my family. You can't talk about them like that."

"I can do what I want."

"You have hurt too many people. You need to stop."

"No one can make me stop."

"I can." Jack advanced towards him.

Roger squeezed Lena's neck, daring Jack to keep coming at him. "Stay back!" Roger warned.

"Let her go." Jack's eyes blazed with an indignation that neither Lena nor Roger had ever seen before. "I mean it."

"Why should I let her go? Why should you care what I do with her?"

"Because I love her."

"That matters nothing to me." Roger turned his back to Jack, dismissing him. Jack tackled him and yanked his hand away from Lena's neck. Roger stumbled and they crashed to the floor. Jack hopped on top of him. Roger swung at him, striking him hard across the face.

Jack landed at Lena's feet. She bent down to help him up, but he pushed her in the direction of Nadia. She scrambled over to Nadia's side while Jack fought with his father.

Roger gained the upper hand, climbing on top of him and punishing him with brutal punches. Blow after blow. Jack deflected a majority of the blows, but Roger took hold of his throat and squeezed.

The scene was total chaos. Janine suddenly appeared from somewhere unknown and jumped into the mix with Roger and Jack. She hopped onto her father's back and attempted to pry his hands from Jack's neck. She was unsuccessful. Jack eventually, and out of pure desperation, head butted his father so hard that he flew off of him. Janine was in the wrong place at the wrong time. Roger landed on her, both crashing against the opposite wall.

There was a momentary break in the chaos. Jack was on the ground gasping for air. Lena crawled over to him and took him into her arms. "Aidan? Are you okay?"

Jack touched his throat; an awful red and green bruise forming. "Yeah," he croaked.

"Stay still, please." She stroked the hair of his beard and glanced in the direction Janine and Roger had crashed.

Janine crawled from underneath Roger and pulled herself to her feet. She held her arm as she limped over and knelt down beside them. "Is he okay?"

"Yes. I think so," Lena said.

Janine went and checked on Nadia. She was in shock. She stared at her parents sitting together just a few feet away. Her eyes were glazed over with an emotion that Janine recognized all too well. There was no doubt in her mind if Nadia was a Chamberlain. The look in her eyes sent chills racing up her spine.

"Sweetheart?" Janine inspected her face. Nadia's eyes twinkled with tears. "Stay here, okay?" Janine got up and hurried towards Lena, but before she could make it there, a hand grabbed her leg and yanked her down to the floor.

She landed on her shoulder, jamming it into the socket joint. She shrieked out in pain as she rolled over onto her back. She saw the barrel of a handgun hovering above her head, with Roger on the other end of it. Roger had taken it from Ty's unconscious body and stalked towards Lena with murderous intent in his eyes.

Janine jumped to her feet. "Dad! What are you doing?" she yelled, placing herself between Roger and Lena. She raised her hands in surrender. "Please, Dad, put the gun down."

"Move out of the way, Janine!"

"Dad, please. Let's talk about this."

"I said get out of the way, Janine. This is between me and her."

"No! It's between all of us." She caught him by the arm as he tried to push past her. He pulled away, yanking her backwards with him. He lost his footing and crashed down on the ground. Janine attempted to wrestle the gun from Roger. They struggled intensely for it.

"Let go of the gun!" he yelled. Janine gripped the gun and yanked on it. "Stop it! Let go of the damn gun, Janine!"

The gun went off. Roger froze; a frown creased his face as he stared into his only daughter's surprised eyes. His eyes widened as Janine's hands loosened their grip.

"Daddy?" Janine gasped, sinking into his arms.

"Oh no," he groaned. He made an indescribable noise as he lowered her to the ground.

Lena raced to her side, pushed him out of the way, and took Janine into her arms. "Oh, my god, what have you done, Roger?" Lena cried. Her heart seized up at the sight of Janine. Roger stumbled away from them and ran for the front exit. He glanced back one last time, before disappearing out of the barn.

Lena held her close to her heart, "Jay? Don't do this to me." She stroked her hair and smiled into those green eyes staring up at her. "Jay?" she whispered.

Janine winced, moving her hand to her abdomen. It was then that Lena noticed where the blood was coming from. Janine squeezed her eyes shut and whimpered. Lena swore under her breath.

"Please, tell me what to do."

Janine took Lena's hand and placed it over her wound. She gazed up at Lena with tearful eyes., "Press," she whispered. "Hard."

Lena pressed. She heard sirens wailing in the distance, sounding like they were getting closer by the minute. She couldn't hold back her tears any longer. Janine clenched the fabric of Lena's shirt, holding on tightly to the only person who truly loved her.

"I'm here," Lena whispered.

"It hurts."

"I know. I'm sorry." Lena put more pressure on the wound. Her stomach turned when she felt the warmth of Janine's blood running over her fingers. She was afraid to look, so she didn't. She glanced over at Jack. He was still laying on his back, groaning, but he seemed okay. He would live.

The police sirens were getting closer. "Did you call the cops?"

Janine nodded.

"You did good, Jay." Janine tried to smile, but she winced instead. Lena pulled her closer and rocked her. She was helpless. "Please, don't leave me." She couldn't lose Janine on the same day she buried Maybelle. That wouldn't be fair at all.

She looked up and saw Nadia standing over them with the same glassy-eyed expression. Lena wondered perhaps if this had pushed Nadia over the edge. She didn't know. All she knew was Janine had just taken a bullet for her.

Her heart couldn't take the thoughts rushing through her mind. Thoughts of Janine when they were little, and as teens, and of all the plans they had made when they were younger. She couldn't take the guilt she now felt for staying away so long and for punishing Janine for nearly twenty-five years. None of that mattered now.

She blinked the tears out of her eyes as she looked down at Janine. Janine was gazing up at her, her eyes shimmering with tears.

"Is she going to be okay?" Nadia asked.

Lena sniffled. "She has to be okay." Janine's body felt like it had gone a little limper in her arms as Lena finally worked up the courage to look where her hand covered Janine's wound. Her stomach lurched and twisted. Nadia knelt down beside Lena and touched her shoulder. Lena looked at her, but she couldn't bring herself to say anything. She just shook her head and looked back down at Janine. Tears streamed down her face.

"I'm—" Janine struggled for her breath, "I'm sorry."

"Shh," she caressed her cheek, "Don't talk, it's okay."

"I'm so sorry," she repeated.

Lena felt a rush of emotions race through her system. Her skin flashed hot, and then cold. Her ears stopped up, and the only thing she could hear were the shallow breaths of Janine as she struggled to breathe.

"I forgive you."

Janine nodded. Tears streamed down her face. She looked frightened. Lena wished she could make this all better and take away any and every fear that she had at the moment. But she couldn't. She couldn't do anything to help her.

Nadia jumped to her feet and backed away from them. Lena looked at her oddly. "Where are you going?" She was confused. She couldn't understand why Nadia was acting so strangely. She knew she couldn't run after her. She couldn't leave Janine like this.

"Where are you going?" she asked her again.

Nadia didn't answer as she looked towards the front of the barn. Police lights flashed. The sounds of cars stopping, and radio chatter let them know that the police had arrived. What would the Archer police say when they came in and found the Chief lying unconscious and the Mayor's daughter bleeding from a gunshot wound?

This was a complete nightmare. Lena knew they would try to pin this on her, and she was prepared for it. As long as Janine got the medical attention she needed, she would take the blame. Nadia backed into the shadows and dashed out of an opening in the back of the barn.

Lena watched the exit where Nadia had gone out, hoping she would return, but knew she wouldn't. The next thing she knew, the police charged through the front. To her surprise they weren't the Archer police. They were State police. Her heart relaxed when she recognized two of them. They were the same ones who led the funeral procession through town earlier today.

The two brothers. She wondered if this was some sort of a weird coincidence or if it had some deeper meaning.

One of them bent down beside Lena and touched her shoulder. "An ambulance will be here in a few minutes," he said. His tone was warm and sympathetic.

"He shot her in the stomach. He shot his own daughter." She choked on her own words.

"Where is he? Where's the Mayor?"

"I don't know. He ran out right after it happened."

The policeman squeezed her shoulder and glanced over at Ty. "And what happened to him?"

"He was trying to hurt me, but," she said nodding her head towards Jack, "Jack Chamberlain stopped him. Jack did that, but in defense of me. Check on him, please." Not knowing how any of this would turn out, she opted not to mention the fact that Nadia was also here when it all happened. It was better this way.

The policeman mumbled something into his radio. She couldn't understand him even if she tried. All she could hear was Janine's breaths.

"Okay. Ambulance is here."

The EMTs came in and transferred Janine onto a gurney. Lena stood aside and let them work on her. Before they rolled her away, she came to her side.

"I'll be at the hospital as soon as I can, okay?"

Janine barely nodded, but she tried. The EMTs rolled her outside and put her in the ambulance. They sped off in the direction of the county hospital. Lena was torn. She wanted to go with Janine, but she really needed to find Nadia. Both would have to wait, because this current scene was utterly chaotic. She had to try and explain what happened. She wasn't even sure if she actually knew.

She caught a glimpse of another set of EMT's checking Jack's vitals. She knew he would be fine. He was strong. He had rescued them. Jack made eye contact with her. She was so proud of him. He smiled at her. And she smiled back at him. She was about to go over to him, when the policeman pulled her aside for a statement.

At least the cavalry was on her side this time. She watched as they waved smelling salts underneath Ty's nose. He sprung to life in the middle of three policemen. They laid siege of him and placed him into custody. He seemed to know his fate. He glared at her as they read him his rights. He kept his head down as they led him out of the barn and into the awaiting car.

At least part of her nightmare was over. It just walked out of the front door, and as long as she was living, it would never walk back in again.

Chapter 26

Roger stood over the bathroom sink and inspected his face in the mirror. She'd scratched up his face pretty badly. How would he explain this to his PR rep? He didn't really care. He'd just tell her the same story he always told her. It was the cat. It was always the cat.

He put his hands underneath the running water and splashed his face. The water stung his cuts and ran off red. He cursed under his breath. His hands shook as he reached for the towel on the rack.

"Looking for this?"

He jumped back to find Linda standing beside him. He snatched the towel from her. "Thanks." He patted his face dry and inspected his face in the mirror. The cuts were deep, so deep that he was certain that he'd have scars for the rest of his life.

"How did you get those cuts?"

"None of your business."

"I said, how did you get those cuts?"

Roger turned to her and frowned. "Why do you want to know?"

"What did you do to them?"

"I didn't do anything." He turned back toward the mirror, but she shoved him against the wall.

"I said, what did you do to them!" she yelled. Her face was distorted, her eyes were wild with anger. "Did you hurt our granddaughter?"

He took her by the arms and shook her roughly. "Don't you ever touch me like that again!" He shoved her against the wall, "I don't have any grandchild. If you wanna call that animal a grandchild, then that's on you, but she is no Chamberlain."

"She's a person, Roger. Just like her mother, she's a person. Did you hurt them?"

"No." He lowered his head over the sink, "But Janine got hurt."

Linda gasped. "Hurt how? What happened?"

Roger squeezed his eyes tightly shut; Janine's voice echoed throughout his head. The look on her face when she realized that he'd shot her was forever etched into his mind.

"What happened?" she shrieked. Linda's entire body trembled. The scent of alcohol seeped out of her pores. "Where is she?"

"Her and Jackson did what they always do. Went crazy because of the Pittman girl."

"What does that mean?"

"I was handling business with the Pittman girls and they decided that they were going to stop me. Your son attacked me. He's not too hurt, but he won't ever try that again."

"Oh my God." Linda ran her hands through her hair and looked nervously around the room. "What happened to Janine?"

"I had a gun. She tried to take it from me. The gun fired. She took a bullet."

"What?" Linda stifled a sob. "Shot? Roger, where is she?"

He glanced over at her, he wished he'd never married her. She was weak. Disloyal to the family name. She was only good as a trophy. She was no good at anything else anymore. His eyes narrowed at her. "The barn." He looked back at the mirror.

Linda made a noise that sounded like a mixture of a groan and a whimper. "Why would you take them there?" She asked, but Roger knew she already knew the answer. The barn was where his "urgent meetings" took place. It was where he went every time he'd disappear out of their bed in the middle of the night. It was where he'd go to relive the moment when he'd achieved absolute power and control over his family.

"You just left her there?"

He looked over at her. Tears streamed down her face, her mouth opened slightly, her lips trembled. He held her eye contact for a few seconds before looking away.

"She's our daughter! How could you leave her like that?"

"Obviously I can't be found there."

"They'll tell what happened!"

"You know what? I don't care anymore. Plus, I run this town. No one will believe them."

"You're insane! I'll tell them what you did!" Linda backed out of the bathroom and ran down the hall. She'd almost made it to the front door when he caught her by the arm and spun her around to face him.

"You will do no such thing!"

"Let me go!" she screamed and swatted at him. The help came running to see what was going on, but with one warning glare from Roger they backed off and went back to their stations.

He slapped her across the face. The force of the blow split her lip. She fell to the floor in a heap. Blood dripped from the newly opened wound. He grabbed her and brought her back to her feet.

"You're going to keep your mouth shut just like you've been doing all these years."

"But we have a granddaughter now, Roger. You can't do this kind of stuff anymore."

"You will keep your mouth shut. Do you understand?"

"I can't keep quiet anymore. You do what you want to do to me, but I can't keep what you've done a secret anymore."

He struck her again, this time harder than the last time. She crashed hard onto the floor. He grabbed her by her blouse and reared back to strike her again, but the front door flew open. He looked up to see Nadia standing in the doorway. She stood there looking at him with the same stone-cold expression that she had earlier at the barn. She stepped over the threshold.

Roger released Linda, dropping her back on the floor. He chuckled under his breath, "Well, well. Who do we have here?"

Nadia said nothing as she stalked toward him with slow and calculated steps. "Get away from her." Her voice was devoid of her usual warmth, the warmth that made her who she was. She'd seen enough of Roger Chamberlain's terror.

"You walk up into my house and give me orders?" Roger stood taller as she drew closer. Roger recognized the look in Nadia's eyes. He saw the same look in his every time he looked into the mirror.

"I said, get away from her."

"You don't even know her and you're trying to defend her?" Roger took a few steps back from her when he realized she had a gun in her hand. The gun he used to drop his own daughter, was the same gun that now rested in the hands of his indignant granddaughter. He knew he should have taken it with him.

"I don't have to know her." Nadia brandished the gun and motioned for him to move away from Linda. When he moved back a safe distance, she bent down and touched her. Linda looked up at her; her face was bruised and bloodied. "Are you okay?"

Linda nodded. Nadia took her by the hand and pulled her to her feet. When Linda was steady enough to stand on her own, Nadia advanced towards Roger.

"Do you even know how to use that thing?" Roger taunted her.

"I don't think you want to find out whether or not I can use it. Now do you?"

Roger nodded and laughed. "Let's talk about this?"

"That's funny, that's the same thing my aunt asked of you right before you shot her," Nadia said calmly.

"She's not your aunt and that was an accident. I didn't mean to shoot her."

Nadia stepped closer. "I'm not going to argue whether or not I'm family, because I know I am. I never thought I was capable of hate, but now I realize I am." She raised the gun at him. He stumbled back. "Because all I feel for you right now is hate. I hate you for what you did to my mother. I hate you for how you treat my father. And I hate you for who you are."

Roger chuckled. "Well, that makes two of us. I wanted a pure lineage, not one that's soiled with you and your mother's black blood."

"You are the one who soiled your so-called lineage, with your hate!"

"It's called preservation!"

"It's called hate."

"Call it what you want, but I know what's important. And that's to make sure the Chamberlain blood is preserved for the future. I will never consider you my family. You're just some bastard child who shouldn't have ever been given a chance to live."

His hateful words stung her ears. She gripped the gun tighter, her face firming up even more. "You will pay for what you did to my mother."

Roger laughed. "Oh yeah? Who's going to make me pay? In case you haven't noticed, I'm the Mayor. No one can touch me."

"You'll be removed the moment they find out how you, Chief Tyson and his sons, raped my mother when she was only fifteen years old. She was only a child!"

"Ha! No one is ever going to find that out. I had to teach my boy a lesson about fooling around with tainted people like her."

"You're a monster!"

"I'll agree to that. But one thing is sure," he stepped closer to her, "Your mother deserved every single thing that I did to her. Every single thing. And I don't regret doing what I did. I'll never regret it. You know why?"

"Why?"

"Because I showed her, and Jackson, and Janine, that what I said was law. And if you broke that law, punishment is what came next. There had to be order. They were running around here rebelling against me and it was all because of your mother!"

"They were just kids, you sick maniac. That's what kids do! They had every right to be friends!"

"That's your opinion."

Nadia pulled the hammer on the gun. He smiled into her eyes, daring her to pull the trigger. "If you're gonna do it, you better do it now, but I don't think you have the guts."

"Oh, I certainly have the guts. But what I don't have is the desire to see you get off that easily for the crimes you've committed."

Roger frowned, "What? What are you talking about?"

Nadia glanced down at her smartwatch and smiled back up at him, "Wouldn't you like to know, huh grandpa?"

The blood drained from his face, "What did you do?"

Before he could say anything else, a half dozen state policemen stormed inside, with weapons drawn, and ordered Nadia to drop her weapon.

Nadia dropped the gun by her feet and raised her hands in surrender. "You did this all by yourself."

The policemen took hold of him and cuffed his hands behind his back. His face burned with anger as he glanced down at her smartwatch.

"Oh, this?" she said. "I recorded everything you said, from the barn until now."

"That'll never stand up in court." He lunged at her but was stopped by the policemen.

"That's not even my problem right now." She removed her watch and gave it to the policeman. "There's a full confession of his crimes on my audio player. I'll help with whatever I can." She turned away from them and put her arm around Linda and squeezed her supportively.

"I am so sorry for everything he did," Linda said.

"Thank you."

"I need to see my daughter. I need to see her."

"Okay," Nadia squeezed her tighter. The warmth had returned to her voice. "We can get the police to take us to the hospital. Do you need medical attention?"

"No. I'm used to it. I'll be fine. I just need to see my daughter." Nadia led her out of the door and to the awaiting police cars.

Roger was about to be put into one of the cars when Nadia walked up to him. She noticed several news trucks set up and filming his arrest. She stared into the coldest eyes that she'd ever seen. "Looks like the world will finally know what you did."

Roger looked over at the news crews waiting near the driveway. He fixed his eyes back on Nadia. "You will pay for this."

"I'm afraid you're mistaken. You are the one who will pay for this and everything else you've done. You'll never hurt anyone ever again."

He spat on the ground next to her feet before they pushed him into the backseat of the squad car.

"We'll see about that," were his last words to her.

The car door slammed behind him and in an instant, he disappeared from her face. His last words left Nadia hoping that the system wouldn't fail them this time.

Roger needed to be locked away for a very long time. She gave no more thought to him but instead, joined Linda in the other squad car and was whisked away to see if Janine had made it to the hospital alive.

Chapter 27

Lena toyed with Janine's necklace in her hands. The first time she noticed it, was the morning after Janine had arrived. It was when they were sitting down for breakfast for the first time together. After she took Janine's hand, the light from the morning sun reflected off it. She remembered thinking that it was an impossibility for Janine to still have the same necklace she'd given her when they were kids. But when everyone closed their eyes for Maybelle's touching prayer, Lena kept hers open and gazed upon it in disbelief. Janine had in fact, kept her necklace all those years.

Lena smiled to herself, remembering how after everyone said "Amen," Janine had caught her staring at the necklace, and what followed was their first silent exchange as adults. It was brief, but it was one that Lena would never forget.

She brought the necklace to her lips and kissed it softly. She sniffled back her tears. Her eyes drifted to her hands; they were stained with Janine's blood.

She grabbed the tail of her shirt and tried to wipe it off her hands as best she could. It was then she realized that she was covered in it also. She hadn't noticed that it was all over her until reality struck her in that moment. Her stomach turned. She couldn't handle the sight of blood, especially not from someone she knew.

She put the necklace around her neck and snapped it on. She sighed heavily and kissed the locket on the end of the chain. She opened it slowly, her heart immediately seizing up inside as she gazed at the tiny photo of her and Janine, dated back to 1994. It was the last one they took together. Back before selfies were a thing, she and Janine had this one. It was her favorite.

She closed it tightly and dropped it inside of her shirt. The door opened up across the hall. She jumped to her feet and walked briskly over to the doctor who'd stepped out of the room. Before she said anything, she observed the doctor's face. His face lacked any emotion whatsoever. He just stood there staring at her.

"Can I see her?"

"I'm sorry, but you may need to give her a couple of hours of rest."

"Is she going to be okay?"

"Yes. The bullet missed vital organs and was lodged in her side, right above her pelvic bone," he said motioning the location of the bullet, "Thankfully she was at just the right angle for it to be a non-fatal GSW."

"Oh, thank god."

"I understand you want to see her, but it's best if she gets her rest. The surgery took a toll on her."

"Okay." She glanced down at her hands. "Can I just sit in there with her, please?"

The doctor sighed heavily and glanced at his watch. "Yes, you can, Lena. I'll have one of the nurses bring you in a more comfortable chair."

Lena frowned. "You know me?"

The doctor nodded. "You probably don't remember, but we were in the same class in the ninth grade. The kids picked on me all the time. One day during lunch period, some guy took my sack lunch from me. Everyone laughed."

Lena searched her memory for that moment he referred to, but she couldn't find it. So much had happened. Too many sad memories blocked out the good ones.

"Anyway, when I was walking home you and the Mayor's daughter pulled up beside me and told me to hop in. It was you, her, Jack, and me and you guys took me to the drive-in for burgers and shakes."

Suddenly, she remembered. He was a lot chubbier back then, but he still looked the same. "Wow, that was you?"

"Yes."

"I'm sorry. A lot has happened, and I can't remember names."

"My name is Byron. Byron Swaim." He glanced down at his watch again. "You left not too long after and I never got a chance to tell you how grateful I was for the kindness you showed to me."

Lena's heart seized up inside of her chest. "Thank you for saying that."

He nodded. "Anything you need, just ask the nurse." He extended his hand to her.

Instead of taking his hand, she hugged him, "Thank you so much!"

"You're welcome." He pulled away and walked down the hallway. Lena watched him walk away and disappear around the corner.

She pushed open the door of Janine's room. She laid peacefully in the bed with her hands resting at her sides. Lena tip toed over and took the seat beside her. She took her hand and kissed it. She held it close to her lips as she fought back a deluge of tears that threatened to come out. Seeing her again after fearing she'd lost her was almost too much for her heart to bear.

She watched her sleep peacefully and there was nowhere else she wanted to be at the moment. In the back of her mind, she wondered where Nadia had run off to. But she also knew that Nadia was smart, and she wouldn't get herself into any sticky situation she couldn't get out of. She closed her eyes and grazed Janine's hand across her cheek.

Lena couldn't believe that Janine took a bullet for her. Janine stirred a little and turned her head towards Lena. Lena sighed and squeezed her hand. When Janine opened her eyes, Lena made sure the first thing she saw was a welcoming smile.

"Hey," Lena said. She kissed her hand again. "Thank god you're okay."

Janine's mouth creased with a smile. "Hi." She looked past Lena and then her head slowly turned, examining the room around her. "Where am I?"

"The hospital."

"What happened?" She tried to sit up and winced in pain. "Ow, my stomach." She reached down and touched her abdomen. Her fingers glided over the gauze dressings before they came to rest at her side.

"Easy now, okay? You've gone through a lot."

Janine looked at her, a frown distorted her face. She seemed to search for the answers in Lena's eyes. "Are you okay?"

Lena nodded briskly. "Yeah, now I am."

Janine dropped her head back onto her pillow. "Where's Jack? Nadia?"

Lena sighed and squeezed her hand. "He's fine. Just bruised up. You know he's just a big ol' bear." Lena laughed softly. "Doctors said he will be just fine. He left to get something to eat in the cafeteria."

"And Nadia?"

Lena shrugged. "She ran off again. And I don't know where she went. I hope she's back at Big Mama's."

Janine groaned. "I'm sorry this all happened." Her voice was weak and low.

"Shh." Lena caressed her cheek. "None of this is your fault." Janine just nodded and turned her head towards the window. Lena tugged her hand towards her and nuzzled it against her face. "You did good calling the State police. Thank you, I wish I'd thought of that."

"Did he hurt you?"

"No. I mean, nothing serious."

Janine turned to face her. She stared into Lena's eyes, saying so many things her lips couldn't put into words. Her eyes filled with tears. Lena reached over and swiped them away.

"Thank you for what you did."

Janine chuckled. "Don't mention it."

"You are insane, you know that? What were you thinking wrestling the gun from your dad like that?"

"Obviously, I wasn't." They laughed together. "It always worked in the movies."

"God, you're so crazy, Jay."

Janine laughed a little more this time, and for the first time, Lena realized how much she'd missed her laugh. She had this infectious laugh that made everyone laugh with her, even if it wasn't funny. Thoughts of their life and time spent together in the past caused Lena's heart to give way to the tears that she'd been holding back all evening. They burst forth without warning.

Janine's laugh hung in the air as she watched Lena cry. She squeezed her hand and smiled at her. "I'm so glad Big Mama called us home."

Lena nodded. "Me, too."

"She would be so proud of us."

"Even prouder of you for what you did."

"I wasn't really thinking about it. I just knew that I didn't want anything to happen to you. I had to stop him from hurting you."

"Thank you, Jay."

"And you know what?"

"What?"

"I would do it all over again if I had to."

Lena smiled and grazed Janine's hand over her own cheek. "Yep, you're totally crazy."

Janine chuckled softly. There was a knock on the door.

"Come in." Lena called.

The door opened slowly, and Jack popped his head around the corner. When he saw Janine awake, he smiled and walked in. He cautiously approached her bed. "Hey. Are you okay?"

"Yes, I'm fine, big brother."

"You got shot."

"I know."

He sat on the edge of her bed and sighed. He glanced over at Lena, their eyes held contact for a few long seconds before he looked away. "They caught Dad."

"They did? How do you know?"

"Mom. She's outside with Nadia. She wants to see you."

"Who, Nadia?"

"Mom."

"Oh." Janine rested her head on her pillow and sighed. She looked at Lena. Lena could tell she wasn't ready to deal with her mother just yet. Lena squeezed her hand.

"I'll go and talk to her for you, Jay."

"You don't mind?"

"Not at all. It's the least I could do after you took a bullet for me. I'll be back in a while, okay?"

"All right."

She took a deep breath. She hesitated at the door when she felt Jack's hand on the small of her back. She turned to see him smiling at her. He was still as gentle and as protective as he used to be. She'd never had anyone since him look at her the way he was looking at her right now. She glanced past him to see Janine watching them with a slight smile on her face.

"Did they really catch your father?" She relaxed a bit more. His eyes comforted her more than she imagined they would. Being here with them, both of them, gave her the feeling of being home again.

"Yes. They told me they got him."

"Where was he?"

"At home."

Lena's gaze shifted to the floor. She couldn't believe they'd really gotten him. Even if he never spends a day in jail for what he did to her, she hoped that he'd answer for what he did to Janine.

"God, I'm so happy to hear that."

"Me too." Jack nudged her out the door while holding it open for her.

When she stepped out of the room, the first person she saw was Nadia. She rose to her feet and waited for Lena to come closer. When Linda saw her coming, she jumped up and ran to meet her.

"Is she okay?" A faint aroma of alcohol lingered on her breath.

"Yes. How much do you know?" Lena asked.

"All I know is that she was shot by Roger."

"Yes. The bullet caught her in the side, luckily missed vital organs."

"Oh, thank god."

"Yeah, she's pretty lucky."

"This is unforgivable!" Linda crossed her arms and shifted her weight on her feet. "He will pay for what he did to Janine."

Lena couldn't help but to think of how ironic this situation was. She laughed lightly and stepped around Linda, coming closer to Nadia. She wasn't going to allow Linda to get under her skin. It wasn't worth it. "She's resting now, but if you give her a couple of hours, she should be ready to see you."

"Oh, okay." Linda grabbed her jacket from the arm of the couch. "I'm going to go to the cafeteria." She walked off without saying another word to them.

After watching Linda walk away, she turned to Nadia and took a stray piece of her hair and tucked it behind her ear. "You okay?" Her tone was tender and soothing.

"Yeah." Nadia's eyes instantly filled with tears.

"Don't cry. It's okay, sweet pea." She pulled her in for a tight embrace. "It's okay, baby."

Nadia buried her face into Lena's chest and sobbed. Lena soothed her, rocking her gently in her arms. Nadia tightened her grip around her mother and continued to cry. Lena allowed her to get it all out. She'd been through so much in the short period of time they'd been in Archer. It was time to start healing.

Jack came up beside them and put his arm around Nadia. She looked up and saw him gazing sympathetically down into her eyes. They stared at each other for a while before Nadia pulled away from Lena. Jack smiled at her and touched her cheek with his hand.

"You want me to go buy you some ice cream?" he said. "There's a machine in the cafeteria."

Nadia chuckled and swiped the tears out of her eyes. He extended both arms, inviting her in for a hug. She hesitated at first, but then she embraced him. He wrapped his strong arms around her, pulling her up into a loving embrace. She cried again; this time harder as her father held her close. He savored this moment with her. He pulled away from her and dried up her tears with a crumbled-up piece of a used napkin.

"Sure." She smiled up at him and he at her. "Maybe chocolate?"

He nodded. "Chocolate is a good choice." He reached into his pocket and grabbed his wallet. He thumbed through the single bills and glanced at her. "Vanilla okay if they don't have chocolate?"

"Yes. That's perfect."

Jack touched her chin and smiled, "I can't believe you're here." He turned to Lena. "You, too."

Lena touched him softly on the arm. "If you have enough left over, would you mind getting something for me too?"

Jack gave her a crooked smile and nodded. "I still like spending money on you."

Lena laughed and patted him playfully on the arm. "Thanks."

He tipped his imaginary hat and disappeared down the hall. Lena took Nadia's hand and sat her down on the couch. She caressed her face softly. "Where did you go?"

Nadia went into the details about what happened after she'd ran out the back of the barn; everything from taking the gun, to running all the way to the Chamberlain mansion, to stopping him from beating Linda. She rambled on and on, and bits and pieces made no sense to Lena, but she continued to listen.

"You went to his house?"

"Yes."

"He could've killed you."

"I didn't think about that. All I wanted was to make sure he didn't get away with what he did."

"He'll get away with it."

"Not this time. I recorded everything he said and did to us at the barn, plus at his house. I got a confession on what he did to you."

"Really?"

"Yes. We got him."

Lena was beside herself. She wrapped her arms around her and squeezed her tight. "You're crazy like Janine."

Nadia laughed. "Well, it was either that or kill him. And I really didn't want to spend the rest of my life in jail, you know?"

"Yeah, I know." Silence fell over them, each moment passing made her heart lighter than before. "Do you want to see Janine?"

"Yes."

"Good, because I know she would love to see you right now." Lena caressed her face and smiled into her eyes.

***

When Janine heard the door open, she looked over and saw Lena and Nadia coming in. Just being able to see them both together and okay after her father had taken them made her feel better. Her heart constantly ached, but for the first time in so many years, the pain wasn't so bad.

She smiled. "Hey." She reached out her hand and Nadia took it. "I'm so glad you're okay."

Nadia sat next to her. "I'm the one who should be worried about you." She smiled and squeezed Janine's hand.

"I'm tough."

"I see that."

Janine tried to push herself up in the bed, but pain streaked through her abdomen, forcing her back down. Lena came around to the other side and slipped her hand behind her. Gently, she lifted her up in the bed, not much, but just enough for Janine to be more comfortable.

"Thank you."

Lena sat in the vacant chair on that side of the bed and closed her eyes. She looked worn out. Her face was scratched up and bruised. Janine couldn't believe her father was the one who damaged Lena's beautiful face, and not only had he damaged her face, but he also had damaged her spirit. As Janine watched her, she realized that the woman who sat in front of her was one of the strongest women she'd ever known, and she loved her so much.

Lena opened her eyes and looked over at her. A smile creased her face, a small yet knowing smile confirmed that they were still connected. Janine nodded and smiled back at her.

"I thought you were going to die," Nadia said, her voice breaking through the silent communication between them.

Janine turned her attention to Nadia and when she laid her eyes upon her, her heart seized up in her chest. Nadia looked at her with so much love. She saw both Jack and Lena in her eyes. She saw his tenderness and her compassion, wrapped up into one beautiful human. Nadia took Janine's hand and pulled it against her chest.

"I love you," Janine said. She surprised herself. The words shot out of her mouth without any hope of being recaptured. But it was okay. She did love this person who was the product of a love that defied all odds.

"I love you too, Janine."

"You can call me Aunt Janine if you want."

Nadia's smile widened as she squeezed Janine's hand. "All right. Auntie."

Janine chuckled and relaxed her head on the pillow. Her head felt like a serrated knife was cutting through it. She felt nauseous. Her stomach started quivering. She clenched the sheets and took a deep breath.

She sat up quickly, ignoring the sharp pain in her abdomen when she did so. "Lena..." She gasped. She panicked; she was sure she was about to vomit all over herself, but Lena was there in seconds with the puke pail. She rubbed Janine softly on the back while she expelled the contents of her stomach. After she was sure Janine was done, she left her side to dispose of it.

She came back to her side and rubbed her shoulder. "You okay now?" She spoke softly and lovingly to Janine.

"I'm so embarrassed." And she was. She was embarrassed about a lot of things. Vomiting in front of them was among the least.

"Don't be," Lena said, "It's all over, Jay." Her words of reassurance accompanied a gentle squeeze on the hand. "It's all over."

Janine understood. She felt suddenly overwhelmed with emotion. She felt her heart rise into her throat, choking sobs from her. Lena wrapped her arms around her, pulling her in close. Feeling the warmth of her embrace and the evidence of her forgiveness pushed her over the edge. She tried to exhale, but what came out was a cry that didn't even sound like her. It was raw, heavy with the weight of nearly a quarter of a century of guilt. It all came rushing out of her soul like an animal being chased by a predator.

The tighter she grasped Lena, the tighter she held her. She wanted to stop crying, to "suck it up" like her father always told her, but there was no stopping the tears once they started. She tried the breathing exercises that her therapist had taught her, but the only remedy that calmed her agitated heart was Lena's gentle caresses and the soft reassurances whispered into her ear.

Lena had always been the only one who could truly calm her down. Lena was her source of peace, her only escape from the horrors she'd seen while living in the Chamberlain household. She let it all out. Lena was her strength when she hadn't anymore to give. For a few moments, everyone else in the world disappeared and it was just them. Two hearts, two best friends, with their love rekindled.

After some time, her tears dried up and she detached from Lena. She looked up at her. She laughed nervously. "Sorry. I don't know where that came from."

"You're such a crybaby, Jay. Always was, always will be." Lena winked at her.

"Guilty as charged."

Lena pulled the covers up over her. She placed the puke pail beside her. "Just in case you get sick again."

"You're leaving?"

"Yeah, I gotta go back to the house and clean up."

"Are you coming back to see me before..." she swallowed the lump in her throat, "Before you leave?"

Lena stood there looking at her for what seemed like hours. She turned and looked at Nadia and then turned back to Janine. "I'll stay until you're released from the hospital, okay?"

Janine couldn't contain the smile that grew wider and wider. "Thank you."

Lena shrugged. "It's the least I can do, you know. You nearly got yourself killed for me."

Janine half laughed; half cried. Lena came back to her bed and pressed her forehead against hers. "Thank you," she whispered, before kissing the top of her head. She turned and motioned for Nadia to join her. Nadia came over and joined in the huddle.

Janine waved goodbye as they left. She didn't feel so alone anymore. They were her family—a sister and a niece who truly loved her, regardless of her inadequacies. Feeling loved was the most satisfying feeling in the world.

She leaned back and turned on the T.V. The first thing she saw was a news clip of her father being led out of the Chamberlain mansion in handcuffs. The news caption read: Mayor of Archer arrested for vicious attack & shooting.

She flipped off the T.V. She didn't need to hear anymore. It was all over.

Chapter 28

Three weeks later...

Lena looked around the house. Everything had been cleaned up. She left everything the way Maybelle would have wanted her to leave it. Neat and clean. She could still feel her here. She sighed and placed Maybelle's apron on the back of the recliner. She grazed her fingers across the fabric, her heart swelled up inside. She missed her so much.

She was never a believer in things happening for a reason, but that one phone call from Maybelle set off a chain of events that no one expected. If she was still here, Maybelle would have sworn up and down that it was the work of the Lord. Lena wasn't too sure about that, but she couldn't deny the events that had unfolded. It was beyond human comprehension of how all of it could've happened the way it did, and when it did.

Her attackers sat in the county jail awaiting prosecution for their crimes; all four of them. After Roger was arrested for his attack on her and the shooting of Janine, others came forward—other women both old and young, and told their stories of being abused by the powerful Chamberlain men. The town was rocked to its knees. Roger was replaced by someone not affiliated with Archer, and the county sheriff took over law enforcement jurisdiction for the town. And it all started with Maybelle's illness and her phone call.

She took a deep breath and headed for the front door. She'd moved Uncle Zeke to Gale's house and promised that she would check in on him from time to time. Just as she was about to leave, the door swung open and in came Janine, followed by Jack.

She wanted to avoid this. This last time together with them. It was hard enough cleaning and packing, with the weight of her decision hovering over her head. She was leaving. She couldn't stay in Archer. There were too many painful memories to remind her. She couldn't make a new life in the same place where her last one had ended.

"Hey," she greeted them. She attempted to walk around Janine, but Janine put her hands up, stopping her escape.

"Wait."

Lena stepped back. "Yes, Jay?"

"Please, hear me out." She took Lena gently by the arms. "Don't leave."

"I have a home in Kansas. I have to get back to work and so does Nadia."

Janine pulled her closer. Lena glanced over at Jack. His expression was dark. She knew what he was thinking, she knew what he was feeling. She was leaving him again. Taking their daughter away.

"I know, but what if you guys stayed here in Archer? With Jack?"

Lena pulled her eyes away from Jack's saddening face. She couldn't bear the look. She couldn't bear seeing the hurt on his face. "I can't. Don't you understand that?"

"If not Archer, then come back with me to Atlanta. Just like we talked about as kids, you know? You and me, living in the city? Nadia could get a transfer and you could still work, doing your photography."

Lena laughed softly. "Now that's where you're wrong. Most of my commissions are in the national parks. I'd be thousands of miles away from them if I relocated here."

Janine took a strand of Lena's hair and tucked it behind her ear. "I get that, but..."

"But what?"

"I don't want to let you go again. Neither does Jack. He needs you."

Lena sighed heavily. She could resist one of them alone but resisting both of them was always hard for her. She had her best friends back and it felt so good and satisfying to return to those feelings before the madness happened. Janine was her soul sister and he—he was her soulmate. Together they completed her.

"Don't do this to me, guys," Lena said pulling away from Janine. "I mean, seriously. It would be nice to hang out more with you two, but I have bills to pay and I'm not as set up financially as you are."

"Lena, please, just stay and—" Her words were cut short by Jack stepping in between them.

He gazed down into Lena's eyes, his own shimmering with tears. "Why?"

Lena swallowed the lump that instantly appeared in her throat. "Why what?"

"You came back and now you're leaving me again. Why?"

"I have no choice."

"You have a choice. Choose me." Lena shook her head and looked away from him. He touched the tip of her chin and lifted her head. "Is it because of me?"

"What? No!"

"Remember we promised each other. We promised it would be nobody else."

"I know."

"I kept my promise. I waited. I didn't think you were coming back." He sniffled and sighed deeply. "But you did. And you brought my daughter."

"I know." Lena held back her tears. She didn't want to hurt him all over again. Why couldn't they understand that Archer wasn't home anymore? "I was never with anyone else. Just you."

"Is it because I'm not like most men? Is that why you don't want to stay with me?"

Lena reached up and caressed his face, running her fingers along his soft beard. She loved him so much, and it was for this reason she existed all those years without intimacy. He cupped her hand, holding it over his scar.

"You are perfect, Aidan."

"Why won't you stay with me?"

"I can't. I'm sorry."

"We don't have to stay at my house. I can build you a new one. I mean, I could pay someone to do it for me. A big one if you want. We can even get you a puppy."

"Stop, please."

"And since you like to cook and I like to eat, I'll make sure our kitchen is big, just like you wanted, remember? What about that?"

Lena squeezed her eyes tightly shut. "Aidan."

"And since Nadia is big, she can have her own guest house so she can stay with us, too. Please. Stay here with me."

"Aidan, I cannot stay here with you." She forced out. "I'm so sorry." She opened her eyes and looked up at him. She wasn't expecting to see this particular expression on his face. It was so alien that she couldn't even place it. All she knew was that he was hurt. Extremely hurt.

He stared at her for what felt like hours, before he broke away from her and stormed out of the door. When he walked out, Lena's heart swelled up with a feeling of loss and longing. She wanted to go after him and then again, she wanted to stand firm with her decision to leave. If she allowed her heart to guide this matter, who knows where it might lead her.

***

Nadia was sitting in the passenger seat of the Equinox when she heard the screen door slam. She looked up and saw Jack racing down the front steps and across the yard. He looked angry or upset. His face lacked the usual brightness that she'd grown accustomed to. She jumped out of the car and came around the front of it.

"Jack!" she called after him.

He glanced in her direction but kept walking. He didn't even acknowledge her, he just walked right past. She caught a glimpse of tears running down his face. She started after him. His long legs and his hurried pace made her have to break into a slight sprint to catch up with him.

"Jack, wait." She stopped running after him when she realized what was happening. She understood now. He didn't want to say goodbye to her. "Dad!" Her heart nearly choked her words right out of her mouth.

He stopped dead in his tracks. He turned around slowly and stared at her; perhaps uncertain if he'd heard her correctly.

She reached out to him. "Dad, please come back." She could barely speak. All she knew was she couldn't let him leave like this. Not when she just found him.

He walked back towards her, his saddened face giving way to that gentle smile that she adored so much. When he came to face her, he took her gently by the arms.

"You called me dad."

"Yes."

"Wow. Why?"

"Because you're my dad, aren't you?"

Jack nodded. "I thought you were ashamed of me."

"No, I'm not."

He took her into his arms and gave her one of the strongest hugs she'd ever experienced. He was so strong and yet so gentle at the same time. It was a perfect combination of the two. She could tell he loved her.

"You and your mom are leaving me," he said pulling away.

"I know and I'm sorry."

"That's what she said."

"Did you ask her to stay?"

He nodded. "Yeah. She said she can't. I told her I'd give her a house. Anything she wants. But she still won't stay."

"There's many bad memories here. I know you understand that?"

"Yeah."

"So maybe the solution isn't here in Archer."

He processed what she had said. It took a while, but eventually he got it. He hugged her tightly again. "Thank you, baby girl."

"Aww."

"It's okay if I call you that?"

"Of course, it is."

"Okay. Great." He started towards the house. "I'm going to go talk to Lena, okay?" He ran back towards the house.

Nadia smiled as she watched him disappear into the house. "Way to go, Dad."

***

Lena was coming out of the bathroom when Jack darted back into the house. He walked right past Janine and straight to her. Her eyes widened with surprise as he faced her and took her hands in his.

"What is it, Aidan?"

He entwined their fingers and pulled her closer. She gasped softly with surprise and frowned at him.

"You always got your way," he said.

"What are you talking about?"

"When we were little, I wanted Skittles, you wanted M&Ms. I wanted Coke, you wanted Pepsi."

"Okay?"

"Pepsi is nasty and so are M&Ms."

Lena laughed softly, her beautiful smile finally shining through. It was the same smile that she had before it all happened.

He chuckled, too. "I wanted you to be happy."

"I know."

"I want to be happy, too."

"I don't know how to make anyone happy right now."

"Just me. Make me happy."

"How? If staying here will make you happy, then I'm sorry but I can't stay here." Lena groaned under her breath. "You think it's easy being here? Do you guys really believe that I'm going to be okay if I have to be faced with the memories? I can't st—"

"Stop!" The tone of his voice was loving, but firm. "Stop talking." Lena snapped her mouth shut and stared at him. He smiled at her and strummed his fingers through her hair. "I love you so much."

She opened her mouth to speak, but he placed a finger to her lips. "I go wherever you go, remember?"

She nodded in response.

"Do you want to make me happy?"

"Yes, I do. But I don't know how."

"I don't want to be here if you aren't."

"What are you saying?"

"Take me with you. I want to go with you."

"You do?"

"Yes. I'll pay for everything. I have money. My money is yours."

"Oh, Aidan, I can't let you take care of my finances like that. That's unfair."

"Not if I'm your man."

"What?" she gasped.

"Let's get married. Let's be a family."

Lena certainly didn't expect him to say this. But oddly enough it was exactly what was needed to be said at the moment. "Married?"

"Yes."

Lena glanced over at Janine who had tears in her eyes. She nodded approvingly and smiled at them. She mouthed the words "say yes."

"I..." She was speechless. She'd already accepted the fact that she would probably be alone for the rest of her life, so this was a shocking turn of events. "You still want to marry me?"

He nodded.

"Even after everything that's happened to me?"

"You're still you and I'm still me."

She thought of all the things she could say to back away from this. She was damaged, although healing, and she hadn't been with anyone since him. She was brand new.

"How do you know that I'll make you happy?"

"Because I know."

"What if you're wrong?"

"I'm not."

After weighing her options over and over in her mind, she finally came to a decision. She sighed heavily and nodded. "All right."

"So, that's yes?"

She smiled. "Yes, Aidan, I'll marry you."

"Woohoo!" He picked her up and swung her around several times before placing her back down on the ground. He bent down and kissed her tenderly on the lips. "Thank you."

She hugged him and rejoiced in the fact that her life had suddenly taken a completely unexpected, yet positive turn.

Chapter 29

One year later...

Janine placed the top on the pot of spaghetti and turned the burner down. She gazed around the kitchen, everything looked very good. Dinner was going to be delicious tonight. After months of trial and error, she'd finally perfected her take on Lena's famous parmesan chicken meatballs and that's what she made the family for dinner tonight.

After everything went down in Archer, life dramatically changed for them all. Janine had resolved to go back to Atlanta alone, but Lena surprised her with an offer she couldn't resist. So, she went back to Kansas with the three of them. And it was the best choice that she could have ever made.

She'd found a quaint studio apartment on the outskirts of Kansas City. She opened up her own dental office in town and hired Nadia to manage her front office. Working together with Nadia strengthened their bond.

"How many patients do I see tomorrow?" Janine asked as she took a seat at the island.

"I think five," Nadia said, "You got the new guy who's coming all the way from Baldwin City to get his extractions done."

"How many of his are we pulling tomorrow?"

"All of them." Nadia took the seat next to her. "Poor guy has really bad teeth."

"Oh man, that'll take two or three hours."

"At least."

"I was hoping to get to the mall on my lunch break. It'll have to be another day."

"What do you need at the mall?"

"Something for your mom."

"Oh, sounds great! Do we have everything worked out for the party?"

"Yes, as far as I know. We've invited everyone that she wanted, so now we're just waiting and hoping she makes it."

"That's excellent. Yeah, I hope she makes it. She told me that the doctor wasn't hopeful that she would."

"Oh, I'm so excited!"

"Me too. You never know, maybe Linda will still be here visiting when it happens," Nadia said with a smile.

Janine nodded her head slowly. She hadn't even thought of that possibility. A few weeks after her father was imprisoned for the crimes he committed, Linda contacted her and informed her that she was going into rehab. Janine didn't really believe her until she received a letter from her on the rehabilitation center's letterhead.

In her letter, Linda expressed remorse for everything she had done to hurt her. She promised Janine that she was going to get better for her children and her grandchild. After six months in rehabilitation, Linda Chamberlain resurfaced sober. Tonight, she was coming for dinner, and breaking bread with her old, and new family.

"Yes, I hope it does happen like that. Mom will be very pleased to be here for the occasion. A new grandchild is a very special thing."

"It certainly is!" Nadia said. "That is until you start having kids. I think Mom is done. So, it'll be up to you then."

"I think not. Never in a million years." They shared a laugh.

Lena walked into the room and eyed them suspiciously. For a few weeks now, she'd walk into a room and the conversation died immediately. She sat down at the kitchen table and rubbed her back. "My back is killing me!" she lamented.

Janine came over to the table and rubbed the small of Lena's back. "The little one must be sitting on a nerve."

"Feels like he's sitting on more than just one nerve."

Janine chuckled and continued to massage her back. "There, is that better?"

"It'll be better when this child is evicted from my womb," she groaned. "Something smells good. What is it?"

"Your meatballs."

"Who cooked them?"

"I did."

"Oh brother!"

Janine increased the pressure on her back. "What's that supposed to mean?"

"Nothing." Lena laughed softly and enjoyed the backrub from Janine. They'd rekindled their friendship and Janine had undeniably reclaimed her best friend status. When Lena wasn't with Jack, she was with Janine. And it just worked.

"You think you're so funny."

"I don't think, I know."

Janine laughed and let that one slide. She'd finally found her laugh again, and it was usually in the wake of Lena's. They were two peas in a pod, as Maybelle always called it, two friends working together for a common cause.

"Is Linda still coming to dinner tonight?" Lena asked. Her voice was softer as she reached over and took Janine's hand.

"Yes. Are you sure you're okay with it?"

Lena smiled. "I know she's changed. I had to really try to put myself in her shoes. I know it must have been hard being married to Roger all those years."

"Yeah," Janine agreed.

"And I know the alcohol had to be the only way for her to cope with the things he did to her. Along with the domestic abuse, he was also unfaithful to her with many women."

"That's true. And now that she's sober, she's so kind and loving. Lena, I promise she will not try to hurt us or her grandchildren. She just wants to be a part of our lives."

Lena rubbed her belly and glanced over at Nadia. "I believe you," she whispered.

Janine squeezed Lena's hand. Over the past year, she'd stopped apologizing as often as she used to, but that didn't take away from the feelings she still had. There was still a twinge of guilt every time she gazed into Lena's eyes or each time she noticed the scar on Jack's face.

"I just want everyone to be happy."

"I think we are. Aren't you happy?"

"Yes."

"I am too. And if you really want Linda to be a part of our lives, then that's what I want too."

Janine nodded and pulled Lena into her arms. "I love you so much."

"I love you too, Jay." Lena held on as long as Janine did, before pulling away. "Now let's hope you don't poison your mother with this cooking of yours."

Janine laughed out loud and pushed away from the table. "You guys are going to get enough of criticizing my culinary skills."

"You mean your lack of?" Lena added.

"Watch it!" Janine warned. "Don't forget I'm the one who's going to be caring for you after you pop that baby out."

Lena mocked fright. "Oh, I'm shaking in my boots." She laughed as Janine sat back down at the table and smiled warmly at her. "What?"

"It's just that I missed this part with Nadia. I'm glad I'm experiencing it now."

"You should try being in this body. It's quite a different experience, I'm sure."

Janine shrugged. "Maybe. But I'm still glad to be here to witness it. I mean, I'm never having kids so it's nice to see it so closely."

Lena arched her eyebrow. "Don't you dare start getting emotional."

"I'm not."

"Sure you're not."

Janine yanked a napkin from the dispenser and dabbed her eyes. "Whatever," Janine said getting up from the table and joining Nadia at the island.

"Told you," Lena chuckled. Now that they'd finally found their laughs again, it was hard to stop.

The front door swung open and Jack stumbled inside. When he caught sight of Lena sitting at the table, a bright smile crossed his face. He dropped everything at the door and walked into the kitchen.

"Something smells good!" He leaned and kissed Lena softly on the cheek. "Did you cook that?"

"No, your sister did."

"Oh..." He grimaced. "I think I'll get a peanut butter sandwich."

"Seriously?" Janine laughed, "I can cook just fine now I have someone to cook for."

Jack knelt down beside Lena and rubbed her back. "Your day was good?"

"Yes, it was."

"What did you do while I was at work?"

"Not a thing."

Jack laughed and snuggled her. "I'm glad you got rest. Our baby is coming soon."

"Yes, he is."

"I'm still thinking of a name. I'm not good with names."

"I know, and it's okay. We still have plenty of time. And if we can't come up with something, we will just name him Jackson the second."

"Yeah, but I want him to be different than me. I want him to be proud of me," he said gazing into her eyes.

Lena caressed his cheek and sighed. "Our son will be very proud of his dad. I have no doubt about it."

"Are you sure? Even how I am?"

"You are the most loving, kindest, and gentlest man that I've ever had the pleasure of knowing and I am so proud to be the mother of your children."

The smile that followed her statement lit up the entire room. He gave her a kiss and pressed his face against her belly. "I can't wait for him to come."

"Neither can I, love."

He caressed her belly, speaking softly to it, "Hey little dude, I'm your dad! I can't wait to meet you."

Lena ran her fingers lazily through his hair and glanced over at Janine. Janine rolled her eyes playfully.

Jack got up and sat in the chair closest to Lena. He pulled a gift box wrapped in shiny blue paper from his pocket. "This is for you."

"Oh? What is it?"

"Open it."

Lena ripped the paper away and opened it. Her breath caught in her throat. "Oh my God, it's beautiful!" She removed the ring from the box and inspected it. It shimmered in the light. It was an emerald cut diamond and sapphire trio. Two sapphires accented the stunning diamond. It was absolutely breathtaking up close.

It was the same one that caught her eye at the mall jewelry store a few weeks back. Jack had asked her if she wanted it, but when she saw the price tag, she declined the offer. Jack never pressed, nor did he say anything else about it, so she assumed it had been forgotten. Was she ever wrong! She handed it to him.

He removed the wedding band from her finger and replaced it with the new one. He was careful as he pushed it onto her finger. It was a perfect fit.

"See. Perfect, just like you."

"Aww." She melted on the spot. She wrapped her arms around his neck and gave him a tight hug. "Thank you so much!"

"Anything for you." He sighed contently. "After dinner, I'll put the crib together."

"Sounds good."

He pulled away from her. "I mean, we can do it together if you want to?"

"Sure, that sounds great." She smiled at him and gave him an Eskimo kiss.

The doorbell rang. Lena got up and walked to the front door. She paused before opening it, turning back to look at them. Jack, Janine, and Nadia were all watching her.

A year ago, she wouldn't have even imagined this. She had everything she could ever want right here; a devoted husband, a loving daughter, and a trustworthy best friend. And her future—their future, nestled securely inside her womb.

She met Janine's eyes and gave her a nod. None of this would have been possible if they hadn't answered Maybelle's call to come home. They wouldn't have experienced the rebirth of their once dead friendship. When they made the decision to forgive, they offered to each other a gift of peace, and paved their way to happiness in its purest form. They were finally free.

The End

"To forgive is the highest, most beautiful form of love. In return, you will receive untold peace and happiness."
~Robert Muller

I hope you enjoyed reading Archer. Please leave a review at your favorite online retailer and let me know what you thought of it. I appreciate all honest reviews.

About Mira Jeffreys

I live in a small town in Kansas. My days are quiet, uneventful, and I love every moment of it. I enjoy long drives, beautiful sunsets, and daily cups of hot coffee. I'm a mom of six beautiful children, & a grandmother of three lovely beings who've completely stolen my heart.

Connect Online

My Official Author Website
www.MiraJeffreys.com

Official Facebook Author Page
www.facebook.com/mirajeffreysauthor

Follow me on Twitter
@MiraJeffreys

Correspondence:
Mira Jeffreys
C/O Better World Press
PO Box 588
Gardner, KS 66030-0588

www.ingramcontent.com/pod-product-compliance
Lightning Source LLC
LaVergne TN
LVHW031536060526
838200LV00056B/4528